ALSO BY MARISA SILVER

Babe in Paradise
No Direction Home
The God of War
Alone with You
Mary Coin
Little Nothing
The Mysteries

AT LAST

a novel

MARISA SILVER

SIMON & SCHUSTER

*New York   Amsterdam/Antwerp   London
Toronto   Sydney/Melbourne   New Delhi*

Simon & Schuster
1230 Avenue of the Americas
New York, NY 10020

This book is a work of fiction. Any references to historical events, real people, or real places are used fictitiously. Other names, characters, places, and events are products of the author's imagination, and any resemblance to actual events or places or persons, living or dead, is entirely coincidental.

First Simon & Schuster hardcover edition September 2025

SIMON & SCHUSTER and colophon are registered trademarks of Simon & Schuster, LLC

Simon & Schuster strongly believes in freedom of expression and stands against censorship in all its forms. For more information, visit BooksBelong.com.

For information about special discounts for bulk purchases, please contact Simon & Schuster Special Sales at 1-866-506-1949 or business@simonandschuster.com.

The Simon & Schuster Speakers Bureau can bring authors to your live event. For more information or to book an event, contact the Simon & Schuster Speakers Bureau at 1-866-248-3049 or visit our website at www.simonspeakers.com.

Interior design by Carly Loman

Grateful acknowledgment is made to *The New Yorker* and *The Atlantic* for publishing excerpts from this work in slightly different form.

Manufactured in the United States of America

1   3   5   7   9   10   8   6   4   2

Library of Congress Cataloging-in-Publication Data has been applied for.

ISBN 978-1-6680-7896-9
ISBN 978-1-6680-7898-3 (ebook)

For Ken, always

CONTENTS

ONE

ARRANGEMENTS

Omaha, Nebraska, 1971

Helene supposed Ruth had been some sort of hippie. Or maybe it all had something to do with women's liberation. She couldn't think of how it might relate to Vietnam, but she was sure that Ruth had found some way to make the connection. Something about imperialism or capitalism. The way she had it, you couldn't buy a pair of shoes without having to acknowledge imperialism, or capitalism, or—what was that other thing she was always going on about?—*advertising*. As if a person had no mind of her own when, in fact, Helene had bought the blue leather pumps with the small gold buckles she was wearing right now because she *liked* navy blue, and because the buckle made things a little more formal, and because, in her opinion, a mature but slightly festive pump was appropriate for the wedding of Ruth, this tall and rashly opinionated girl, to Tom, Helene's otherwise responsible son.

Whatever the girl's reasoning was, nothing about this wedding was appropriate. For one thing, it was taking place in a public park in the middle of winter. All right, she conceded, it was the end of March, but all it took was one look outside the car window, where sooty patches of snow clung to the grassy verge, to know that the lamb had not replaced the lion in Omaha, Nebraska, a city Helene had never been to before, and from the grim looks of it, one she would never need to visit again. For another, Ruth and Tom were not going to be married by a rabbi but by a judge who was, according to Tom, somebody one of Ruth's sisters had heard about.

She wanted to speak of these things now, to commiserate about the weather, and the judge, and everything else about this unconventional wedding, but she barely knew Ruth's mother, who was driving, tapping her fingers impatiently on the wheel to let Helene know she'd rather be doing anything else than taking her on this errand. Evelyn Turner. Which was certainly not an authentic name, Helene thought. Of course, there had been a time, years ago, when she hadn't liked the idea of being saddled with the name Simonauer for the rest of her life, but it had become something to be proud of, hadn't it? A declaration. Especially after the war. At any rate, she'd met this Evelyn Turner only hours earlier and now she was allowing herself to be driven (a little recklessly, she thought, as the woman turned left into a line of not-distant-enough oncoming traffic) to a florist shop so that Helene could perform her "job" for the wedding.

Which was how Tom and Ruth had put it, back in Cleveland six months ago, when they told her that she would be in charge of the flowers. "You have such good taste," Ruth had said. This might have been a compliment or not. It was hard to tell with the girl, who always seemed to be saying one thing and meaning the very opposite. Whenever Tom brought her to the house, she wandered through the rooms, complimenting the decorative bowls on the coffee table or the silver vases on the dining room sideboard, but Helene knew the girl was judging her, one object at a time.

After Tom and Ruth described her meager role—they were not even having a rehearsal dinner for her to host, which seemed to Helene the least they could do on her account—Tom had looked at her with such eagerness. He wanted her approval, not only of this idea that her sole contribution to the wedding should be a few bunches of flowers, but also of his choice of wife. Helene did the best she could. Hadn't she gone out of her way to compliment Ruth's outfit that day? Those bell-bottom slacks? That—what was it called—poncho?

"I thought maybe you could pick out my bouquet, too," Ruth had added, uncharacteristically demure. *Bouquet* was such a genteel word that Helene wondered if irony was involved. Tom, touched by Ruth's sudden shyness, took her hand just the way he'd taken Helene's two years earlier, at his father's funeral. Then, she'd been stunned by the sudden reversals in her life. Her husband dead. Her son acting as her protector. The whole thing had made her feel claustrophobic and she was relieved when the service was over. But, oh—the expression on Tom's face as he waited for her to agree to the wedding plan. He reminded her of nothing so much as himself as a little boy when, after behaving badly, he'd look at her with those dark, wet eyes, desperate for her to reassure him that she loved him despite his naughtiness.

Once Ruth came into the picture, Helene let go of her assumption that her son would wed one of the perfectly reasonable Cleveland girls he'd dated in high school or college. Those girls, sensing Tom's devotion to his mother, courted Helene's favor with deference and a suitable restraint of personality. She'd also let go of the idea that the wedding would take place in the darkly potent sanctuary in University Circle with its domed ceiling, its difficult pews, and the provocatively obscure choir loft that, if it didn't approximate heaven, made a person feel at least proportional. But she had not come to terms with the fact that any normal idea of a wedding, one a mother might reasonably expect, had been jettisoned.

For instance: Ruth had decided that she would not walk down an aisle. In fact, the folding chairs would be arranged in the park so that there would be no aisle at all. *I'm not*, she said, *a sheep to the slaughter!* She also decided that the idea of being given away was, in her word, *gross*. Which seemed, to Helene, a funny way for a young woman about to finish a PhD in Germanic and Slavic languages to express herself. *Gross* was the favorite word of every child Helene tutored at the afterschool reading program where she volunteered. *This snack is gross. This homework is gross.* And even, from one particularly distractable eight-year-old boy: *You smell gross.*

Which she most certainly did not, she reminded herself, as Evelyn accelerated through a yellow light. Helene brought a hand to her ear, ostensibly to adjust her large pearl earring, but really so that she could sniff her wrist and assure herself of the fact that her smell was, and had been for nearly thirty years, the unimpeachably floral scent of L'Air du Temps.

Evelyn pressed the cigarette lighter below the dashboard. "Do you mind?" she asked.

"Not at all," Helene said, though she did. The car already smelled strongly of residual smoke that would certainly become trapped in the fibers of her good wool coat. She grew increasingly uncomfortable as Evelyn glanced away from the road to fish a cigarette out of her purse, put it between her lips, then reach for the lighter. She guided the glowing coil to the tip, steering with one hand by making small, sharp motions back and forth as if she were driving by feel.

"My husband died in a car accident," Helene said. She'd taken to using this explanation with strangers. It allowed for a straightforward sympathy without the diminishing effect of the excitement people felt when presented with a truth that beggared belief. A car crash had the added advantage of making Helene a double victim, first of the loss, and then of the car companies, or the gasoline companies, or whoever it was that benefited from a highway speed limit more suited to race car drivers than actual people. In the two years since Emil's death, she'd become a hesitant driver, heavy-footed with the brakes, as if she believed the story herself.

"Yes," Evelyn said. "Ruth mentioned it." She drew deeply on her cigarette before she put her hand back on the wheel.

An accident. *Well*, Evelyn thought, exhaling a stream of smoke, *that was one way to put it.* According to Ruth, the man had been crushed to death by a tree. Sitting in his car. In his own driveway. Not so much an accident as lousy timing. But then, timing was the whole kit and caboodle, wasn't it? Look at Ruth. Two years ago, she met a young man on the street, and now they were getting married. If either she or Tom had been at that same spot five minutes earlier or five minutes later, Evelyn would not be driving around with a woman who clutched her purse on her lap as if she thought Evelyn might steal it.

She drew smoke deep into her lungs. The cigarette was a good choice. It made silence more acceptable. More than that, smoking made her feel farther away from the woman whose ample hips took up the other half of the bench seat and threatened to brush up against her own every time she took a curve. Well, maybe that was an exaggeration, but Tom's mother was solid as a block and she sure knew how to fill a space. Even when she'd arrived at the house that morning, a complete stranger, she behaved as if Evelyn were lucky to take her coat and offer her a cup of coffee.

Evelyn pulled a right turn a little faster than was strictly necessary, and Helene grabbed the handle on her door. The woman wore the sort of hairdo that most people had given up on a decade ago, Evelyn thought. A set. A teased and sprayed bubble that had you sleeping like a mummy for a week between appointments so it would hold its shape. She wasn't as tall as Evelyn had expected given that Tom was well over six feet. He must have gotten his height from the dead father. Although, who knew? Ruth was much taller than either she or Frank, taller than her sisters, who called her "stork" when she was young. This was nasty, but also true, because Ruth had those long, impossibly thin legs that went right up to her hips without flaring. She had a habit of holding her head high with her chin slightly forward. Ever since she was a little girl, she stood this way. As if she wanted to be the first one to see what was coming.

Anyway, the smoking allowed Evelyn not to bother herself with the kind of conversational jawing that would allow this woman to report back to whomever she would report back to in Cleveland that *Ruth's mother was a lovely woman.* Evelyn was not a lovely woman. She didn't try to be and never had. Smart—yes. Able to smell when someone was trying to put something over on her—you bet. Especially once Frank died (of very un-accidental heart disease, thank you very much) and it seemed like every other repairman were either flirting with her or trying to charge her double, or both. People thought a woman lost half her brain when her husband died. In fact, Evelyn had never felt quite so sharp.

No doubt, Helene was waiting for Evelyn to say something consoling about the dead husband. She was probably hoping that the two of them could make some sort of friendship based on their shared bad luck. Well, Evelyn wasn't interested in the sisterhood of widows. She hadn't been when Frank died six years earlier, and she wasn't now. All those women inviting her to lunches that ended in teary hugs. Their tedious belief that the world had given them a bum steer. People died. It happened every day of the week. You pulled up your big-girl pants. You got on with it.

She wasn't wild about the idea that Tom's mother would be living in her home for the next two days. It was going to be awkward. They would have to, inevitably, have *conversations* about God-knows-what. Evelyn would need to get dressed before she came out of her bedroom because she'd be damned if the woman was going to see her in her bathrobe without makeup. Wasn't there such a thing as a hotel? The house was full enough as it was. Ruth and Tom had been spending the week leading up to the wedding in Ruth's old room. They'd pushed the twin beds together, which was fine by Evelyn. She wasn't born yesterday, or the day before that. But apparently Helene was, and now that she was going to be staying over, Tom would sleep on the pullout in the basement. Paula and that husband of hers would be driving in from Lincoln later in the afternoon, so that took care of Paula's old room. Ruth would get her bedroom to herself before the wedding—fair enough. But inconvenient, because it meant that Helene would have to take Naomi's room, and Naomi, home from Kearney State for the week, would have to sleep with Evelyn. Thinking about it made Evelyn shudder. She hadn't shared a bed with another person since Frank, and the idea of sleeping next to her twenty-four-year-old middle daughter, of hearing her breathe, of their bodies accidentally touching in the night—well, she and her girls weren't in the habit of hugs and cuddles, were they? And what was wrong with that? Evelyn hadn't gotten that sort of thing from her mother and she'd turned out just fine.

She glanced at her watch. It was already one-fifteen. She should be home boiling two dozen eggs and peeling beets. She should be dragging the leaves for her dining room table out of the garage, ironing napkins, and cleaning her serving platters, which she hardly used. There came a point in life where you just said to hell with all that pretending and you dished food right out of the pots you made it in. There came another point where you didn't even bother to bring the pots to the table, and you told Ruth, Naomi, and Paula to fill their plates at the stove. And then, you gave up on the whole thing and told your daughters that if they wanted to eat, they could pour a bowl of cereal. This happened when Frank stopped feeling strong enough to come downstairs for meals. Cooking, sitting at the table with her girls, and listening to them talk about their plans for the weekend or who stole whose eye shadow made the charade of a family dinner feel like she was holding on for dear life when dear life had already let go.

Stopping at a red light, she suddenly felt exhausted. She'd lain awake half the night before, listening to Ruth and Tom argue. This morning, the two of them were overly considerate as they made breakfast, apologizing when they got into one another's way. *Do you want your eggs runny or firm?* Ruth said. Had Evelyn ever heard her daughter ask such a question? Ruth would decide what kind of eggs she wanted, and that's what everyone else would get. But there she was, fluttering around the kitchen, doing a bad impersonation of Donna Reed. It was a terrible thing to watch. Well, whatever they'd fought about was none of Evelyn's business. Ruth and Tom would work it out or they wouldn't. And even if they worked it out now they'd come up against it again, because the first problem in a relationship is always the last problem. Evelyn had warned her girls about that. She'd sat through enough dull conversations with her friends as they complained about their husbands for the very same reasons they'd whined about them from the start. Sure, you could teach a man to lower the toilet lid after he did his business. But people did not, fundamentally, change. She and Frank hadn't had any marital problems, but his father died of the very same heart disease at the very same age. That bomb had started ticking on day one.

Except whatever was going on with Ruth and Tom *was* her business because Tom was supposed to take his mother to Sonya's shop for the flowers. But then Ruth, still busy making up for the night before, decided that she and Tom had to spend the day before their wedding together, driving around to see her childhood haunts, which left Evelyn with the job of chauffeuring this—

Was the woman saying something now?

"I'm sorry?" Evelyn said.

"What?" Helene said.

"Did you say something?"

"No."

"I thought I heard—"

"You didn't."

Helene hoped she had not inadvertently spoken her thoughts, which were less than charitable. She'd mentioned her husband's death, and Evelyn Turner offered nothing in return. No kind thoughts or an acknowledgment that Helene's letting go of her only son not two years after Emil's passing or traveling to Omaha and putting her life in the hands of a fast-driving cigarette fiend so that she could make her meager contribution to this patched-together wedding should be counted as acts of heroism. "And I was sorry to hear that Ruth's father has also passed," she said. "Tom told me everything, of course," she added, not wanting to be the only one whose life was discussed in absentia.

"It wasn't a surprise," Evelyn said. "He was sick for a long time."

"But you can never really prepare for these things, can you?"

"Of course you can," Evelyn said, taking the final puff on her cigarette then stubbing it out in the ashtray. Helene watched as Evelyn did something that made it look like a tongue of smoke was licking her nostrils. It was a trick of some kind, Helene thought, and it was meant to be belittling in the way of all tricks.

"Here we go," Evelyn murmured, turning in to a shopping center, where small stores flanked a supermarket called Hinky Dinky.

Hinky Dinky, Helene thought as Evelyn parked the car. Tom was marrying a girl who came from a place where people said things like, *I have to run over to Hinky Dinky's*. This whole thing was impossible.

The temperature had dropped since they left Evelyn's house, and once she was out of the car, Helene pulled at the lapels of her coat to protect her neck. She should have worn a scarf. She had a good constitution, but she was also fifty-seven years old, and it was foolish for a person to take unnecessary risks. Evelyn looked younger, with her tight skin and her slim figure. Maybe she was one of those dieters Helene read about in magazines at the hair salon. Women who did nothing but eat grapefruit morning, noon, and night. She was wearing a lightweight trench coat and—how had Helene not noticed this before?—the woman's legs were bare! She was not wearing hose! With a mother like this, it was no wonder Ruth thought that getting married outside in the freezing cold was a fine idea. And it was also no wonder that Evelyn Turner appeared to be unbothered by the fact that *her* assigned task for the wedding was to prepare egg salad sandwiches and her "famous borscht" for the postwedding luncheon at her house. That's how Tom had put it back in Cleveland when Helene, coming to grips with her assigned task, asked what Ruth's mother's job would be. He and Ruth had smiled at one another, sharing some private knowledge about this soup, and Helene realized that Tom had begun to adopt Ruth's family lore as his own. Could he boast about his mother's famous anything? Most of what he'd eaten during his childhood had been prepared by Erna, who was a wonderful cook. Helene chose the recipes, of course. But you didn't brag about your mother's meal plans, did you?

Famous borscht. She wanted to say those words out loud. She could say, *I hear you're making your famous borscht* and let the implication sink in, but she was too busy trying to keep up with Evelyn, who walked quickly across the parking lot toward a florist Helene knew nothing about. She'd spent her entire adulthood developing relationships with the people she did business with. Her florist in Shaker Heights, her hairdresser, her dry cleaner, her mailman. These people knew her customs and tastes. They sent notes to remind her when it was time to think about the Passover flowers or store her coats for the summer. And in return, she always remembered to ask about someone's ailing mother and give their children little holiday gifts. These were gestures. But they were important. They were how things worked. Wasn't that true when, just the other day, Paul—no, it was Jeffrey now—had pulled up in his mail truck just as she was backing out of the driveway, and she'd bothered to stop and ask after his son in the army? And couldn't she be sure that on a day of rain or snowfall, Jeffrey would bring her mail right to the door rather than leave it in the mailbox?

But now she was going to have to buy flowers, probably the most important flowers she'd ever buy in her life, from a perfect stranger. Who, the minute Helene stepped foot in the store, came flying out from behind the counter and threw her arms around her.

"Helene! It's so nice to finally meet! Evvy has told me so much about you!"

Helene's confusion and the shock of being manhandled by

this stranger put her in a frozen state where all she could do was wait out the embrace. "I'm not sure how much she could have told you," she said when the woman finally released her. "We've only just met."

"Well, she certainly told me about Ruth and Tom," the woman said. "Your son," she added, raising her voice as if she thought Helene might be deaf, or daft, or both.

"I'm aware," Helene said.

"Don't mind Sonya," Evelyn said. "She's the enthusiastic one."

And suddenly, Helene understood. Evelyn had not just brought her to any flower shop, but to one owned by her very own sister.

Sonya suddenly clapped her hands to signal a transition. "So, what were you thinking?" she said. "We figured four arrangements for the park to define the space. And then we bring them back to the house. That way you don't even have to bother with a centerpiece."

"Kill two birds," Evelyn said.

"It's cheaper that way, too," Sonya said. "Although don't worry on that score. You're getting the family rate."

Did she wink?

"I'm prepared to pay whatever the flowers are worth," Helene said.

"Well, that's just it, isn't it?" Sonya said. "What's a thing worth? You read the market, consider profit margins and your overhead, then you set a price. But there's more to it, isn't there? There's the emotional piece. A man buying flowers for his wife on Valentine's Day doesn't want to look like a penny-pincher, does he? He doesn't want me to think he's trying to get away with something. And the funny thing is, his wife's not going to have any idea how much he paid for those roses. But he walks out of the shop a little puffed up knowing how much he spent."

"Men," Evelyn said.

Helene thought it was distasteful to talk about money this way. When she'd bought the very shoes she was wearing, she and the salesman had talked about all sorts of things: that the shoes would complement the dress she'd wear to the wedding, that Tom had been hired by an investment firm in downtown Cleveland straight out of business school, that the house he and Ruth had picked out was not in Shaker, but it wasn't too far away. By the time she walked out the door with her shopping bag, she couldn't remember money changing hands.

"And then you think about the competition," Sonya continued. "What their prices are set at. You know, here's a funny thing: you have two flower shops side by side—and I've seen this with my own eyes—and one sells the same tulips as the other for a few dollars less. Nine out of ten times a customer will pay the higher price at the other shop. And you know why? Because they think there must be something wrong with the cheaper bunch."

"You can't make a fool think smart," Evelyn said.

Sonya went to the cooler at the back of the shop and took one fully arranged vase of flowers after another from its shelves, then placed them on the counter near the cash register. Helene realized that her contribution to the wedding was more insignificant than she thought. All the decisions had been made. The approving smile on Evelyn's face told her everything. Helene was nothing more than a checkbook.

Sonya described the roses and chrysanthemums that made

up the arrangements, telling Helene which flowers would let off a scent, which bore some significance to the occasion. "Forget-me-nots," she said, laying the tip of her finger on a petal. "A nice sentiment for a wedding, don't you think?"

"I think if they're worried about forgetting each other they have some things to work out," Evelyn said. "Which I think they do, by the way, given last night's performance. I could barely sleep."

"Those were just the jitters," Sonya said.

"Maybe," Evelyn said.

Helene had no idea what they were talking about, but she refused to ask and betray her ignorance. "My son is very loyal," she said.

"Oh, we all like Tom," Evelyn said. "Don't worry about that."

"I brought him up very well," Helene said.

"Very," Evelyn said.

Helene felt that she was being mocked. "I'm afraid to say, none of these arrangements are what I was thinking of."

"Oh," Sonya said, disappointed. She looked at the flowers sadly, as if she were worried their feelings were hurt. Then her expression shifted and she became avid and alive to the challenge. "Not a problem," she said. "The customer is always right. Tell me what you have in mind."

The truth was that Helene had given no thought to the flowers at all. She felt Sonya and Evelyn waiting for her answer. She looked at the four vases, all of them bulging with stems and buds and greenery.

"Something not quite so . . . busy," she said. "And less . . . red."

Evelyn sighed. "I'm going to run over to Hinky's. I need paprika."

"Her egg salad really is delicious," Sonya said after Evelyn was out the door. She had a wry sort of smile on her face, as if she could read Helene's thoughts.

"The borscht," Helene said.

"I know what you're thinking. Stains."

"I didn't want to say."

"Well, at least the bride isn't wearing white," Sonya said in a tone that made Helene sure that she, too, thought the peasanty nightgown-looking dress Ruth had chosen was a mistake. They were quiet for a moment.

"So," Sonya said, gazing at her rejected bouquets, "what should we do?"

For the first time all day, Helene felt that someone was on her side. "Maybe you can show me your more exotic flowers," she said. "Things you don't see all the time."

"Well, to tell you the truth, we don't carry anything that unusual. It's not what people here are generally looking for."

Helene heard a small defeat in the woman's voice. She understood the way in which Sonya's bright gregariousness was only a cover for a more long-standing yearning.

"Most people aren't very imaginative, I'm afraid," Sonya said. "They want to play it safe."

"Roses are safe," Helene said. "Carnations are safe."

"Carnations!" Sonya said. "If I have to do another arrangement of carnations for a funeral, I'll shoot myself!"

"Then we'll know what flowers *not* to have at yours," Helene said.

Sonya laughed. Helene felt pleased with herself. She walked

over to the cooler and opened the door. "Let's have a look," she said.

"Just don't blame me for the orange daisies and the baby's breath," Sonya said, her ebullience returning.

Helene spent the next ten minutes pulling various stems from buckets and laying them side by side on Sonya's worktable. It was a job to try to make something unique with what the woman stocked, arrangements that people would talk about years from now: *Remember those stunning flowers at Tom and Ruth's wedding? Did you know his mother chose them?* And that was the point, wasn't it, she thought as she circled the worktable, placing one stem at a time into the vases, stepping back, judging, adjusting. A wedding was all about what would be remembered.

The door opened, and Evelyn came back into the shop.

"Got the secret ingredient?" Sonya asked.

Evelyn waggled the small paper bag in her hand then took in the new arrangements. Her impassivity made Helene feel that she needed to account for her choices, to explain that the stalwart willow bark was meant to symbolize, she thought, and Sonya had concurred, the strength of marital commitment. But now she was becoming angry. Why should she have to justify herself to this woman? What had she to prove to someone who thought a wedding lunch of soup and sandwiches was a good idea, a woman who didn't have enough control over her daughter to get her to hold her wedding in a temple, wearing a white dress, and standing in front of a rabbi, for heaven's sake?

"Are we done here?" Evelyn said, looking at her watch. "I've got to get a move on."

"I haven't chosen the bouquet," Helene said.

"What bouquet?" Evelyn asked.

"Ruth's bouquet." It wasn't until this moment that Helene realized that, whether the request had been sincere or not, it was odd that Ruth had asked her to pick out the flowers that she would hold on her wedding day. Wasn't this something a mother and daughter would want to do together? Clearly, Evelyn was not as lucky as Helene to have a child who still cared about her opinion. She felt sorry for the woman now, and she thought it would be a generous gesture to include Evelyn in the selection. Magnanimous, really! But what was the woman saying now?

"Oh, yes. Ruth and I decided it would be nice for you to pick out the bouquet," Evelyn said. "Seeing as I've got three girls and you have only the one son."

Was this true? Was this what had made Helene suspicious back in Cleveland when Ruth had asked? Was the girl's flattery and diffidence only a strategy she and her mother had come up with together?

"Well, let's see what we've got here," Sonya said, walking back to investigate the cooler. "I've got just enough purple nemesia. Which we could mix with the sweet alyssum. Very delicate. I use that for a lot of my brides."

"Ruth isn't like a lot of brides," Helene said.

"And why's that?" Evelyn asked.

"Well, just look at her plans for the wedding! She wouldn't want to carry something you see all the time in advertisements. Or something expensive, what with capitalism. Ruth isn't that kind of girl, is she?"

The women fell silent. Sonya looked down at the floor as if preparing herself for her sister's anger. She was the cheerful one. That would have to make Evelyn—well, she *was* looking a little grim.

"I don't know what kind of a girl Ruth is," Evelyn said finally.

Helene wasn't sure what the woman meant, whether she was making fun of Helene, or if she was truly confounded by her daughter. Helene thought of what she could say in response: that Ruth was obviously intelligent, and that if she was no beauty, she was certainly pretty enough with her long chestnut hair and her dark eyes. And she had thick eyelashes, didn't she? That was nice. But she couldn't bring herself to do it. She just couldn't get past the fact that it was her fault that Ruth had come into Tom's life. Helene had put something into play that had gotten completely out of her control.

"Well, haven't I just had the most wonderful idea!" Sonya said, picking up her scissors.

Helene and Evelyn watched in silence as she pulled out a few yellow and white flowers from the refrigerator, gathered them into a bouquet, filled them out with eucalyptus leaves, cut down the stems, then secured everything with a white satin ribbon. She found a small glass vase and filled it with water. She announced that she would bring the arrangements to the park the next day and set them up before the ceremony. "But this goes home with you," she said, handing the vase to Helene. "Ruth will want it once she's dressed."

Helene took the vase. A simple bouquet for a simple wedding. That's how Tom and Ruth had put it when they told Helene that they had invited only six guests. Ruth would have her sisters, somebody's husband, her mother, and her aunt on the bride's side of the aisle, while Helene would be alone on the groom's side. Well, there would be no aisle, she reminded herself as she paid for the flowers. But there were always sides. There were sides, and people took them.

By the time they left the shop, it was two-thirty and the sun was hidden behind thick clouds. Evelyn knew the weather wouldn't hold. She wanted to get back to the house and not just because of all the work she had to do. She wanted to be in her home, where she knew what was what. She would make egg salad and sprinkle paprika on top. She'd cut the beets and the onions, carrots, and cabbage and, while the soup simmered, she'd go upstairs to her bedroom, close the door, and lie down. She would make sure to tell the girls not to bother her. Helene would have to fend for herself. The woman was a disturbance. Evelyn needed to be undisturbed.

While Evelyn drove, Helene held the vase with the bouquet in her lap. The car filled with the sharp, medicinal smell of the eucalyptus, which reminded Evelyn of the menthol rubs she used to massage into her girls' chests when they were stuffed up and achy with fever. Those smooth, narrow chests. Ruth had been so skinny that Evelyn could practically spread her hand and reach from one side of the girl's rib cage to the other. Ruth wouldn't remember getting those massages. The past was the past. And a Vicks rub didn't guarantee affection. It hadn't been true what Evelyn said back at Sonya's shop. She and Ruth had never talked about giving Helene the job of the bouquet. They'd never talked about the bouquet at all. Ruth had made that decision on her own. She'd always been self-sufficient. She'd slipped out of Evelyn's fingers as soon as she could walk and talk. She seemed to have no use for her mother beyond food and other basic needs. Ruth used to wait for her father to get home from work to announce a good grade on a test or the fact that, once again, she'd been voted the best reader in her elementary school class. There were times when Evelyn thought that her oldest daughter didn't take her into account at all.

But it was fine. Evelyn wasn't upset. Not a bit. Dealing with the bouquet would have been one more thing to add to the list, and frankly, when Evelyn tried to imagine Ruth asking her to pick it out with her—well, it was a little much. Like something out of a bad movie. No, that's not the way she raised her girls. You get yourself involved with all that sappy mumbo jumbo and that's when the plumber thinks he can pull a fast one and charge you double. No. You keep your head on straight.

Something struck the hood of the car. She thought that the wheels had kicked up a rock and she worried about a dent. But then hail started falling thick and fast. It was impossible to see clearly through the windshield. The light turned green, but the car in front didn't move. Traffic stopped in all directions. No one honked a horn. Everyone knew that it would be only a matter of minutes before the hail stopped and the day would proceed as if nothing had happened. But in the meantime, the noise and the way all the light had gone out of the sky made the car feel cut off from the world. Evelyn glanced at Helene, wondering if she would have something to say about the storm, but the woman looked deflated. She'd loosened her grip on the vase, and the waterline sloped dangerously toward the rim. Evelyn started to say something to warn her, but she didn't. There was no point to it, really. There was no point to any of it. Ruth was getting married. And a bunch of flowers, or whether the egg salad had a kick of paprika in it, were no guarantee of anything.

They had both lied. Helene, about the circumstances of her husband's death. Evelyn, about the bouquet. And what did it matter? They had done their jobs. They had delivered two people into the world who met because of an accident of time and place. The wedding was the next day. The day after that, Helene would go back to Ohio, and she and Evelyn would not be necessary to one another again.

TWO

HUNGER

Omaha, Nebraska, 1937–1940

When she was fourteen years old, Evelyn Margolis stood in her backyard and waited for a boy to shoot an apple off her head. The rifle fired, the apple fell, and for a moment, Evelyn wasn't sure if she was dead or alive. It was as if God had plucked her out of time, dangled her while he considered his options, then dropped her back in place. She was excited, not by her survival but by the thrill of that moment when she might or might not have existed at all.

It turned out that the boy, Anders Karlsson, from the next farm over, had missed. It was only that Evelyn had startled at the noise of the shot, and the apple rolled off her head. The bullet was probably buried in the small field beyond the yard where her father tried and, in those droughty years, mostly failed to coax cabbage and turnips from the dirt.

The back door of Evelyn's house flew open and Anders took

off running as her mother crossed the yard in what seemed like one giant bound, her heavy breasts riding beneath a loose housedress.

"*Who are you?*" Ida screamed in a spray of spit, grabbing Evelyn by the shoulders. "*Who Are You?*"

Later that night, Evelyn lay in bed in the room she shared with her younger sister, Sonya. Sonya slept easily, her belly full of the stew Evelyn hadn't been allowed to eat, having been sent to her bedroom without dinner. She was starving, but this was nothing new. Her growth spurt coincided with years of chipped beef on toast, mashed potatoes on toast, cabbage soup, and cabbage pie. She was hungry all the time. At school, she barely listened to her teachers and thought, instead, about what she could eat next and when she could eat it. The only class she paid attention to was math because she understood numbers and how to work them. Algebra equations were nothing to her, and she was always first with her hand in the air to give her answer. Still, her teacher only called on the boys. When she complained, he told her that it didn't make sense for him to give her the opportunity.

"There's no future for a know-it-all like you," he said.

After that, a feeling of unrelieved want settled into Evelyn's character, a hollow desire that was only momentarily satisfied by pinching a Big Hunk from the counter at the market or by letting a boy aim a rifle at her head.

As she waited for sleep, she thought about how unfair it was that her mother hadn't gone after Anders Karlsson. *Who are you?* she might have shrieked at him. *An idiot? A murderer? A Jew hater?* Because there were plenty of those around. When Sonya and Evelyn walked to school in the mornings, a gang of kids pitched pennies at their feet. But her mother hadn't said anything to Anders. She hadn't even made Evelyn's father demand an apology from Mr. Karlsson. By that time, Ida had given up on Maurice Margolis as any kind of useful husband.

Who are you?

Evelyn had the feeling that her answer to that question, and not the lousy aim of a boy pretending to be William Tell, would make the difference in how her life turned out.

She lived on the small truck farm her grandfather had planted on the eastern outskirts of Omaha. The successful enterprise was ruined by the Crash and the parched years that followed. Many farmers in the same position as Maurice gave up and moved their families closer to the city, taking work in factories and mills. Evelyn's teachers would call the roll each morning and one week Anna Nillson wouldn't answer back. The next week it would be Davey Russo. Empty desks remained empty; people had lost faith in the farming way of life. Still, Maurice refused to leave. He said that if God let something bad happen, he would eventually balance it out with something good.

"You and your Almighty," Ida would grumble. Her faith was a conditional thing. She invoked God when she thought he would be useful, cursed him when he wasn't. In moments of real fear, when Sonya or Evelyn fell ill, or when her change purse was empty, she'd become strict, lighting the candles on Friday nights, or not eating on Yom Kippur, as if she could pull a fast one on God with a furious display of devotion.

When they were not bickering about the futility of the farm, Evelyn's parents avoided one another. Her father inspected the dry field or puttered with equipment in his shed while her mother did battle with the dust that slipped in beneath the window sashes, or sat at her sewing machine, patching rips, taking out waistlines, and lowering hems to make the family's clothing last. But in Evelyn's opinion, her mother's real preoccupation was the management of her daughters. Sonya was a good-natured, obedient girl who did what her mother told her. Evelyn, with her restless hunger for food, for change, for some jolt that would make her feel her life, became the focus of Ida's criticism. *Don't shout, I'm not deaf! Speak up, I can't read lips. This, you call clean?* When she could escape her mother's rage, Evelyn joined her father in the field, taking comfort in his calm resignation. But when he crouched down to lay his hand on the dry earth and she saw his lips move in prayer, she felt ashamed.

By the time Evelyn was sixteen, Ida decided she'd had enough.

"We're moving to the city," she announced one night at dinner. She'd already found a job. "You got a Singer, they give you work," she said with a shrug, but Evelyn could tell she was proud. She'd been hired to tailor men's suits and shirting at a haberdashery in the Near North Side of Omaha. "And I already got the rent money, so you don't have to worry about that," she said. She'd written to her sister in Kansas City, who'd married a mortician whose work didn't rely on the markets or the weather. Evelyn was astonished by her mother's cunning. All the while she was daydreaming about stolen chocolate bars and trying to find ways to feed the other kind of emptiness she felt, her mother had secretly rearranged her future.

"There's nothing for you here," Ida said to Maurice, which was her way of inviting him to join them. When he shook his head, something softened in her expression. "Your faith will kill you," she said.

Two weeks later, Ida, Evelyn, and Sonya were set up in a two-room apartment in the city furnished with a couch, a bed, and a dresser whose drawers smelled like other people. Ida slept in the bedroom. The girls slept in the apartment's main room, one on the couch, the other on its cushions arranged on the floor of the kitchen that was just half a refrigerator, a sink, and a stove set against one wall. The apartment wasn't big enough for a table, so the three ate their dinners on the couch, holding plates on their laps. They shared a bathroom at the end of the landing with the other tenants on the floor. The walls of the apartment were thin, and Evelyn could hear the toilet flushing, the neighbors yelling, and the buses, cars, and trucks that rumbled down the street below. Her mother complained about the noise, but Evelyn was amazed that the lives of strangers were taking place mere feet from her own.

Ida was energized by the change, by her job, and most of all by her weekly paycheck—the first money she'd ever earned in her own right. She became fluent in the language of her new world. At night, she'd tell Evelyn and Sonya about floating chest pieces, lashed hems, and undercollar melton. Evelyn had the feeling that her mother was determined never to say the words *fertilizer* or *irrigation ditch* ever again. Ida happily complained about her coworkers' sloppiness, or how much time Mr. Abromowitz in 3R took in the bathroom each morning, just as she had complained about the endless dirt in the farmhouse, or her stubborn husband. Evelyn knew that pointing out the failings of others magnified her mother's sense of worth. Ida warned her daughters about the dangers of traffic, about pickpocketers, and about single men who loitered on sidewalks and who were *up to no good, and don't make me spell it out.* Evelyn and Sonya were allowed only to run short errands to the corner market and to ride the bus to their new school.

Central High was enormous, a city of teenagers who behaved with an assurance that made them seem like they knew more than Evelyn did, not just about history or chemistry, but also about how the unspoken world worked. The way they moved down the halls in their bright saddle shoes or slid into their desk chairs seemed sophisticated, and Evelyn felt that everything about her, from her home-sewn dresses to her tired-out clodhoppers, marked her as the hayseed she was. She was mostly alone for the first month, but then she made a friend—a plush and laughing girl named Lena, who walked beside her during the passing periods and filled her in on the hierarchy of girls and the boys with one-track minds who sat next to Evelyn in English class and passed her notes about the things Romeo wanted to do to Juliet while their teacher read passages from the play out loud.

On the first Sunday of every month, Evelyn, Sonya, and Ida took two buses out to the farm to visit Maurice. In order to survive, he was slowly selling off parcels of the land at rock-bottom prices. The buyers were not farmers, he admitted, but real estate speculators who were planning to let the land go to seed while they waited for the city to spread eastward. He'd held on to a quarter of an acre to farm, he said proudly, but Ida was unimpressed. During these visits, she cooked pots of soups and stews so that he would have something to eat and cleaned the house, all the time narrating her efforts with her customary put-upon sighs. While she worked, Evelyn and Sonya sat with their father, telling him about their life in town. He responded with astonishment, as if they were telling him stories of exotic travels. Evelyn, in turn, let him know what a relief it was to spend the day on the farm, how Omaha was filled with the smells of rotting garbage, and how hobos relieved themselves against the sides of buildings.

"All the time!" she said. "Right in front of the world and everybody!" She knew her exaggeration was an apology and she wondered if his wide-eyed reactions were his.

When she was back in the city, crammed into the two small rooms with her sister and her perpetually fussing mother, Evelyn was gripped by a familiar hunger. She'd finally stopped growing, and her body was filling out. Her nipples ached. When she walked down the halls at school, the tops of her thighs rubbed against one another, creating a feverish sense of readiness. Her clothes hugged her in complicated and insinuating ways.

"I can't even raise my hand in class," she complained to her mother one morning, lifting her arm to show how the front of her dress gaped at her chest and her belly, revealing her anemic-looking slip.

"Stop eating so much," Ida said. "Suck in your gut."

The truth was that Evelyn barely ate at school. Lena had taught her how to smoke and at lunchtime, they'd share a cigarette in the girls' bathroom, inhaling greedily. Evelyn babysat for a family on the second floor of the apartment building, and she saved up enough to buy a pack of Lucky Strikes. At night, when her mother shut herself into the bedroom, Evelyn slipped outside the apartment, went down to the sidewalk, and smoked. She loved the way smoking marked time in a personal way. The rate at which her cigarette burned was a sign of her impatience or her ease, or even her desire for things she couldn't name. The sidewalks were mostly empty at night, but when cars passed and their headlights swept over her, she felt exposed in a way that was exciting and dangerous.

When Evelyn came home one afternoon with safety pins holding the front of her dress together where the buttons had popped off, Ida got her tape measure and told Evelyn to hold out her arms. Evelyn was disappointed that her mother's solution was to sew her another dowdy-looking dress from leftover men's shirting fabric she took from the garbage at work.

"No one dresses like this," Evelyn complained.

"You better believe they don't," Ida said. "They'd be lucky to have a professional like me sew their clothes."

"But professionals do make their dresses, Ma! They get them at the department store."

"You know what this department store is? They take the same clothes I make, the same clothes somebody else makes, they put them in their big window and charge double!"

The argument went on for days, until Evelyn brought home a newspaper advertisement for a seventy percent markdown at Brandeis's. The picture showed a model with a dress that was on sale for four dollars and ninety-nine cents. "Your time is worth more than the cost of this dress," she said, and then proved it, showing her mother a piece of paper where she'd done a calculation. Flattered by the recognition of her value, Ida gave in.

The following Saturday, the three of them took the bus to South Sixteenth Street, where the J. L. Brandeis & Sons building took up nearly an entire block. Its stone face was layered with designs that changed floor by floor, a flamboyance that delighted Sonya and Evelyn, but darkened their mother's mood. None of them had ever been inside a department store, and once they walked through the heavy doors, Ida grabbed Sonya's hand and warned Evelyn to keep up, as if she were leading her daughters through a dangerous neighborhood rather than the elegant displays that filled the lobby floor. Evelyn hung back, dazzled by the sharply dressed women who tried on scarves and jewelry and lipsticks. She could tell that serious business was taking place, and that the choice of a hat signaled something far more important than pleasure or even beauty. The women who posed in mirrors with their cheeks sucked in and lips pursed were making important decisions about who they wanted to be.

She caught up with her mother and sister just as they were heading toward a stairwell. "Ma, there's an elevator," Evelyn said.

"What, you're too fancy for stairs now?" Ida said, and pushed through the door. Her breathing grew labored as she climbed and she let out irritated grunts, letting Evelyn know just how much effort she had to expend to satisfy her foolish daughter. Evelyn kept her mouth shut. A dress hung in the balance. Once they reached the fourth floor, Ida marched them through Ladies' Dresses to the sales rack in the back. She picked through the options quickly, scoffing at prices, quibbling with the quality of seams, handling the garments like pieces of raw meat she was inspecting for gristle and bone. Any dress that Evelyn and Sonya admired, their mother dismissed. Finally, she pulled a dress off its hanger and held it out. "Put this on," she said.

"Where?" Evelyn said, but then understood. "Right here?"

"Where else?"

"But, Mama, people will see," Sonya whispered, looking behind her at the women who were shopping the full-price racks.

"People will see there's not much to look at," Ida said.

Miserably, Evelyn turned toward the wall and slipped off her blouse. She drew the dress over her head, then reached underneath and stepped out of her skirt. The dress was a terrible shade of dishwater. The bodice was covered by ruching that hid the shape of her chest. The only appeal was a thin green belt that clasped at the front with a small metal fitting. Ida zipped up the dress, then turned Evelyn around to face her. With no mirror, Evelyn could judge the poor effect only from Sonya's expression.

"It won't fall apart tomorrow," her mother said.

"It's gray," Evelyn said miserably.

"Gray is good. No one notices a gray dress. You can wear it every day."

Evelyn groaned. Her mother gave her a murderous look. Once Evelyn had changed back into her blouse and skirt, she and Sonya followed Ida to the register where she handed the dress to the salesclerk as if it were a clump of dirty laundry.

"It's a lovely dress," the clerk said as she shook it out and laid it on the counter.

"If it was lovely, somebody would have bought it full price," Ida said, handing over her money.

"Oh, you never know," the woman said, winking conspiratorially. "Even bargain shoppers can find treasures."

"I paid you already. You don't need to give me the bunk." Ida took the shopping bag and her change.

Mortified, Evelyn followed behind her mother and sister as they headed toward the stairs. Just as they passed the elevator, a bell sounded, and the door slid open. Three well-dressed women stood inside, holding their shopping bags.

"Going down," the elevator operator said.

Ida hesitated. Her eyes darted back and forth as if she were trapped.

"Madam, in or out?" the operator said.

"What are you girls waiting for?" Ida said, pushing Evelyn and Sonya ahead of her into the elevator. "They'd die if I didn't tell them to take a breath," she announced to the assembled women. The doors closed. As they descended, Evelyn watched her mother's gaze flit between the dial above the door, where an arrow slowly marked the passing floors, and the white-gloved hand of the operator manning the control. Suddenly, Evelyn understood why her mother had been so determined to huff and puff her way up the stairs. And just as quickly, it dawned on her that her life had been built on a great misunderstanding. She'd allowed her mother to define the terms of her existence, but Ida Margolis, for all her bitter certainty that she understood the world better than everyone else, was terrified of an elevator.

The following week, Evelyn returned home at the end of the day with the news that she'd found a job. An elderly widow who lived in one of the big houses on West Farnam had posted an advertisement on a bulletin board at school.

"I did the interview right there in the vice principal's office. On the telephone," she said.

"A job to do what?" Ida said.

"Whatever she tells me to do. I'm her assistant."

"What do you know from assistant?"

"I have to go to her house once a week," Evelyn said, ignoring her mother. "On Saturdays."

"How about you assist me on Saturdays instead?"

"How about you pay me?" Evelyn said.

"Don't be smart."

"I am smart. That's why Mrs. Brandeis hired me."

Evelyn watched her mother's expression as she worked her way from recognition to disbelief.

"Like the department store," Ida said finally.

"The same as the department store," Evelyn said.

For once, her mother was speechless.

The job changed everything. Evelyn would arrive home at the end of a Saturday, and her mother and Sonya would be waiting to hear about the events of her day. Evelyn described Mrs. Brandeis's house, its dark, paneled library, its elaborate carpets, its chandeliers, and its quiet.

"I've never been anywhere so peaceful in my life," she said, her statement helped out by the grinding flush of the toilet down the hall. She told her mother and sister about the dumbwaiter, which brought Mrs. Brandeis's tea from the basement kitchen to the first floor, about the powder room with its fancy mirror etched with the image of a swan. There was a conservatory with a glass dome, she said, where plants and flowers grew year-round. Her mother blew out her lips at these luxuries, but she was riveted. As the weeks passed, Ida began to speak to Evelyn differently. She asked her opinion about choices that needed to be made. Did Evelyn think they should treat themselves to *Gone with the Wind*? Did she think the weather would hold out for a picnic in Hanscom Park? The shift in the household dynamic gave Evelyn the queasy pleasure she'd once felt stealing a candy bar.

Because what she knew, but what her normally suspicious mother had failed to comprehend, was that Mrs. Brandeis did not exist. Or if she did, if there was such a lady who lived in a fine home somewhere in the city, the daughter or granddaughter of whoever it was that built the famous store, that woman had not hired Evelyn to do anything. Not filling out name cards for her dinner parties, not helping her place orders for silk stockings, not writing thank-you notes to the many people who sent her birthday gifts. Mrs. Brandeis was Evelyn's invention, the details of her life culled from the magazines Evelyn and Lena read at the newsstand where they bought their cigarettes. Mrs. Brandeis was the solution to both the problem of her mother's control and her own restlessness.

Sonya, whose desire to please masked a strategic mind, was a trustworthy co-conspirator. At the beginning of the deception, Evelyn worried about the risk of using the Brandeis name, one their mother could look up in the phone book if she ever became skeptical. Sonya argued that recognizability made the lie believable. And there was something else Evelyn banked on, too. The incident in the elevator had taught her that her mother's disdain for excess masked her sense of inferiority. If she suspected something, she'd never have the nerve to contact a person like Mrs. Brandeis, even if it meant catching her daughter in a lie.

"And how was Mrs. Brandeis today?" her mother asked each Saturday night, eager for news.

"I cleaned her diamonds," Evelyn said one week.

"Soap and water?" her mother asked.

"Dish detergent," Evelyn answered, having read about the method in *Woman's Day*.

"Mrs. Brandeis's intestines are giving her a bad time," she reported after another day of "work."

"Oh no," her mother said worriedly. "She should try bicarbonate."

"I'll tell her."

Her mother nodded, pleased to know that her expertise might become important to this great woman's health.

On the subject of money, Evelyn hedged. Mrs. Brandeis hadn't paid her yet, she told her mother, after she'd worked a month of Saturdays, but she promised that she would.

Her mother flew into a rage. "If she doesn't pay you, then she thinks you're nothing. Worse than nothing. You don't go there one more time unless she gives you what she owes."

Sonya came up with the solution: Evelyn started a small business at school doing math homework for bad or lazy students. Having observed her classmates stumble through theorems and proofs, she would make just enough mistakes so that the teacher never caught on. Two Saturdays later, when she returned home at the end of the day, she showed her mother the two ten-dollar bills Mrs. Brandeis had given her. She expected her mother to take the money; she'd made it clear that the minute Evelyn graduated, she had to get a job and pay for her keep. But instead, Ida told her to find a safe place to hide her earnings. She watched approvingly as Evelyn taped the bills to the underside of the couch.

"Now you're somebody," Ida said.

At first, Evelyn would leave the house on Saturday mornings with great anticipation, knowing that she had an entire day to herself. She spent hours exploring the city. She rode the streetcar down Harney, wondering what secrets lay behind the stony expressions of the other passengers. She'd get off on a whim, then linger in front of shop windows, as captivated by her reflection as she was by what was on offer.

If the day was fine, she'd buy a bottle of Nehi, find a bench, then drink, and smoke, and watch the passing parade of cars and people. In bad weather, she'd sit in the public library for hours, reading magazines, sometimes falling asleep in one of the soft leather chairs. She might go to Henshaw's and nurse a cup of coffee, mixing in the free creamer and sugar so that it tasted almost like a milkshake. She would pretend to read the cafeteria menu or a newspaper someone had left behind, but mostly she studied other people. A woman sitting alone stared at her hands on the table so intently that she seemed to be wondering at something they'd done—a mad embrace? Evelyn wondered. A murder? An old man and woman sat across from one another and shared a piece of pie while they talked. There was nothing remarkable about them except for the fact that they were having a conversation. She'd never seen her parents talk just for the sake of it.

On an unexpectedly cold and wet April day, she passed the Hotel Fontenelle. She was poorly dressed for the weather in a lightweight jacket and, imagining the warmth inside, she slowed down in front of the entrance. The doorman opened the door for her, stood aside, and put his hand to the brim of his cap in greeting. And suddenly, she was standing in the double-height atrium, with its squared-off marble columns and its dark carpet. A seventeen-year-old girl named Evelyn Margolis might reasonably visit the library to check out a book for a school project, or stop at a cafeteria for a warm drink, but there was no reason for her ever to set foot in a fine hotel. She waited for someone to kick her out, but no one did. Not the bellhop, or the man at the front desk, or the maid who was emptying ashtrays. She had the strange feeling that she might not be Evelyn Margolis at all. She could be someone else, an invention no less possible than old Mrs. Brandeis herself. She could be the young woman who was now slipping off her jacket and who was now taking a seat in a finely upholstered wingback chair. She could be the young woman crossing her legs so that one fell alluringly against the other like the models in fashion magazines, the young woman who held her chin thoughtfully in her palm and tilted her head just so, as if she were thinking about her plans for the night ahead, or an important book she'd read, or nothing at all. People left the hotel, the men carrying briefcases, the women, alligator purses. People entered, carrying suitcases and shopping bags. This was a place of comings and goings. A thrilling place of constant change.

"Is this seat taken?"

A man stood near the matching chair that was set at an angle to hers. He was stocky, but he wore a suit in a style and fit her mother would not have been able to criticize. The jacket was broad at the shoulders. The wool tapered at the waist, then draped over his hips. He wore a tweed tie, a *cravat*—that was the word Mrs. Brandeis would have used, and it was a word that whoever Evelyn was right now would use, too.

"Or maybe I've got it wrong and you're waiting for a friend," the man said.

"I don't have a friend," Evelyn said, which sounded a little pathetic. She thought of Lena and wished she were there with her. Lena would surely whisper some sly mockery in Evelyn's ear as the man hitched up his trousers, creating a pouch of cloth at his crotch, and took a seat.

"I'm down from Bismarck," he said.

She nodded. She didn't know what Bismarck was.

"And you? Where abouts are you from?"

"Shangri-la," she said.

"Ah," he said, seeming to understand something.

She thought maybe she was in trouble now, and that her dumb joke had given her away. She started to gather up her jacket.

"Now look at me chasing you away when you have as much right to sit here as I do. How 'bout I buy you a drink to make up for it. Something hot to take the chill off. A toddy. I bet you wouldn't say no to a good hot toddy."

Evelyn would say she'd never had a hot toddy. Evelyn would leave, go out into the cold, and wander around until it was time for her to go home. Evelyn would make up more stories about Mrs. Brandeis to satisfy her mother's sad curiosity. And then Evelyn would lie awake that night, restless and unsatisfied. But here, she was not Evelyn, was she? She was a young woman talking to a man in a handsome suit. She was someone he found interesting enough to invite for a drink. She had never had a drink in her life, but today she could be a person who said:

"Why, yes. A hot toddy sounds like just the thing."

As they stood, the man held out his hand and introduced himself. "Howard Mahoney. From Bismarck." He repeated the word as if they were starting all over again with new rules. His cool, thick hand shaking hers, his other hand tipping his hat the slightest amount, just as the doorman had. She'd entered this place, and a series of secret codes were taking her farther inside, down a hall, through a door.

And now they were sitting at a small table in the bar. She warmed her hands around a glass mug filled with an amber-colored liquid that was garnished with a cinnamon stick and a lemon slice. The man had ordered a drink that came in a V-shaped glass. He held the long, narrow stem with surprising delicacy, his stubby little finger extended. He'd taken off his hat and balanced it on his knee. His wavy blond hair swooped up from his forehead and peaked like icing. His skin was freckled, his eyes bright blue.

"I don't even know your name," he said.

"Juliet," she said.

"I guess that makes me Romeo," he said, winking.

The wink made her wonder if he knew she was lying. But he didn't seem to care, and so she didn't care, either. Juliet didn't care. She took another sip of her drink. Juliet did. She began to feel relaxed, and her thoughts loosened. The drink tasted lightly of honey, and she drank it quickly. Howard caught the attention of the bartender, and moments later she was sipping the second drink of her lifetime. She felt lightheaded but not in the way she did when she smoked. The feeling was not one of privacy but of a kind of overwhelming connectedness, as if she were filling in a picture of herself, but her pen bled over the edges, and she was spilling into the world around her, the people at the bar, this man across the table. Everyone in the hotel, on the street. All of Omaha.

"How about something to eat," Howard said a little later. She didn't know how much later.

"What a marvelous idea," she said, sounding like the actress in the movie she and Lena had sneaked into at the Ritz Theater. The name of the actress floated toward her, and she reached out and grabbed it. Rosalind Russell. She was Rosalind Russell now. How easy it was to turn into someone else!

40

And then it was later still, and she was taking the last bite of a club sandwich, and Howard was saying, "Boy, you were hungry," and she was saying, "I'm always hungry." And then they were in the elevator, and she was leaning against him, her head on his shoulder, his arm around her waist. And as the elevator operator closed the door and pushed the control handle to the right, she thought, *I'm not scared of elevators.* And when the elevator doors opened, she followed Howard Mahoney down the hall to his room and waited while he unlocked the door. It was the neatest room she'd ever seen. The bed was made up without a wrinkle. The nap of the carpet was as smooth as fur. Just like at Mrs. Brandeis's house. She laughed.

"I sure love that laugh," Howard said.

And when he unzipped her gray dress, she thought, *Yes,* and when he reached under her slip and his fingers moved inside the elastic of her underwear and she felt the warmth of his hand cupping her, she said, "Yes."

By the time she arrived home, she'd thrown up twice. The first time was when Howard Mahoney saw the blood on the sheet. "A virgin hooker," he said with disgust. "If you think I'm paying for that, you've got another think coming." She started to heave, just making it to the bathroom in time. When she came out, he was dressed in his trousers and his undershirt. She found her clothes on the floor, turned away from him, and dressed quickly. She couldn't do up the zipper all the way, and her hands were shaking so much she couldn't buckle the little green belt. He looked at her and shook his head.

"Jesus," he said. "Even my mother wouldn't wear that dress."

Outside the hotel, she was so confused that when the door-man opened the door of a taxi that was idling at the curb, she got inside and gave the driver her address. As the car pulled onto the street, she threw up again. The driver yelled at her. She cried and apologized. She took off her jacket and used it to try to clean up her vomit, but the driver said she was just going to make it worse. He pulled to the curb and told her to get out. Freezing cold, she walked the rest of the way home. She was no longer drunk. She felt like a vacuum had sucked out her insides, and that the slightest wind coming from a passing bus might knock her down. When she finally reached her building, she cupped her hand over her mouth, exhaled, and smelled her rank breath. More vomit than alcohol, at least.

The story she told her mother: She'd come down with a stomach bug while at work. Mrs. Brandeis had put her to bed in one of her luxurious guest rooms. When Evelyn started to feel better, Mrs. Brandeis had her driven home by the chauffeur. She'd thrown up in the car. "I tried to clean it up," she said, holding out her jacket.

"Oy vey," Ida said, wrinkling her nose. "You better boil it to get the smell out."

The following Saturday, Evelyn told her mother that she felt queasy.

"You got the Kotex?" Ida said.

"It's not that. I just feel funny is all. I don't think I should go to work today."

Ida put the back of her hand on Evelyn's forehead. "You're fine," she said.

"I'm tired."

"Tired nothing," Ida said, pushing Evelyn toward the door. "If I don't go to work when I'm tired, you'll be sleeping on the street before you know it."

The sun was out. The cold snap of the previous week had given way to a mild temperature. Still, Evelyn knew she couldn't spend the day walking. There would be no pleasure in the solitude, no sense of freedom in deciding to go one place and not another. And what if she saw that man again? Probably he was back where he came from, that city that sounded like a bee sting, a word she didn't even want to say to herself because it reminded her of everything that had happened, the sweet sharpness of the drink, the novel taste of bacon in her mouth, the feeling of being turned inside out when he'd pushed himself into her. Instead, she took the two buses out to the farm. She had not seen her father in a while. The bad winter had given her mother an excuse to stop the Sunday visits. Maurice had driven his truck to the city to see them a few times. The four of them ate a meal, Evelyn, Sonya, and their mother sitting on the couch, her father sitting on the wooden chair borrowed from the Abramowitzes down the hall. Afterward, they listened to *Fibber McGee and Molly* on the radio. Her father laughed so hard at the crazy ideas McGee came up with that he became teary. Evelyn didn't remember ever seeing her father give himself over to happiness like that.

When she reached the farm, her father was so frantic with gratitude for her surprise visit that she wished she hadn't come. He hurried around the house, folding a newspaper, clearing a book off a chair and a plate and glass off the kitchen counter. It was as if he were embarrassed by the signs of his life. He offered to make her coffee. She said he didn't have to bother.

"How about I fix us some soup?" he said, opening the freezer, where a few containers of the food Ida had cooked for him months earlier were caked with ice.

"Don't worry about all that, Papa," Evelyn said.

"I don't get many visitors," he said.

By now, he'd sold off the final parcel of land. All that was left was the house and the small yard, where she'd once stood with an apple on her head and her eyes squeezed shut, unable to imagine just how ruinous her desire could be. Her father brought her outside, eager to show her the small garden he'd started. He'd just planted broccoli. When the weather was a little warmer, he'd put in tomatoes and then beans. "It's not much," he said.

"It's nice, Papa."

He explained to her how he nurtured some of his seeds in small containers in the shed, and how, during the last cold spell, he'd covered his plants with his sweaters so that they didn't freeze.

"All my clothes, they were out here," he said, laughing at himself. "A crazy man, your papa."

She looked beyond the yard at the land that used to be his. This year, the rains had come. Even untilled, the earth looked rich. If her father had been able to hold on to the farm, his God would have rewarded his faith.

When it was time for her to leave, he walked her to the door. She wanted to say that she missed him. She wanted to say that she wished that she and Sonya and their mother had never left, and that everything was still the way it was. But she didn't know if that would make him happy. And despite everything that had happened, she didn't know if it was true.

44

The following Saturday, she left for her job but returned home an hour later.

"I have bad news," she told her mother and sister. "Mrs. Brandeis died."

Her mother's hand flew to her mouth. "When? How?" she asked.

"Yesterday. She had a heart attack," Evelyn said.

Sonya looked down at her shoes, and Evelyn wondered if she'd gone too far. She could simply have said that Mrs. Brandeis didn't have work for her anymore, or that she had broken a piece of fine china and had been fired—her mother would have believed that. But she needed to end things once and for all.

Ida sat down on the couch. "That poor woman," she said quietly.

Suddenly, Evelyn began to cry. Huge, ugly, heaving sobs.

"Come here," Ida said, pulling Evelyn onto her lap. Evelyn put her arms around her mother's broad back and pressed her face against her soft shoulder, letting her tears and snot fall.

"It's some life," her mother said. "No matter who you are, it's some life."

On Monday, Ida came home from work with a yahrzeit candle. Evelyn and Sonya watched as she fit it inside a drinking glass, lit it with a match, and cupped the glass in her hands.

"*Neir Adonai*," she said, but then stopped. "That's all I remember. My *tata* did the whole thing every year for my mother. The candle. The prayer. Every year since I'm seven years old until the day he died."

Evelyn stared at the small white flame and thought about her father. He didn't seem sad, or even diminished. In fact, as she'd watched him crouch down over his garden, pulling up weeds and packing loose dirt, he'd seemed even more himself, as if his losses had chiseled him into a truer shape. Her mother had chosen to turn her back on the farm and her husband and the humbling of failure. Evelyn had despised her for that. But her mother had been carved out by loss, too.

For a long time afterward, Evelyn felt as if she were grieving. For whom or what, she wasn't sure. Mornings, she woke on the couch or the floor and after a moment of forgetfulness a heaviness settled in. She went to classes, but she had no interest in them, even in math. She enrolled in a typing class. She applied for and got a secretarial job at a lumber company on North Twenty-Fourth Street. She'd start in July.

On graduation day, the principal announced the senior prizes. The math prize went to a boy whose homework Evelyn had done a few times. That was easy money. He was good at math, but lazy. All it took for her forgery to pass the teacher's notice was to get all the problems right. She was awarded a certificate for being the fastest typist in the class. When it was time to receive her diploma, she stood up from her seat, climbed the steps to the stage, and shook the principal's hand. Then she went back down the steps, sat next to Lena, and waited for the ceremony to end. She looked at the certificate. She was Evelyn Margolis. It said so right on the diploma, written in fancy script. She wondered how much more she would need to lose before she knew who that person was.

THREE

THIS IRINA

Wheeling, West Virginia, 1938; Cleveland, Ohio, 1969

The middle of the three Harker children, Helene was a relativity. She was less rare than beautiful Louisa and more reliable than impulsive, but adored, Victor. Suddenly finding herself an only child at age twenty-five did not lay these comparisons to rest. She would always be less lovely and more predictable than ghosts.

Louisa sliced her finger when she was cutting a rose. By the time the flower opened, sepsis had traveled through her bloodstream, and she was gone. A year later, Victor fell off the roof of their father's cotton mill. At eighteen, he was a charming rascal who armed himself against his preordained future running the mill with alcohol and imprudence. But there was no bottle on the rooftop, and there were no glass shards scattered on the ground below. Victor was sober when he died, the doctor said. Still, everyone put the blame on drink, and Helene's parents allowed it. How else to explain a boy whose reckless ebullience came hand in hand with nights of private weeping?

This was in Wheeling, West Virginia, in 1938, when the war was a loudening sound.

Helene's parents emerged from their grief as shallow versions of themselves. Her father pushed the mill to further prosperity, not because of the desire for more success (for who was there to inherit the business now?) but because, like the workings of his spinning machines, his mind was set to productivity. Her mother took up her rounds of afternoon visits, but she did everything without the zeal that had once animated her social ambition. There was no daughter who could benefit from an auspicious marriage now. Helene would stay home to take care of her parents as they aged.

Helene had a bump on her nose, imprecise lips, and an obdurate figure. Sturdy ankles obscured the tendons whose harpstring modulations on more slender young women signaled a physical pliability. Her days fell into the unsurprising rhythms of an old maid's. It was up to her to keep the house alive to the moment. She put up decorations for Hanukkah, Purim, and Sukkoth, and made sure the housekeeper kept the windows clean and the porch swept. She had the furniture reupholstered when the material grew so feeble that it split to reveal cushions as wan as her parents' faces. Trying to imagine a future for herself, she began to study for a teaching certificate. She'd been a good student, and being around children would make up for the fact that she wouldn't have any of her own.

One Saturday afternoon, the dour and stoop-shouldered doctor who had pronounced Victor dead telephoned the house. His German accent was thick, and Helene called her father to the telephone, imagining the *qvistion* this man wanted to *isk* had something to do with an overdue bill. After listening for a minute, her father handed the telephone back to her with a look of surrender. He understood that he and his wife were about to weather their third loss.

Aside from the awkwardness of what connected them, Helene was skeptical about her suitor from the start. Not because he was ten years her senior, or because she was two inches taller and more than a few pounds heavier, or because his grave and formal courtship seemed more like an act of diplomacy than ardor. She was suspicious because he didn't have two names. Her father, born Henryk Horkheimer, had become Henry Harker. The family's tailor, Jack Ayers, had been Jakob Arensdorff. But Dr. Emil Simonauer had only ever been Emil Simonauer. That she had detected a melancholy second thought in his gaze when he asked for her hand—well, who was she to argue with last chances? But the fact that she would be Helene Simonauer and not, say, Helene Simon, made her sense that her marriage, rather than propelling her into a new and optimistic future, would put her at the mercy of a threatening undertow.

Emil had already been offered the position in Cleveland when he proposed. Helene was delighted to boast to her friends that the job was a promotion: her fiancé would be the head of internal medicine at a metropolitan hospital. His stature justified the age difference. She was marrying someone already well established, while the young, admittedly handsome and excitingly brash husbands of her friends were only beginning their climbs. It would not be until later, after she understood the landscape of her new city, that she'd realize that Emil's hospital was in a poor section of town, and that the advancement came with a cut in pay. Her disappointment was offset by the fact of her father's wedding gift: a small house that she would fill with the dowry of beautiful furnishings and linens that had been meant for Louisa.

Helene and Emil had a modest wedding in November and left for Ohio on the same afternoon. Emil's car broke down outside of Canton, and they arrived in Cleveland late and exhausted only to find that the furniture and household items had not yet been delivered. Prudent or cheap—she didn't know her new husband well enough to say—Emil didn't offer to take her to a hotel. Instead, they made a bed on the floor out of clothes they pulled from their suitcases. Her anxious expectation about her wedding night was forestalled. The house was cold. They slept in their coats. They woke the next day to a winter sun that lit up the dust on the floor. Their newness to each other was an embarrassment, and they were polite as they adjusted their clothes and turned away to hide their morning breath. When Helene heard Emil urinating in the bathroom, she understood that marriage would require willful ignorance.

She was relieved when he left for the hospital. She put on her coat and walked down the block, hoping she might run into a neighbor who would invite her into a community of wives. But the few women who were out were apparently not in the habit of greeting one another the way people were in Wheeling, where a trip to the corner could occupy a full hour, and when you returned, you knew the gossip of the day.

The furniture arrived that afternoon, but it was not until weeks later that Emil got up from his twin bed and lay down in hers. Her mother had given her a book full of euphemisms that edged up to but didn't quite land on the facts, but nothing could have prepared Helene for the strangeness of Emil moving on top of her or the shock of his release. He looked as if he were in terrible pain, his eyes squeezed shut, his mouth stretched and frozen. The book talked about "pleasure," which she'd equated to the satisfying twinges she sometimes felt when she put her hand between her legs. But seeing her husband so excruciatingly possessed, she knew that the word had a more troubling connotation.

Afterward, Emil thanked her.

"You're welcome," she said politely.

He went back to his bed and slept.

A missed period later, Helene sat on the toilet in the restroom outside Emil's office and collected her urine. She looked away when she handed him the warm cup, but he didn't seem bothered by the transaction, and when he left her alone in the office to take the sample to the lab so that it could be injected into a mouse or a rat—she'd tried not to listen when he described the process to her—she realized that, to Emil, her pregnancy was a clinical situation. During the next nine months, he monitored her closely. The attention was reassuring, but when he put his stethoscope to her stretched belly or when he gave her a cream for the hemorrhoids she'd been ashamed to admit to, she wished she had a husband who knew nothing about anatomy, one who did not use words that made her shrivel, like *anus* and *discharge*.

After the birth, Emil kept track of her cycle and visited her bed infrequently and only when she was least likely to conceive. "I'm an old man," he said, two years later, when she brought up the possibility of giving little Thomas a sibling. Although Emil was only thirty-eight, he looked much older, and she had to agree. She wondered if he'd ever been young.

Thomas was her joy and her fixation. Other than making decisions regarding his son's health, Emil left the raising of the boy to her. The days were long and filled with worries—had she overheated the formula? Had she underdressed him for the weather? Was he sleeping too much? Too little? She hired a Polish girl from the east side to clean and cook, but Erna, the oldest of six, knew how to care for a baby, too. She had a quiet way of taking charge when Thomas had a tantrum, or when she sensed that Helene needed a break. The two of them laughed at Thomas's manly burps and the silly face he made when he squatted down to make in his diaper. Helene was grateful to have someone to share these things with (although she didn't share how that grimace reminded her of nothing so much as her husband when he relieved himself in another way). When he started to walk, Thomas would hear Emil's car pull up the driveway, wait for the front door of the house to open, then run full tilt toward him. There was always a moment, right before Emil remembered to put down his doctor's bag and catch the boy in his arms, when he looked as if he'd forgotten that he had a family.

When Thomas was in grammar school, he brought home a Mother's Day card he'd made where he'd written, *My mother is the best parents a boy ever had*. Helene felt proud and humiliated by the truth, laid out in Thomas's lopsided scrawl.

She was in her bedroom when the tree went down. It was May 25, 1969: her fifty-sixth birthday. She'd celebrated with a quiet lunch with Emil and Tom, who had driven home for the weekend. He was finally getting his MBA in Columbus after dithering away a few postcollege years doing a tour with the

Peace Corps in Guatemala, then taking art classes at the museum. Emil sat at the head of the table, wearing a suit, even though it was Sunday. He was on call, but the truth was that he'd never been comfortable in casual clothes. Tom had been mortified when his father showed up at one of his high school wrestling matches looking, he complained to Helene, like an undertaker. It was her job to interpret father and son to each other, and she reminded Tom about the comfortable life he had, courtesy of his father's hard work.

"Why do you pretend it's his money?" Tom said.

She'd slapped him across the face.

Although there had been opportunities for Emil to move to hospitals where he could have earned more or even gone into private practice, he was dedicated to his patients and chose to stay. There were occasional pay raises, but he refused them, preferring that the hospital put the money toward improvements. Excess made him uncomfortable. It was all Helene could do to convince him to buy a new suit when his became shiny with age. Tom was right: the money was hers. Once her mother died, her father sold the mill. Soon after, he was gone, too, and his savings went to Helene. She convinced Emil that they needed to move to a bigger home, and she found one on Weybridge Road. There had been some awkwardness at the bank when they took out the mortgage on the house and the loan officer pushed the papers across the table for her to sign. She couldn't help but take the look the man gave Emil as pity. After that, she had all her money signed over to Emil's account and she ceded financial decisions to him. "Ask your father," she'd say whenever Thomas wanted a new baseball bat or a board game he and his friends were excited about. She didn't buy herself a cardigan without first knocking on the door of Emil's study at home, then stepping into the shadowed room, where Emil sat at his desk reading medical journals. Taking a seat opposite him as though she were one of his patients waiting for good news or bad, she discussed the potential purchase in detail, as if he cared that cashmere never lost its fashionable currency. "That sounds fine, dear," he'd say, and she'd leave the room, satisfied that she'd been given permission to spend his money, which was her money in disguise.

To her friends, she referred to Emil as The Doctor to remind them, and herself, of his greater value.

As it turned out, Emil's attire at the birthday lunch was justified: as soon as she had cut into the molded salmon crisscrossed with strings of pimento that Erna had prepared in advance, he was called into the hospital. Helene and Tom ate the meal alone. When they were finished, she brought out the cake she'd bought at the bakery, as she did each year, telling the woman behind the counter what message to write on the icing. This year: *Dear Mother and Wife.* Tom sang heartily, and Helene blew out the candles. Afterward, he left to visit old high school friends, and she went upstairs to rest. She slept deeply and dreamlessly, then woke to the noise of a powerful wind, as if she were in the middle of a sudden and violent squall. She had the unnerving sensation that she didn't know where she was. The room was too bright. Where were the thickly leafed branches that shaded the balcony windows? She got out of bed, opened the French doors, and stepped outside. She tried to make sense of the fact that the white oak in the yard had fallen over. And then she tried to comprehend that the trunk of the tree lay across the crushed roof of Emil's car, and that the unmoving figure inside it was her husband, who had returned at just the wrong moment.

After the funeral and the shiva, Helene encouraged Tom to go back to school. He was unsure, worried about leaving her alone. He watched her constantly, as if he thought she would fall apart at any moment. The truth was that she had no idea what she felt. She'd teared up at the funeral, but only when she watched Tom greet the well-wishers. Her son, so gracious and grown. But she couldn't seem to grasp what it meant that her husband was dead. She imagined she would miss him, but she had no idea in what ways. Would she miss the predictable disappointment of turning over at night to see Emil buttoned up by sleep? Would she miss deciding not to tell him about the many things that had gone on in her day, because what seemed meaningful to her at the time—a nice conversation with the mother of one of Tom's friends, or the pride she felt when she'd been elected to the women's steering committee at the temple— became forlorn in the retelling? There was no important drama to any of it. There were only some things, and then other things, a haphazard collection of moments that added up to a day. Helene's and Emil's lives had run parallel to one another for so long, their connection like the strip of carpet that separated their beds.

Tom's concern was sweet, but it was also a burden. She didn't want to hurt his feelings, but she wanted him to go.

"You know, your father was the one who took care of the bills," she said at breakfast, when he'd been home for a week.

Just as she hoped, something shifted in him. "Just forward them to me at school, Mom," he said with self-assurance. "I'll take care of everything." Later that afternoon, to her relief, he drove back to Columbus.

A few weeks later, she sat at Emil's desk in his study, preparing a packet of bills to send to Tom. This was the first time she'd gone into the room since her husband's death. The shades had always been kept at half-mast, and the room, lined by wooden bookcases and lit by floor lamps, had the imminent quality of twilight. It was she who'd created the sacrosanct aura of the room when Emil had been alive. Tom was never allowed to play in here. When Erna cleaned, she knew not to rearrange the papers on the desk, which, Helene warned, might be research critical to the health of The Doctor's patients. Earlier that week, Helene had phoned the family lawyer and her banker to arrange for Tom to be able to sign checks and so forth, so along with the bills, she was sending him the plush leather checkbook binder, the one she'd bought for Emil in order to create a sense of occasion when he did the work of the family finances. She opened the desk drawer, aware of the sober drag of the runners, which dignified the simple gesture, picked up the binder, and saw that beneath it was hidden—yes, she felt their clandestine nature almost instantly—a small bundle of letters.

They were tied together with red-and-white bakery string. She tried to imagine Emil searching through the kitchen drawers to find what he was after. That room was her province—hers and Erna's—and he would not have known where to look for a teacup much less the collection of ribbons and string that lived in the drawer to the left of the one that held the sharp knives. It was the string, wrapped several times around the letters horizontally and vertically and then knotted, that made her know she was in the presence of something dangerous. For a moment, she thought she should leave the packet where it was, just as she'd left Emil's shirts hanging in his closet and his ties on the rack. But then she went to work loosening the knot.

56

There were four letters. No envelopes, but she guessed that the letters must have been sent to Emil at work. How else to explain why she, who took in the mail each day, had never seen them? She unfolded the first one. The handwriting was unfamiliar, but she recognized the language. She didn't speak or read German, but she'd seen Emil's medical degrees, and there had been a few German books on her parents' shelves in Wheeling, even though they spoke English solely and adamantly. The letter was dated July 26, 1939, eight months after her wedding. She quickly opened the others and saw that they were all signed by someone named Irina. Helene had the unnerving feeling she was being watched. She carefully folded the letters, wrapped the bakery string around them, put them back where she'd found them, and laid the checkbook on top. The unpaid bills could wait. The felt runners were like a finger held to lips. *Shhh*, they warned as she closed the drawer.

During the next few days, she avoided the study. Friends called, offering to visit or inviting her to lunch. She declined and kept herself busy answering condolence notes and arranging for the personal items in Emil's office to be sent to the house. Finally, unable to put the letters out of her mind, she phoned the university, and was put through to the foreign languages department. The secretary there listened to her request, then called out to someone who must have been in the room with her. In a matter of seconds, Helene was talking with a graduate student, who introduced herself and agreed, for a fee, to translate.

"You can just drop the stuff off in the department office," the young woman said unenthusiastically. "I have a cubby."

A cubby! The word brought back Tom's kindergarten, and an overeager teacher who'd written, *Tommy!* on the name tag he had to wear on the first day of school. Helene had let her know that her son could be called Thomas, or Tom, but that The Doctor drew the line there. Helene grew agitated. The idea that she ought to devote a whole morning going to a part of the city she hardly knew, that she'd need to find her way around an unfamiliar campus and probably ask a stranger for directions, that she'd have to wait for the secretary to get off whatever phone call she was on in order to point out this girl's, this Ruth Turner's *cubby*—it all made her angry.

"The work will be done at my home. In Shaker Heights," she added, to let the girl understand the dynamics at play.

"Shaker," Ruth Turner said. "I should charge you double."

"If you can't manage it, perhaps you can give me the name of someone who can," Helene said.

"I'll be there on Saturday. Give me your address."

She was a tall girl, taller than most men, which would make things hard for her in the marriage department, Helene thought, three days later, as she watched Ruth Turner get out of a hideous-looking yellow car. Helene stood in the dining room, peering through a crack in the curtains she'd kept drawn since Emil's death, not to indicate a house of mourning but because she felt exposed by his absence. She didn't like the idea of people being able to see her sitting alone at the table eating her dinner. *There's that woman*, she imagined them saying, *eating all alone again*. Or maybe she was the one saying it; the consequence of widowhood seemed to be an acute self-consciousness. The girl yanked down her black-and-white-striped slacks so the waist hugged her narrow hips. She slung her bag over her shoulder, then took giant strides up the walkway with what Helene now realized were extraordinarily long legs. She'd be better off in flat shoes than in the heeled sandals she was wearing, Helene considered. That slouch was no compensation. She watched the girl reach for the doorbell, but when the familiar triplet chimes sounded, she startled.

"Sorry I'm a little late. I had to borrow a car," the girl said by way of a greeting. Helene was sure this was a rebuke for her having told the girl to come to the house, but she was not about to apologize. Ruth Turner peered past her into the foyer. "Where's the stuff you want me to work on?" she said.

"Letters," Helene said. "As I told you when we spoke on the phone."

"Okay. Letters. Where are they?"

"Are you in a hurry?" Helene said.

"As a matter of fact, yeah. I left somebody in bed. I'd like to get back home before he gets out of it."

As she led the girl inside, Helene congratulated herself on not reacting to the provocation. And where was it written that in order to prove you believed in all this free love nonsense, or whatever the girl was trying to put across with that swath of skin where her pants did not meet her skimpy shirt, you could not bother to compliment someone's home or put your purse on the front hall table like a civilized person?

"This is my husband's study," Helene said, her hand on the doorknob. "He has recently passed."

"Oh, you're sad, then," Ruth said. Her expression registered none of the forms of solicitude Helene had become used to, those beagle-like stares that singled her out and gave her a sense of importance.

"Wait here," Helene said as she opened the study door. She'd planned how this would go. She wanted the girl to be aware of the seriousness of the room and so understand Emil's status. She would do her work, though, at the kitchen table. But the girl followed her right over to Emil's desk. "Oh!" Helene said, holding out her arm as if to bar her from coming any closer, but she was too late. Ruth had pulled out the desk chair and sat down. Helene watched helplessly as the girl reached into her bag and pulled out a spiral-bound notebook.

"Forgot my pen," she said. She pulled open the center drawer and found a pencil. "You ever notice," she said, examining the sharpened tip, "how everyone keeps things in the exact same places? Pens and pencils always in the middle drawer. Loose change always in a bowl by the front door. I mean, I could probably go to a house in Outer Mongolia and know where to find the paper clips."

Helene immediately thought of the glass bowl filled with coins sitting on the front hall table. "I doubt that Mongolians use paper clips," she said.

"This is it?" Ruth held up the packet of letters Helene had earlier placed on Emil's blotter, and before Helene could say anything, Ruth reached into the leather box on the desk that held (of course) a pair of scissors and snipped through the string. She looked up at Helene. "It's gonna take me a few," she said.

Thrown by the girl's boldness, Helene realized she'd been dismissed and left the room. She wasn't sure what to do with herself. She went into the den and straightened the pillows that were already straightened. She went into the dining room and adjusted a chair. Erna came each weekday to cook and clean. William came to rake the leaves in the fall, shovel the driveway and walkway in the winter, and mow in the summer. The window washer came twice a year. The plumber, the electrician—

they all came when something needed to be done. The truth was, she'd arranged things so that the house had little need for her at all, and now with Tom grown, and Emil gone, even less so. She lived mostly between the kitchen, the dining room, and her bedroom. Occasionally, at night, she sat in the den and tuned into *Family Affair*, or *Julia*. She'd never watched shows like these when Emil was alive, but sometimes, lying in bed after watching an episode, she found herself thinking about the characters as if they were real people with problems that worried her.

She contented herself that the girl's estimation of the time it would take to do the job ("a few") was turning into more than that. She climbed the stairs to her bedroom, sat at the foot of her bed, and waited. She didn't know for what. The sound of the study door opening? The girl calling out for her? *Yoo-hoo.* Or, more likely, *Hel-lo-o*, the three sarcastic notes rising and falling with her scorn. What she was not prepared for was that, when she finally got impatient and went downstairs, the girl was gone. She'd left the letters on the desk alongside some pages ripped from her notebook where she'd written her translations in a surprisingly excellent cursive. The chair was pushed in, the pencil placed—Helene checked—back in the drawer. She'd left an invoice, marking down the time it took her to do the work, the total, and an address where Helene could send a check. Helene was disheartened to see that something that had seemed so important was worth only twenty dollars. She went into the dining room, split the curtains, and peered out. The yellow car was gone.

She returned to the study and picked up the translation of the first letter.

July 26, 1939

Dear Sir,

*I am writing to you to ask if you would be so kind
as to send us the papers and boat tickets we need.
   We are very eager to come to America, as you
might imagine!*

Humbly, Irina

Ruth was the only female PhD candidate in Germanic and Slavic
languages, and she knew that the other graduate students despised
her. She hadn't been much liked at college or, for that matter, in
high school. She'd always been the smartest one in class and she
was targeted for any perceived weakness. By seventh grade, she
was five feet eight, a social disfigurement the other girls didn't
hesitate to point out. In high school, it was her flat chest, and the
fact that she must have been easy, for how else to explain the way
boys were drawn to her despite her obvious defects? At Smith,
most of the girls were smart and took themselves seriously. Still,
she was considered standoffish and arrogant. No one understood
that she held herself apart because she was a scholarship student
from Nebraska (the mention of the place caused girls' expressions
to go blank) who didn't have the money to go out to a restaurant
in town or join her roommate, Penny, for a ski weekend in Vermont. Ruth was unfamiliar with the manners of East Coast girls
who mixed cosmos in their dorm rooms and whose fathers had
bought them horses for their sixteenth birthdays, or sailboats,
or both. She had thought it would be a relief to come back to

the Midwest for graduate school, but it turned out that the men in her program mitigated their fear of her academic prowess by commenting on her looks every chance they got.

The problem of having a brain in a body was sometimes exhausting, sometimes thrilling, but always, Ruth thought, as she parked the car in front of Beverly's building, the source of an annoying self-awareness. She not only had to summon the boldness to speak up in class and defend her ideas, but also had to think about what she wore, how she sat, whether she swayed her hips too little or too much. At least there was Beverly, the department secretary, who would roll her eyes when some ass commented on Ruth's lipstick (*Hey, Turner! Can you quote Heidegger with that mouth?*). Beverly always told her when there was a departmental bar crawl Ruth had not been invited to so that she could show up and claim as much time sucking up to her drunk professors as the rest of them. Beverly also alerted Ruth before she posted applications for conferences on the department bulletin board. And it was Beverly who let her borrow her car whenever she needed it. Ruth hid the key in the wheel well and started to walk the six blocks to her apartment.

Helene Simonauer had irritated her from the start. As soon as Ruth pulled up to the house, she saw the movement of the curtains in the bow window and knew she was being watched. People were always amazed by what she took in, but there were people who were seen, and therefore saw little, and others who were barely seen and saw much. Conventionally (and conveniently) beautiful people lost the habit of curiosity early on. From the time they were darling little girls and handsome little boys, they understood their principal role in life was to be admired. Ruth's sister Naomi was that kind of girl. With her genetically surprising blond hair, her rosy complexion, and a fatally agreeable personality, she was, without a doubt, the least inquisitive girl Ruth had ever met. Her new boyfriend, Mitchell, an equally charmed specimen, ferried her around with his hand on the middle of her back as if she were a car that he didn't want to get dinged. Little Paula (oh, how Ruth loved to call her that and watch her youngest sister's face practically blister) was dark haired and sharply pretty with her flashing eyes and her curves, which was probably why Jim Bicks, that surly (but, okay, handsome) fool agreed to marry her right out of high school. But her looks were undermined by the fact that she was always angry. She'd just announced she was planning to go to law school. A good choice: once she got her degree, she could get pissed off at people for a living.

Ruth had a face that was pleasant enough at first or second glance, but whoever bothered to look at her a third time might notice that her left eye opened wider than her right, and that her smile rose higher on one side than the other, which made her seem capable of only a skeptical happiness. Her mother, not normally generous, had handed down high cheekbones to all three daughters, but whereas the sharp planes augmented Naomi's and Paula's beauty by catching light and shadow, Ruth's cheekbones only accentuated her long, narrow face. As a teenager, she'd felt miserable about the way she looked. Her mother was no help, or rather, Ruth didn't ask for her sympathy. What could she expect from a person who could swipe on a perfect coat of lipstick without the help of a mirror, and whose idea of a snack was a stick of gum? Good old Evelyn's self-control made it impossible for Ruth to imagine that she'd be particularly consoling. Once, Ruth admitted to her father that she thought that she wasn't pretty. He'd taken her face in his hands.

"You are a treasure," he said.

Which wasn't what she wanted to hear. But her father's hands on her cheeks and the warmth of his gaze were comforting and, for a time, she let herself believe in his belief.

When Ruth came downstairs each morning, she felt her mother's quick gaze as she judged Ruth's outfit or the state of her complexion. Her criticisms were implicit. A capable if joyless amateur seamstress—she'd learned from her own mother—she was always running up a dress or a skirt for Ruth or her sisters from a Butterick pattern. Whenever Ruth put on a finished outfit, her mother would fold her arms across her chest and tilt her head, as if she were trying to figure out how something so right could look so wrong.

In college, Ruth went to New York City and saw *Jules and Jim*, and she learned the term *jolie laide* as it applied to Jeanne Moreau. She liked the idea that she, too, might be confusingly beautiful and smart and undeniable. Those high school girls had been wrong—she didn't lose her virginity until college. It was high up on the list of things she wanted to accomplish in her freshman year, and she managed it with a boy from Amherst whom she never saw again. She developed a taste for sex. She was good at it. It made her feel powerful. But the minute a boy professed to have feelings, she'd lose her footing, and suddenly her height, her small breasts, and her long face would remind her that she was more Modigliani than Moreau.

Knowing that Helene Simonauer had spied on her did not make Ruth feel like one of those watched people, only like what she was: a financially strapped graduate student in a piece-of-shit borrowed car who had to scrape together money in whatever way she could—babysitting faculty children (including those of the professor she'd left in her bed that morning), tu-toring the older ones who had not inherited their parents' IQs. This translation job had hardly been worth it, but she couldn't afford to be choosy. After she'd taken in the size of the house, she planned to say something about getting reimbursed for the travel time, but then the woman said that thing about her dead husband. And then Ruth read the letters.

She was relieved that Professor Evans (she enjoyed his discom-fort when she called him that) was gone by the time she got back to her place. She wasn't interested in small talk over coffee at the junk-shop desk that doubled as her dining table. She never really knew how to make the transition between the skilled and transac-tional person she was in bed and whatever the men were expecting her to be when she was out of it. Grateful? Besotted? Softened into mush by their ministrations? She just couldn't do it. Anyway, she was too distracted for sex now. That woman had watched her, and then Ruth had translated those letters, and now she had the feeling she was being shadowed by something she couldn't name.

Oct. 14, 1939

Dear Sir,

Thank you for sending the money with your cherished letter. I have taken proof of your generous sponsorship to the immigration office, but they will not issue any more papers for now. Food is growing scarce. Will we ever see each other again?

Irina

"I'm no fool." Helene said this out loud as she reread the translation of the second letter. As if people were congregated in Emil's study with her—her girlhood friends, who'd thrown her a wedding shower while whispering about her less-than-desirable fiancé, or women from the temple who, over the years, had begrudgingly voted her onto committees because of The Doctor's generous checks at fundraisers, which were her generous checks signed by Emil. And somewhere, in the background, was Tom, not adult Tom, but the little, smooth-faced boy who squealed with delight when he heard his father's car coming up the driveway, who was satisfied with a hug, a pat on the head, and the occasional game of toss in the yard. Thinking of Tom, she allowed for other explanations. Emil's parents were both dead by the time he and Helene married, and he had no siblings. But surely he had a distant relative or acquaintance, someone he was not particularly close to, someone who would address him as *sir*.

But she couldn't really convince herself of that story. This Irina was connected to Emil in some other way. Helene knew it. The formality of the salutation was contradicted by the signature. The *I* was written clearly, but the rest of the letters successively flattened until all that signaled the final *a* was a small bump. And there was no last name. *You know who I am*, the signature said. Or rather, and this was worse: *We know each other*.

Emil had been an unsurprising man. For three decades, he woke up, ate a bowl of oatmeal and a soft-boiled egg, then did his setting-up exercises—ten deep knee bends and twenty jumping jacks. Sometimes, he passed gas, which embarrassed her, although he never excused himself. During the years when their life had been occasionally intimate, his efforts were practical, a necessary biological exertion. She had never felt comfortable displaying her pleasure in front of him and so she made certain convincing sounds and movements and kept that part of her life to when she was alone in the bath. Even so, for a few days after they had intercourse, Helene could convince herself that there was a private feeling between them.

She knew women who took pride in their ability to read between the lines. The unusual adjustment of the passenger seat in Milt Goldman's car was all that it took for Marilyn to ask for a divorce, for instance. But there had never been the scent of a strange perfume lingering on Emil's clothing and no one ever hung up when Helene answered the phone. There was nothing surprising about her husband. When a collar frayed, he asked her to replace the shirt with the exact same style. The same was true for his ties, his shoes. She didn't care about expensive clothes and jewelry, but she was determined to appear to be a woman whose husband cared for her material comfort, and so she bought those things for herself, telling her friends that Emil had surprised her with the fat beads of coral or pearl that her jeweler had recommended to offset her ample bust. When one of Emil's patients showed his gratitude by giving him two tickets to see the Indians play, Helene drove her husband and son downtown, took a photograph of the two of them standing in front of the stadium, and then sat in the stands with Tom, while Emil went to work. She had the photo framed and displayed on the wall of his office so that when he consulted with patients, they would know how much greater a man he was for being able to balance a dedicated practice with the responsibilities of family. When she slapped Tom that day, it was not because of his teenage impudence, but because she had been so successful in inventing the stories that defined her life that she'd come to believe in them.

But then, what were these letters?

The phone rang. It was Tom, calling from school.

"I'll mail you the checkbook in a few days," she said. "I've been very busy."

"That's good, Mom," he said. "It's good that you're busy."

"Life marches on," she said.

"I guess," he said. "But do you ever get the feeling that you shouldn't be doing what you're doing? I mean, tonight, I'll probably go out for a beer. Tomorrow I'll go to classes. I don't know. It feels strange."

Sometimes, when he was little, and she lay next to him in his bed reading him a story, or when she sat with him over lunch and patiently listened to him tell a knock-knock joke, she was nearly moved to tears by her luck.

"Well, I can't say that I'll be going to classes or getting a beer," she said.

"Very funny, Mom," he said. "It's just that sometimes I forget that I'm sad. How can you forget a thing like that?"

Will we ever see each other again? In another context, the line would be melodramatic. The sort of thing she'd overhear if she was passing by the kitchen and Erna was watching one of her daytime programs on the small television while she cooked. But there was no melodrama in 1939, was there?

"Mother?"

"Hmm?"

"Are you listening?"

"Yes. Of course."

But she wasn't. She'd started to reread the translation of the third letter.

February 2, 1940

Dear Sir,

I believe we will not last much longer.
*   Please. If you do not think of me, think of the*
child.

Irina

Ruth sat in a carrel at the library, ostensibly working on her thesis, but thinking about her mistake. It had been bothering her for days. It was the kind of error an undergraduate in one of the beginning German classes she taught would make. It's true that she'd rushed through the translations once she realized the scope of the work and how little she'd earn. But that was no explanation for her having written *the* child when it was *our* child. *Unser Kind.* She didn't get things wrong. She couldn't afford to. The men in her department might get away with occasional sloppiness, but her work had to be impeccable.

It wasn't the worst mistake, she reasoned. You could infer mutual possession in combination with the intimacy of the notes. For one thing, despite writing, *Dear Sir,* Irina used the informal "you," although the Simonauer woman wouldn't know that. But how could a person read the phrase *If you do not think of me* without understanding the implication that, in some other circumstance, the man she was writing to, this man who Ruth was certain was the dead husband, might have thought of her a lot.

The Simonauer woman had hovered over her at the desk practically vibrating with impatience and officiousness. Even when she was finally alone, Ruth could hear the woman pacing the house, which reminded her of her mother in the days after her father's funeral. No sooner did Ruth get up from a chair or a couch then her mother would rush over to puff up a cushion or wipe a nonexistent smudge off a side table. Her anxiety was obliterating. Finally, one night at dinner, as her mother started to blot a drop of condensation that had slipped from Naomi's water glass, Ruth reached out and grabbed her wrist.

"Stop it!" she'd said. "Why can't you ever just stop?" And then she was shrieking, and she had no idea what she was saying. The next morning, her mother came up with that insane idea that she should see a psychiatrist. Not Naomi, who couldn't stop sobbing. Not Paula, who wouldn't come out of her bedroom, even to eat, so that they left plates of food outside her door as if she were a prisoner. No, it was only Ruth who needed to see a doctor, even though she'd managed everything—writing the obituary that ran in the newspaper, taking her sisters shopping for appropriate funeral dresses. She'd been as bloodlessly efficient as her mother had taught her to be, but now Evelyn Turner, who didn't believe in a bad mood, much less mental illness, decided that because Ruth had yelled at her, she needed professional help.

The psychiatrist was an old man, heavily bearded and gutted. He was avuncular, but in a mechanical way, as if he'd taken a class in bedside manner and were going through some checklist in his mind: look the patient in the eye; nod while listening; make a small sympathetic sound here and there. The room smelled so assertively of wet fur that Ruth kept looking around for a dog or a cat, but there wasn't one, which made the smell more worrisome. The doctor asked her how she was feeling with so much syrup in his voice that she had burst out laughing. She explained that her father had been sick for many years. "For most of my life, he was going to die," she said.

She didn't tell him that the death came as a relief. She didn't say that, as he grew sicker, the anticipation of his dying had preoccupied most of her high school years, that she avoided sports and clubs so that she could get home each day as quickly as possible. She didn't tell him that she once believed her presence by her father's bedside was what kept him alive. Nor did she admit that she had fully intended to go to college in Omaha so that she could continue to live at home. But then her father figured out her plan and forced her to apply to schools out east. When her mother called her at Smith a week earlier, she'd stood in the dorm hallway, unable to reconcile the fact that girls were passing by, carrying textbooks and field hockey sticks and care packages from the mail room, while she was holding a phone and listening to her mother tell her the terrible news. It was then that she finally understood her father's urgency: he'd wanted her to go as far away as possible so that there would be no chance she would watch him die.

She also didn't tell the doctor that her relief had been short-lived. And that now what she felt, from morning until night, was rage, and that grabbing her mother's wrist had been an act of enormous self-control.

Instead, she engaged him in an interesting discussion about

the mourning rituals of different cultures, which she knew something about because she'd read Claude Lévi-Strauss for an anthropology class. As she suspected, the doctor was so dazzled by her intellect that he began to try to match her with the sorts of obscure references that the bright girls at college used to impress their professors. And then, the session was over.

"He says I'm fine," she had told her mother when she returned home.

"Of course you are," her mother said, as if the doctor's appointment had been some frivolous idea that Ruth had cooked up on her own.

She knew she wasn't going to get any more work done in the library, so she started to pack up her notebooks. She could go weeks or months without thinking about her father. But then, suddenly, when she was walking out of a lecture, or brushing her teeth, or when she'd been translating those letters, she thought of the afternoons when he'd come home early from the lumberyard, no longer able to put in a full day, and he'd sit with her and talk about the books she was reading—*Anna Karenina* and *The Magic Mountain*—or she'd listen as he told her about his childhood in Odessa. The weaker he grew, the more he told stories of his past. By then, she'd become captivated by languages, had studied Latin, and had taught herself a passable French. Sometimes he'd slip into his native tongue, and she'd try to grasp the rudiments of Russian.

Remembering her father, she decided as she left the library, was probably why she'd made that sloppy error. Because rather than focusing on possessive articles, she was thinking that no matter what her father had wanted for her, she'd always know that the biggest regret of her life would be that she'd been in a dorm room drinking cocktails and trying to fit in with rich girls when he died.

At the end of the week, Helene went into the study to get the checkbook. She was due at the salon at three and she'd have just enough time after her appointment to get to the post office before it closed. Tom would have the current crop of bills and the checks, and she wouldn't have to open that drawer in Emil's desk or, frankly, go into that room again. Whoever Irina was, Emil could be commended for trying to do a good turn for someone during a horrific time. Further proof that The Doctor was exemplary. She'd find a way to slip the information into conversations with people when she decided to start seeing them. In fact, she thought, one day she might find some time to send the letters to an organization that collected that sort of thing for posterity. Really, if the letters were important it was because they were an invaluable piece of history.

Just as she was getting into her car, she saw the awful yellow jalopy pull up to the curb. Did the girl come to collect her payment in person? Did she think Helene couldn't be trusted to put a check in the mail? Helene put her car in gear, but now the girl was practically loping up the driveway. Soon enough, she was leaning down next to Helene's window, looking out of breath and a little crazed. Helene rolled down the window a quarter of the way.

"I'm glad I caught you!" the girl said.

Helene was pleased to see how awkward she looked as she tried to line up her face with the narrow opening. "As you can see, I'm just on my way out," she said.

"You're busy, then," Ruth said.

It was just the way she'd said, *You're sad, then*. This unsettling confirmation of the obvious felt like ridicule. "I've already sent you the money," Helene said. "You should get it any day now."

"Oh, no problem about that," Ruth said. "I was just wondering if we could talk."

"I'm in a bit of a hurry," Helene said.

"Where are you going?"

The girl's forwardness took Helene by surprise, and before she could stop herself, she mentioned her hair appointment.

"I could come," Ruth said.

"To my salon?"

"Oh, yeah. That's weird," Ruth said. Her laugh was overly boisterous and not attractive. "But, I mean, gosh, I could," she said.

It was the *gosh* that did it. There was something so disarming about the word coming out of the girl's mouth that Helene found herself agreeing to the proposition. Was this widowhood, then? This surrender to absurdity? Ruth trotted around the front of the car, and, in no time, Helene was driving the two of them down Shaker Boulevard.

Just as she had not complimented the house, Ruth said nothing about the Chrysler, whose interior was beige and immaculate. Helene never ate in her car, for one thing, and she was always careful to put her shopping bags in the trunk so that should there be a leak from a crate of strawberries, or blood seeping from a butcher-wrapped cut of meat, the upholstery would not stain. She noticed that the girl's knees were pressed up against the glove box, but there was nothing to do about that. If Helene adjusted the bench seat, she'd be too far from the steering wheel. Tom used to tease her about the way she looked when she drove. She insisted on keeping her hands in the ten-and-two position, which made her elbows stick out like chicken wings, he said. She felt belittled by machinery, and she didn't want to distract herself with talk, so she succumbed to the girl's prattle. In this way, she learned that Ruth was from Omaha, that her father had worked in a family-owned lumberyard, and that he died when she was in college. He was an autodidact—this was Ruth's word, and Helene was hardly going to admit that she wasn't quite sure what it meant.

"But old Evelyn kept her shit together after he died," the girl said.

Helene sighed. "There are so many other words in the English language to choose from."

"Touché," Ruth said. "Anyway, my mother kept things going. I mean, she didn't have a giant house she could sell or anything like that. She's a secretary. She types ridiculously fast. They gave her a prize for it in high school."

"Well, I'm sure that's nice," Helene said.

"Not really," Ruth said. "It's a 'good for you' prize. You know how many times I get complimented for the fact that I do my grading on time? It's complete bullshit. Excuse me—crap."

The salon was up ahead. Helene turned on her blinker, grateful that the metronomic *click-clack* seemed to make the girl stop talking. She pulled into a parking spot. "Here we are," she said, but then realized that simply arriving did not signal an end to things. Because now the girl was getting out of the car and following her into the salon. And then, Helene was introducing her to Debbie, her stylist, and Elsie, who washed her hair, both of whom must have thought that Helene was delighted to be bringing them a new client. She'd let this girl into her home, let her sit in Emil's chair and read those letters, and now the girl had gained control of her life!

"Debbie," Helene said. "It seems to me that Ruth is in drastic need of a haircut, don't you think?"

"I'm fine," Ruth said.

"Oh, it looks to me like you haven't had a good cut in quite a while," Helene said.

"I don't need one."

"Don't worry, dear. It'll be my treat." Helene was pleased when she saw Ruth flush. Who had the upper hand now?

Once Debbie finished Helene's cut, she led her to the domed dryer and adjusted the settings. Ruth, turbaned after her wash, sat in Debbie's chair. Debbie unwound the towel and began to study the girl's hair, running her fingers through it, examining what Helene was certain was an awful case of split ends. As Debbie investigated, she glanced over at Helene. *What a feral cat you've brought me*, her raised eyebrows seemed to say. *Oh, don't I know it*, Helene's eyebrows responded. Satisfied, Helene picked up a copy of *Ladies' Home Journal* and pretended to read about tapioca.

Debbie took a long time with Ruth's hair, which might have given Helene some satisfaction, but by the time both cuts were finished, and she bought a new can of hair spray for herself, and paid and tipped Debbie and Elsie, whatever advantage she thought she'd gotten by orchestrating the girl's makeover felt hollow. She didn't feel triumphant, only tired. She wanted to go home.

Outside, Ruth stood by the locked passenger door, sliding

a palm over her smooth hair while Helene opened the trunk to put the bag with the hair spray inside. She let out an inadvertent sound, and Ruth came around the back of the car.

"It's nothing," Helene said, looking at the checkbook. "It's too late for the post office, that's all."

"My mom had one of those binders," Ruth said as she and Helene settled into the front seat. "It was command central when she did the books for my dad and my uncle's business. Piles of receipts and all that."

What Helene wanted to say as she drove back toward her home was that she really didn't care about Ruth's mother, and that she wished this girl would stop taking surreptitious glances at herself in the side mirror and pursing her lips in a way that she must have thought was attractive but that only made her look like she'd eaten a lemon. She wondered about this fast-typing, capable mother who hadn't even taught her daughter to say thank you when someone paid for her to get a haircut at an excellent salon. Fifteen minutes later, Helene pulled into her driveway. She got out of the car and took the hair spray from the trunk. She watched for a moment as the girl headed toward her car, and then, feeling finally relieved of her, she walked to her front door. Erna would be cooking dinner, no doubt. Helene had left a note for her to roast a chicken with some vegetables and a few small potatoes. She was already imagining sitting alone in the dining room, carefully cutting the meat, bringing a bite to her lips, dabbing the juice with her napkin, aware that she was being watched by ghosts old and new—her brother and sister, her mother and father, and now Emil.

"Wait!" Ruth called out.

What? Why in the world was the girl coming up the walkway? And once she reached Helene, why was she at a loss for words?

"Is there something else?" Helene said.

The girl reached into her bag, took out a folded piece of paper, and held it out. "I'm sorry," she said as Helene took it. Then the girl turned and walked quickly to her car.

Helene must have looked off when she came into the kitchen because Erna immediately filled a glass from the tap and handed it to her. This small gesture made Helene feel weak, and she sat down at the kitchen table while she drank.

"Dinner will be ready at six," Erna said.

She always served dinner at six. Not a minute before or a minute later. But Helene knew what Erna meant. When Tom started going to school, and their time and conversations were not taken up with his care, Helene and Erna often found themselves in the house together for hours at a time. Certain boundaries were indirectly established. When Erna was cooking, the kitchen was hers.

Helene left and walked through the dining room. Something wasn't right, she thought. And then she realized that Erna had opened the curtains for the first time since Emil's death. No, Helene thought, as she hurried over to close them. She wasn't ready for this. She wasn't ready to be the person she had become. But just as she was about to pull the drapery cord, she looked outside and was surprised to see that Ruth's car was still there, and that Tom's car was now parked in front of it, and that the two of them were standing on the sidewalk, talking to one another. Tom made a gesture with one hand. Ruth threw back her head and let out that laugh of hers. Helene couldn't hear it from inside the house, and yet, somehow, she could.

At least the girl had been discreet, she thought later. Erna had gone home, and she and Tom were eating dinner. All that Ruth had told him was that Helene had hired her to do some organizing.

"I can help you out with that while I'm here," he said gamely.

"Don't you have classes?"

"I thought you could use some company," he said. "I don't like you being alone."

After dinner, they watched the news, then he challenged her to a game of Scrabble. When she won, he asked for a rematch. She understood that his visit wasn't so much about her. He was the one who didn't want to be alone, and so she played game after game until, finally, he went upstairs to his room. When she heard his door close, she went into the study, gathered the letters and the translations, and brought them up to her bedroom. She put them in a hatbox in the back of her closet.

She sat down at her vanity table and looked at herself in the mirror. Debbie had done her usual good job with the set Helene had begun to favor, a proper cut for a woman her age. There were times, though, when she missed the long hair of her girlhood and the part of her life when she'd start and end each day sitting just as she was now, working the horsehair bristles of her brush through her hair. The repetitive strokes had loosened her mind, and sometimes she would imagine a young man coming up behind her. He would put his hands on her shoulders. They would watch each other in the mirror.

She took off her malachite choker and the matching earrings and put them into their designated compartments in her jewelry box. She closed the lid. She took a dab of Pond's and rubbed the cream into her hands, moving them over and under each other, her fingers twining and untwining until the moisture was fully absorbed. She screwed on the cap of the jar, taking a small pleasure as she always did in the smooth workings of the seal. She took her tweezers, leaned toward her mirror, and plucked the recalcitrant hairs from her chin. She studied her face. When she thought about herself, she was every age she'd ever been. A child forcing Louisa and Victor to be the make-believe students so that she could be the make-believe teacher; a sturdy teenager playing lawn tennis in the park; a young married woman, relieved that she had not been passed over and that she was not living in Wheeling, trying to convince her parents that the fact of her existence was reason enough for them to come back to life. But confronted with her fifty-six-year-old face, she realized that she was only who she was at this moment: a woman who'd invented the life she wanted to live, but who had not, until now, fully understood its terms.

She'd read the final letter so many times that she had it memorized. Now, watching her reflection, she recited it out loud.

> *Remember that this is our last chance to survive.*
> *We are begging you, falling on our knees. Have you*
> *already half forgotten us?*

Half forgotten. It was an exact description of Emil. Just like when little Tom ran into his father's arms. Just the way Helene felt when she lay in her bed, waiting.

This last letter bore no signature. It was as if the woman

knew that all was lost, and that her name no longer mattered. Soon, she and her child would disappear from the world. *Our child.* Their child.

In the months and years to come, Helene could sometimes convince herself that it didn't matter about Irina, or whether she had been loved by Emil in a way that Helene had not. She would never know the circumstances that led him to leave her behind and come to America. She would never know what he did in the face of these desperate requests. Sometimes, when she needed to reinvigorate the notion of the unassailable man she'd invented, she would convince herself that Irina was a spurned lover, and that Emil had left for his new life before knowing there was a child. Or that perhaps the baby belonged to someone else, and the woman was preying on Emil's guilt out of desperation. But then there was the fact of the war, and the truth that, whatever the woman's motivation had been, she and her child likely didn't survive. And so, it was impossible to make Irina the villain of any story. In the end, all Helene would ever have were questions. And, despite her desire to make her success in life apparent with her cashmere sweaters, and her beads, and her fine house, there were only ever questions. Why did the prick of a flower poison her sister? Why, on a muggy summer night, did her brother leap into the darkness?

It would come to her: the memory of Emil, standing by her hospital bed, holding Thomas for the first time. The clinician in him vanished as he worked to tame his emotions. "Thom*as*," he said, his accent landing hard, the sibilance like the residue of smoke. "*Thom*as," she said, correcting him.

Maybe this was not the first time he'd held a child of his, but it was the first time he'd held Thomas. This was not a question. This was true.

And sometimes, she remembered a day so long ago, when Thomas was a year old. Erna had taken him for a walk in the stroller on that warm afternoon. Helene was rarely alone in her home, but now that she was, she didn't know what to do with herself. Sweating in her blouse, she climbed the stairs to her bedroom and took it off, thinking she'd change into a fresh one. But the brief pleasure of the air on her chest and arms was enough to make her unhook her brassiere and let the straps slide off her arms. Then some urgency seized her. She needed to cool her whole body. She unzipped her skirt and let it fall to the carpet. She stepped out of her slip and her underwear. Still hot, she opened the French doors. The hint of a breeze drew her onto the balcony, which was shaded by the white oak she'd admired so much when she and Emil had first toured the house. She lay down on the cool stone. The soft flesh of her shoulders and buttocks provided a cushion against the hard surface. She felt the heavy air press down on her like a body. She heard the distant sound of an airplane engine. At first it registered as a pleasant reminder of the ongoing world, but soon the noise grew louder as a small plane passed overhead. It flew so low and slowly that she thought it might be possible that the pilot could see her. Still, she didn't move. She imagined that later, this man would tell someone what he'd seen out his window. There was this lady, he'd say. This lady on her porch in all her glory. Just lying there for all the world to see.

FOUR

THE HANDOFF

Cleveland, Ohio, 1978

Helene was cold. She hadn't put on her coat, which was foolish, given the weather, but she didn't think the exchange would be so drawn out. Evelyn had pulled into the driveway minutes earlier, but it was taking forever for Francie to get out of the car. And now what was going on in there? Evelyn was turning around in the driver's seat to say something to Francie. As if she wanted Helene to believe that she had to convince the girl to get out of the car. For heaven's sake. Didn't the woman have a job to get to? Tom and Ruth had scheduled their trip to Bermuda to take advantage of Evelyn's three-day holiday weekend. The plan was for Helene to keep Francie for the final four days. The small burden of the extra day was offset by the not-unpleasant sense of martyrdom Helene felt, and by the fact that getting less time with Francie would put Evelyn at a disadvantage. Helene had not been happy when the woman moved to Cleveland just after Francie was born. If Ruth was so confounded by a baby, wouldn't a simpler solution have been to hire help? But Ruth wanted her mother nearby. Which was nice enough, Helene supposed, but also irritating because it meant that Francie had to be shared.

Finally, the back door opened. Francie slid out of the car and started toward the door, carrying her little red suitcase in one hand and a paper grocery bag filled with who-knew-what in the other. Evelyn's car continued to idle in the driveway as if she thought Francie would encounter some danger. Helene held out her arms and was pleased when Francie walked into her embrace, although she was always taken aback by Francie's skimpiness. Even in her thick winter jacket she felt breakable. She wondered if Evelyn had fed her enough.

Once inside the house, Helene took Francie's bags and put them by the foot of the stairs. "Look at you! You must be frozen," she said. Francie's little hands were red. Why didn't Evelyn make sure she was wearing her mittens? She helped Francie off with her snow jacket and her boots. "Run into the kitchen and ask Erna for a hot chocolate," she said, and felt a clutch in her throat when Francie actually ran down the hall. Such a dear, literal girl. A bit more nervous than you'd expect a five-year-old to be, what with the way she ducked her head and looked up at a person with those dark, worried eyes. She always seemed certain you were about to tell her she'd done something wrong. Well, Helene thought as she hung up Francie's jacket in the coat closet, with a mother like Ruth always making declarations about everything from the evils of sugar to the nutritional value of homemade yogurt, it was no wonder the girl was daunted. Having made no use of her PhD, Ruth had taken to motherhood as if it were another course of advanced study at which she needed to excel. She read books about it, for heaven's sake! As if a person needed to learn what was bred in the bone. Tom seemed to go along with everything. *Ruth says* was the beginning of almost any sentence having to do with his daughter. Recently Ruth had glommed on to a book that advised parents to listen to their children. Now when Francie acted up during one of Helene's Friday-night dinners, instead of sending the girl from the room until she could straighten herself out, Ruth would interrupt the table conversation, take Francie by her shoulders, and bring their faces close together. "I'm listening," she'd say. "Tell me what you are feeling." Well, what the girl was feeling was obvious to everyone. Children were not that difficult. They were either tired, or hungry, or tired *and* hungry. Occasionally, they were ill. Of course, Helene never said what she thought. Tom would defend Ruth, and Ruth—well, Helene would never be fully comfortable around her. Not after the business with those letters. Once they started dating, Ruth told Tom about them, of course, and naturally he'd asked to see them. Helene explained to him that she'd finally gotten rid of them along with all those files and medical encyclopedias that lined the shelves of Emil's study, and his ties, suits, and shoes, too. Tom understood. Of course he did, and he never brought up the matter again. Ruth didn't, either, but her silence, like so much else about her, was full of potential.

Helene carried Francie's bags up the stairs and put them into Tom's old room. As she unpacked the case and transferred the clothes into the bureau drawers, Francie appeared at the door, her upper lip darkly mustached. Helene licked her thumb and cleaned the chocolate off the girl's smooth and springy skin. The gesture gave her a topsy-turvy feeling in her stomach because she had done this same thing a hundred times when Tom was a boy, probably standing in this very spot.

"I made you a present, Grandma," Francie said. She up-ended the paper bag, and what looked like garbage fell onto the carpet. Francie knelt and started weeding through crayon drawings and bits and pieces of cut-up construction paper until she found what she was looking for and handed it proudly to Helene. It was a floppy—something or other. Some kind of not-quite-square-shaped woven thing.

"What a pretty little . . . mat!" Helene said.

Francie looked down. "It's a pot holder, Grandma."

"Well, of course it is," Helene said. "I see that now."

"I made one for Mommy and Daddy, too," she said, rummaging through her pile, then pulling out another equally indeterminate-looking item. "Nana has a kit. And I made a bookmark, too," she said, holding up a rectangle of clumsily embroidered mesh.

"You sewed this?" Helene said, taking the bookmark.

"Nana taught me."

Of course this was the kind of thing Francie did over at Evelyn's apartment, Helene thought. The woman was handy. She'd sewn that wedding dress of Ruth's. Well, it was hardly a wedding dress, but the flower print had been somewhat demure. And when Evelyn had first come to Cleveland, and Helene had gone out of her way to ask if she would like to contribute something to a fundraising auction, the woman had constructed that enormous floral centerpiece made entirely out of candy. Sunflowers crafted out of butterscotch, and carnations made with those red-and-white starlight mints. It had been a big hit and sold for far more than the opening bid. People had come up to Helene all night to rave about Evelyn's ingenuity.

"This is a monkey," Francie said, holding up a drawing she'd made that looked, surprisingly, very much like a monkey.

"You are a very clever girl," Helene said.

"What are we going to do today, Grandma?"

Helene looked at her watch. It was only nine-thirty. The day loomed, and she had nothing in mind. Francie often stayed for an overnight after a Shabbos dinner, but in those cases, there wasn't much that needed to be planned. She went to sleep soon after her parents left, and they picked her up early the next morning. Helene hadn't thought that in agreeing to watch Francie for four days, the girl would need a full calendar of events. But what else should she have expected? Ruth and Tom were always going on about giving Francie "stimulating" experiences. When they came to collect her on those Saturday mornings, they'd be running off to a children's pottery class, or to something called eurythmics, where Francie marched around a dance studio with other children for forty-five minutes, clapping. It was hard to tell if Francie liked all these activities. Tom had invited Helene to join the family at a performance of *Little Red Riding Hood* at the Play House. When the actor portraying the apparently dim-witted woodcutter climbed the risers to pick a child to help him find Granny and Red, he landed on a chin-quivering Francie. How awful it had been to watch the poor girl go through the whole thing. Onstage she was clearly terrified and wouldn't even tell the man her name. He'd had to do some quick improvising to make up for the fact that he'd chosen the wrong sort of child.

She opened Tom's closet and set Francie's empty suitcase on the floor next to the boxes filled with his report cards and the essays she'd kept because he'd gotten A's. She'd saved his wrestling trophies, of course, and a baseball mitt, and a pair of skates from that winter when he'd taken up ice hockey. She should carry these things up to the attic, or better yet, tell Tom to sort through it all and take what he wanted so she could get rid of the rest. But then the room would somehow cease to be his old room, wouldn't it? It would be just another room in her house. The thought gave her a chill.

She and Francie cleaned up the mess on the floor, and then she announced that Francie could watch her Ruth-sanctioned one-hour-a-day of television. Once that was over, it would be nearly lunchtime. After eating, they would go to the grocery store to pick up whatever it was that Erna needed for dinner. Then they could go to the tailor—Helene wanted to have the waistbands of a few of her skirts let out. That would put them back home by about two-thirty, which would leave three and a half hours before dinner. That was a long time, but the girl ought to be able to entertain herself. My God, Helene thought, suddenly overwhelmed as she looked down at Francie, who was sorting her art projects into piles. If worse came to worse, Helene would offer Francie some non-sanctioned television. Then it would be time for dinner. Then bath, story, and bed.

The first day passed easily enough, but the following morning, Helene woke with a feeling of dread. She glanced at the clock. It was only six-thirty. The day spread out in all its emptiness. Erna wouldn't arrive until nine, which meant Helene had two and a half hours to fill. With what? She couldn't simply put

Francie in front of the TV. It was one thing to give her an extra half hour here and there, but Francie would surely report to her parents what sorts of things she did at Grandma's, and she would just as surely tell them that all she'd done was watch TV, because that was the forbidden thing. She wouldn't remember to tell them about the perfectly nice bedtime story Helene had read to her the night before about those very flexible Chinese brothers, or that Helene had let Francie try on her necklaces and clip-on earrings, or that she'd been allowed to clomp around in her grandma's shoes. Of course, she wouldn't need to give a rundown of what she did at Evelyn's house because she had the evidence: pot holders.

Three more days. Children were exhausting.

She could still remember from so long ago what she'd felt that time she left Tom with Emil and Erna and drove down to Wheeling on her own. Even though she was going to see her ailing father for what she knew would be the last visit, she was nearly giddy with relief. The hours alone in the car gave her a glorious feeling of being unleashed. She knew she should hurry to her father's bedside but once she crossed into West Virginia, she stopped at a small roadside restaurant. She hadn't even been hungry. But it had been rare and wonderful to sit in a booth by herself with her cup of coffee and a piece of strawberry rhubarb pie. When the waitress came for refills, she'd complimented Helene's hat. Helene remembered the thrill of saying, "I saw it in a shop window and I don't know what came over me! As if I need more hats!" And then that wonderful moment when the waitress laughed in a knowing way because, of course, what woman didn't understand wanting something for no other reason than the pleasure of possession. The knowledge that you had something beautiful sitting in your closet made you feel that there were possibilities. For instance, one day you could put on that hat and turn into a woman who ate alone in restaurants and exchanged confidences with waitresses.

"Grandma?" It was Francie's little voice coming from the other side of the bedroom door.

"Come in, darling," Helene said.

The door slowly opened. And there she was, her hair a mess, her flannel pj's twisted around her nonexistent hips. Helene lifted her quilt and Francie ran around Emil's bed and climbed into hers. Helene gathered her close.

"You have big bosoms, Grandma," Francie said, laying her head on Helene's chest.

Some decades-old humiliation took possession of Helene: she was seventeen and attending an afternoon tea dance, the only girl left sitting when the small band struck up "Embraceable You." She started to tell Francie that it wasn't nice to say things like that, but then Francie turned over and tucked herself into the curve of Helene's body, her little bottom nestling against Helene's soft belly with the rightness of a puzzle piece snapping into place. *Oh!* Helene put her arm around Francie and closed her eyes. When they next woke, it was almost nine, and Helene had an idea.

"Let's go ice-skating!" she said, throwing off the covers and getting out of bed.

"I don't know how to skate," Francie said quietly.

"Then you'll learn!" Helene said. "It'll be fun. Did you know your daddy learned to skate when he was your age?" This wasn't strictly true. The hockey had been a high school fancy. But Francie needed persuading. She looked anxious, but that was just like her, wasn't it? Maybe it was all those choices Ruth was always giving her. What did she want for breakfast? For lunch? Did she want to wear her red sweater or her blue one? This must have been another thing she read about in those books of hers. Helene was old enough to know that every decision you made trailed second thoughts in its wake. What sort of child-rearing expert had decided that a five-year-old should confront regret?

She heard the familiar sound of a car door slamming: Erna's husband dropping her off as he did every day on his way to work. "Run downstairs and ask Erna to make you some oatmeal," she said.

"With butter?" Francie asked, and then, in a whisper, "And sugar?"

"Lots of sugar," Helene said as Francie scrambled out of bed and ran from the room. How bold of her to go against her mother's dietary rules. How wonderful that the two of them could share this secret rebellion.

Helene went to the window and raised the shade. The light had barely pierced the cloud cover; the day would be chilly and grim. Oh, those days of having to stand in the cold and watch Tom's hockey games. She was never happier than when he dropped the sport, even though she had Emil give him a lecture about the importance of perseverance. She felt less eager for the outing with Francie, but the long day ahead felt threatening, as did that bag filled with crafts.

By the time Helene and Francie had both eaten breakfast and Helene had showered and dressed and then made sure Francie put on her warmest clothes, it was past ten. She slipped on her coat and her gloves, then helped Francie into her jacket and boots. "Put on your mittens," she said.

"I forgot them at Nana's."

"Oh, for heaven's sake," Helene said. Which was not the right thing to say, because Francie looked like she was going to cry. And it really wasn't her fault. Evelyn should have noticed. "It's nothing to worry about," Helene said, although now they would have to stop off at the five-and-dime to buy a new pair. This irked her, she realized as she settled Francie into the back seat of her car, because she was having to use her time with Francie to make up for Evelyn's mistake.

Once they were at the store, they discovered that the only mittens in Francie's size were black. Francie refused to wear them, insisting that they were meant for boys.

"Mittens are mittens," Helene said.

But Francie was adamant. She wanted the blue pair.

"The blue ones are too big, darling," Helene explained. "Look," she said, fitting one of them onto her own hand. "This is for grown-ups."

"I want the blue ones," Francie said.

There was something stubborn in her determination, and Helene considered pressing her point, but then she thought about Tom and Ruth and that business about Francie's having a say about everything. Fine, let her make a poor decision and suffer the consequences. That was part of making choices, too, wasn't it? She paid for the mittens at the register, removed the tag, and handed them to Francie.

"Oh, thank you, Grandma! I love them!" Francie said.

"Aw, what a doll," the cashier said.

And suddenly Helene's irritation evaporated. The woman

had noticed the wonderful relationship Helene had with her granddaughter. She saw that Helene was adored.

The skating complex was jammed. Helene and Francie walked into a chaos of piped-in organ music, people shouting to one another, and the racket of buzzers and bells coming from arcade games. Helene grabbed Francie's hand and pushed through the crowd toward the sign for skate rentals. Once she'd paid for a pair in Francie's size, she steered Francie to an empty spot on a bench.

"Slip off your snow boots," she said.

Francie, overwhelmed by the crowd and the noise, did as she was told. Helene bent over awkwardly and fit Francie's feet into her skates, then finally gave up and knelt on the cold concrete. "Now you're ready," she said once she'd laced up the boots. She got back to her feet and checked her stockings. Her knees were red, but her pantyhose were no worse for the wear.

"Aren't you going to skate with me, Grandma?" Francie said apprehensively.

"Me?" Helene said, laughing. "Oh, dear. No one needs to see me break my neck!" Francie's eyes grew wide. "That's just a figure of speech, sweetheart. I've just worn the wrong clothes, haven't I? I can't skate in this dress."

"I don't want to do it anymore," Francie said.

"Of course you do. Look at everyone," Helene said, gesturing toward the rink. "They're having a marvelous time!"

"I don't want to."

Something hardened in Francie's plea, her fear turning into strategy. Helene had noticed this at those Friday-night dinners, too, the way Francie's complaints about the food or about an itchy turtleneck solidified into a stubborn determination. Sometimes Helene wondered whether Francie cared less about the vegetable she was refusing to eat than she did about getting her parents' attention. The business at the five-and-dime had been a mistake. This time, Helene was not going to give in. She adjusted the ridiculously large mittens over Francie's hands and stuffed the cuffs into the sleeves of her jacket. Eventually, Francie got to her wobbly feet and let Helene guide her to the edge of the ice. A whirl of skaters circled around the oval rink. A couple glided by arm in arm, their movements graceful and coordinated. A woman who, Helene thought, looked far too old for her tiny skating skirt, executed a spin in the middle of the ice. Kids fell, laughed, got up, and fell again. Everyone was more or less skating in the same direction, but when some teenager got out of hand and went the wrong way, an official wearing a black-and-white-striped shirt blew his whistle to deliver a warning.

A little boy in a bright blue parka pushed past Helene and Francie and stepped onto the ice. He hugged the side board as he tried to move one foot in front of the other.

"See?" Helene said, pointing to the boy. "He's just learning, too!" Right then, a skater flew past at such a startling speed that Helene pulled Francie back to protect her. The man bent low as he expertly threaded his way around the slower skaters, one arm behind his back, the other sweeping side to side. He didn't bump into anyone, but a skater fell in his wake as if the man's wind speed alone had toppled him.

Maybe Francie was right, Helene thought. This was too much—the speed, the angry sounds of skates scraping against the ice, that shrill whistle. And now they were playing that awful disco music. Skaters lined up in rows and tried to do some kind of dance in unison. But just as she was about to tell Francie that they could leave, Francie walked onto the ice. She took two or three tentative steps then started to lose her balance. Helene reached out as if she could prevent the inevitable, but Francie went down. Helene was terrified that someone would run into her, or over her, but the other skaters managed to avoid a collision and continued on their way. Which made Helene angry. Were people so heartlessly intent on their own good time that they couldn't bother to help a child? She started to wave her arms, trying to capture the attention of the official, when the woman in the short skirt skated toward Francie and, in one seamless move, lifted her onto her feet, then sailed on, never breaking her stride.

Helene tried to get Francie's attention to let her know that she'd seen the calamity and that Francie should come off the ice. Surely, she'd want to go home now. Helene did some quick calculations. They could go out to lunch and then maybe Francie deserved a special trip to the toy store. But Francie wasn't looking her way because she was trying to skate again. She took a few steps, fell, got herself back on her feet, and kept going until her short, jerky steps became slightly longer and steadier strides. And then, for the first time, she glided! Left foot. Right foot. And all in an even cadence that had less to do with the thumping beat of the music than with some rhythm that was Francie's own and that separated her from the frenzy around her. It was an astonishing sight. Francie must have learned steadfastness and determination from Tom, who had learned it from Emil, who had given him that talking-to after Tom quit the hockey team, a lecture that had been Helene's idea. So when it came down to it, Francie was skating, was now halfway around the rink, and all because of Grandma!

But—oh look! Francie's little hands were bare. Her mittens must have slipped off. Helene would have to find a way to get them back. Maybe someone from the staff would pick them up. That referee person. Because it wouldn't be a good lesson for Francie if they just left the mittens there. You had to take care of your belongings no matter how ill fitting they were. That was the consequence of making a bad choice. But none of that mattered really because Francie had learned to skate! She would tell her parents about this, about how she'd been scared but Grandma had told her to try and now ice-skating was her most favorite thing to do. And Ruth and Tom would be grateful. Because, really, what good was knowing how to embroider a bookmark in this day and age when a girl like Francie should grow up to have an important job? She could be a doctor, or a lawyer, for heaven's sake. And those things would take the kind of persistence she'd learned when she was only five years old and her beloved grandmother had taken her ice-skating for the first time in her life. Look at her! She was so beautiful, swinging her arms, her strides getting longer and more confident. And, oh! She fell. But no matter. She would get up again and—

But why was the man in the black-and-white-striped shirt blowing his whistle five times in a row? And why did the other skaters begin to slow down as if they all knew that five whistles was a special signal to stop? And why wasn't Francie getting up? The official skated over to her and leaned down. What was he saying? He straightened up and spoke into his walkie-talkie. And then a woman's voice came over the loudspeaker. "Will the person responsible for Francie Simon . . . Simon"—there was some rustling of a microphone—"Francie Simon-something . . . please identify themselves."

*　*　*

Evelyn arrived at the hospital barely a half hour after Helene called her. Helene didn't think it was necessary for both of them to be there, but when she'd reached Ruth and Tom at their hotel in Bermuda, the first thing Ruth said was "Call my mother *now*." It was a little insulting, but before Helene could assure Ruth that she had everything under control, Tom had taken the phone to let her know that they were going to catch the first available flight back home. By the time Evelyn arrived at the emergency room, Francie had already come back from her X-ray and had been given some medicine for pain that put her to sleep. There was nothing for either Helene or Evelyn to do but stand by Francie's bed and wait for her to wake up.

"It's just a mild fracture," Helene explained authoritatively. The doctor had used the word *broken*, but the nurse had said *fracture*, which Helene thought sounded less drastic.

Evelyn brushed a few hairs off Francie's forehead. "She must have been so scared," she said.

"She was very brave. She hardly cried," Helene said. "And we got here in no time."

In fact, the drive had been harrowing. Francie had howled in the car and asked over and over for her mother. Helene got lost trying to find the hospital, and then, when she finally reached it, she had to circle it twice before she saw the entrance to the emergency room. Once she carried Francie inside, a nurse started asking her a battery of questions about Francie's health. Did she take any medications? Did she have any allergies? What was the name of her pediatrician? Helene knew the answers to all these questions—no, no, and Dr. William Baylor—but still, she'd felt as if she were being cross-examined.

"She doesn't even need surgery," she said to Evelyn. "She'll wear a splint. The wrist will heal on its own and that will be that."

"You took her ice-skating?" Evelyn said.

"Yes, I did. She was very excited about it," Helene said.

"I didn't know she knew how," Evelyn said.

"Now she does."

"Not that well, I guess," Evelyn said.

Both were silent.

"That was a joke, by the way," Evelyn added. "If I had a nickel for every time one of my girls sprained an ankle or broke a finger. Well, I wouldn't be rich, but I could buy a pack of chewing gum."

"Tom never broke a bone," Helene said.

"Well, Tom is—what's the opposite of wild?" Evelyn said.

The opposite of wild is tame, Helene thought. Which sounded like an insult. Well, if a tame child got through his youth unscathed, if he grew up to be a man who had the good sense not to fall to pieces like his wife, demanding her mother come to the hospital to make sure Helene was not—what?—doing more harm to Francie?—then tame seemed to be a very excellent quality, indeed.

"By the way," Helene said. "Francie left her mittens at your apartment."

"I didn't notice," Evelyn said indifferently.

Helene thought of the speech she could give about how a million craft projects could not make up for inattention, but she said nothing because of course here was Francie lying in a hospital bed with a broken arm. Helene had taken the high road when the woman moved to Cleveland, including her in her Friday-night dinners, offering to introduce her at the temple, although Evelyn didn't have more than a High Holiday interest in any of that. When Francie was a newborn and Helene would go over to visit, Evelyn would be there more times than not holding Francie while Ruth rested. And so it was Evelyn who would ask Helene if she'd like to hold the baby or if she'd like to give Francie a bottle, and it was Evelyn who would take the baby from her when Francie started to fuss, as if Helene didn't know how to calm a child.

Francie stirred and then opened her eyes. Her gaze was un-focused, her expression vacant. She hardly looked like herself. Helene was frightened, certain something had gone terribly wrong. She was about to ring for a nurse when Francie spoke.

"Nana?" she said.

"Yes, darling. I'm right here," Evelyn said. She sat on the bed and drew Francie to her chest.

"Careful!" Helene said, fearful that Evelyn would crush the broken wrist. But Francie pulled her uninjured arm out from under the hospital blanket and hugged Evelyn. She started to cry. In the car her sobs had been filled with panic. Now the sound was—well, she sounded relieved.

A young doctor came into the room and, with the help of a nurse, splinted and wrapped Francie's arm from the elbow to the wrist. He said that they would wait until the swelling went down to decide whether Francie would need a cast and that she'd have to come back in a week for more X-rays. He-lene signed the discharge papers while Evelyn and the nurse sat Francie on the edge of the bed, helped her slip her good arm into her snow jacket, then closed the jacket around the sling.

"It's time for us to go back home, dear," Helene said.

"I want to go to Nana's," Francie said.

"You're staying with me now," Helene said, trying to keep her voice from reflecting her distress. "All your clothes are in Daddy's old room, remember?"

"I want to go to Nana's," Francie repeated fretfully.

"I have to go back to work, honey," Evelyn said, glancing at Helene. Helene thought she detected an acknowledgment of the ridiculous way the girl had been raised to believe that she ought to decide such things for herself. "And you love your grandma's house," Evelyn said. "I bet Erna will make you something special to eat."

"She's making a coffee cake," Helene said. "Your favorite."

The two helped Francie off the bed and led her toward the doors of the emergency room. Evelyn stayed with Francie just inside while Helene went out into the cold and got her car from the lot. She drove it around, then waited while Evelyn helped Francie into the back seat, gave her a kiss, and closed the car door. Helene glanced in the rearview mirror. Evelyn stood where she was, watching them drive away. Helene knew she ought to feel justified, but instead, she felt sheepish, as if she'd gotten away with something.

When Helene and Francie returned home, Erna said that Tom had already called. He and Ruth would be back the following afternoon. They'd come straight from the airport to the house. Of course they would want to see their daughter as soon as possible, Helene thought. But it was hard to avoid thinking that their urgency had something to do with not wanting Francie to be with Helene, the unreliable caretaker, any longer than necessary.

Francie seemed fine during the afternoon. She proudly showed off her sling to Erna. Helene read to her and they played rounds of Go Fish, games that went slowly given that Francie had only one good hand to work with. Helene had to help her go to the bathroom the first time, but after that, Francie managed on her own. She seemed hardly bothered by her injury. She ran around the house and ate a peanut butter sandwich and a slice of coffee cake. But as the painkiller she'd gotten at the hospital began to wear off, she started to whimper. Helene took her upstairs and gave her the double dose of liquid aspirin the doctor recommended. She helped Francie out of her clothes. She buttoned her pajama top over her sling as best she could then held out the bottoms so Francie could step into them.

"I can do it, Grandma," Francie said, her voice disarmingly mature as if her injury had hastened some understanding about what it would take to survive the world and its random disasters.

After she tucked Francie into Tom's old bed and turned off the light, Helene looked across the landing. Her room seemed very far away.

"I'll leave both our doors open and the hall light on," she said. "You just call out if you need me and I'll come as fast as I can."

"Okay," Francie said sleepily.

Still, Helene couldn't leave the room. What would happen if she was asleep and didn't hear Francie's little voice? Or what if she did hear but in the time it took for her to get up and cross the hall, Francie suffered?

She sat at the bottom of Tom's bed. "I'm just going to stay with you for a while," she said. Francie mumbled, but she was nearly asleep.

Helene thought about what had gone on at the hospital when Evelyn convinced Francie to go home with her grandma. She believed there had been a moment of kinship in Evelyn's glance, a recognition of Ruth's and Tom's foolishness and Francie's indulged defiance. Now she realized she'd been wrong and that there had been a familiar insincerity in Evelyn's voice that Helene recognized. It was the same tone she had used when Tom was young and she told him little lies to move him past a disappointment. *Your father is so sad that he can't build a snowman with you today. Dad called to wish you good luck in the match!* Most likely, Evelyn didn't have to go back to work at all. She'd only pretended this was the case so that Helene would have to reckon with her manipulative generosity. Sitting in the dark, Helene understood that Evelyn had come out the winner. Helene had maintained her dignity, but it was Evelyn, holding their weeping granddaughter, who'd been reassured of Francie's love.

FIVE

MARY LOU'S BLUFF

Cleveland, Ohio, 1980

"So, how about it, Sal?"

"If you're going to ask me again, I think you should at least use my name."

He called her *Sal, Sally Mae, Skin-n-bones, Dolly, Winner.* In bed, he called her *Fox.* Evelyn loved it, and she hated it, and she loved hating it, and hated loving it, but she kept all that to herself. It didn't do any good to tell a man what you were thinking. Burl offered his arm as they walked across the parking lot. Gentlemanly maybe, or simply insulting, the way it assumed that a woman couldn't make it from here to there without falling on her face. But Evelyn took his arm. It was confusing to be all these people—Sal, and Fox, and the woman who despised charm, and the woman who was, right now, feeling a pleasant sense of—oh, for God's sake, was it *pride?*—to be heading into the racetrack on the arm of a man who wanted the world to know that he had been chosen by her.

The clubhouse at Thistledown was a shrine to disappointment. It was Saturday morning and too early for a crowd so there was no hiding the smattering of yesterday's losing tickets on the floor. And yet there they were: those intrepid men (and they were almost always men) arriving first thing and staying well past the point of hope. They consulted their racing schedules as they stood in line at the betting windows, looking, Evelyn imagined, the way men did when they used a urinal and were forced to attend to a private need in full view. Burl ignored it all as he steered her toward the paddock. He was betting on making himself her second husband.

"I think my odds are good this time around," he said.

It always went like this. The comparison amusing, insulting, and a little bit exciting in a disheartening way. "That's optimistic, what with my record." she said.

"That was a failure of luck not skill. May the man rest in peace."

"Frank's not resting. He's dust or whatever comes after dust," she said.

"Don't speak ill, Dolly."

At six three, Burl was nearly a foot taller than she was and a hundred pounds heavier. As they walked, his binoculars bounced against his gut. In bed, the give of her mattress took the edge off the mass of him as did his unexpected athleticism and fine-tuned adjustments. Afterward, when he slept, he always seemed smaller, his expression as loose and uncomplicated as a boy's.

They reached the paddock just as the horses were led in

by their handlers, who paraded them around in slow circles. Evelyn knew that Burl's respect for Frank had little to do with chivalry and everything to do with fate. He was always taking its measure, trying to outguess it. Which was, as far as she could tell, a complete misunderstanding of the whole idea. Fate plowed toward its destination without paying attention to how smart you were. At any rate, she had her doubts that she was fated to marry Burl Moran, retired appliance salesman and owner of one-sixteenth of a thoroughbred horse.

Burl patted the sweat on his brow with his handkerchief then tucked it neatly into the breast pocket of his plaid sports jacket. His fussiness about his clothing and his cleanliness—she'd never known a man to sand dead skin off his heels—were ways, she understood, of trying to control fate, too.

"There's my girl, my sweet thing," he said, nearly swooning as Mary Lou's Bluff entered the paddock. His voice always crumpled into baby talk at the sight of his horse. Well, Evelyn reminded herself, not exactly his—Burl was part of a consortium of investors, most of whom didn't even live in Ohio. She liked to tell him that he owned half of the horse's left ass cheek. But mostly she didn't tease him because his love for the animal went beyond Mary Lou's moneymaking ability. It was something loyal and incorruptible. It made her nervous.

Mario, Mary Lou's groom, stopped the horse in front of Burl to let him nuzzle her snout. Burl's lips were moving and Evelyn knew that he was reciting his little prayer or pep talk, or whatever it was he said to Mary Lou each time she raced. Evelyn could never make out what he was saying, but she knew to keep quiet until he was done because if she distracted him, he'd have to start all over again. Francie was funny that way, too. On the first of each month, she wouldn't talk to anyone until she said, "Bunny, bunny, rabbit, rabbit" three times fast. If she forgot, if she said even so much as "Mommy" before remembering to say those words, her eyes would grow fearful and glassy. Ruth or Tom would have to reassure her that they were not going to die and that she was not going to die and that Nana and Grandma were not going to die. Evelyn had never known a child who thought about death as much as Francie did. At seven, her worries had resulted in a mystifying set of behaviors. She'd snap her fingers five times and if one of those snaps didn't create the right clicking sound, she'd have to begin the whole thing again. Burl was Francie's greatest cheerleader. She was only a kid, he said whenever Evelyn became frustrated by Francie's quirks. She'd turn out fine. Sometimes, Evelyn let herself believe him. After all, if anyone knew about faith it was a gambler with a superstitious heart.

"Looking good, my sweet girl," Burl twittered as Mario continued to walk the horse around the ring. The animal's muscles shifted and rolled beneath her mahogany coat. "Take your time," Burl said. "I'm a patient man." Evelyn didn't know if he was talking to the horse or to her. Mary Lou's Bluff lost more than she won and this was Burl's fourth proposal in two years.

She watched the other bettors who studied the horses, a not-much-to-look-at bunch in yesterday's wrinkled pants and, on this humid morning in late May, guayabera shirts that were already sticking to their backs. They licked the tips of their pencils, then made notes on shreds of paper cupped in their palms. She wondered if they were writing down anything meaningful or if they were scribbling nonsense, trying to let others know that their systems were foolproof. Burl was always telling her to look for signs: Was that gelding sluggish or alert? Did the paint just look you in the eye? Did Mary Lou have the look of eagles? Burl could tell her all about racing histories and length of stride, but she knew what thrilled him was the gut choice that defied any statistics and even his crazy ideas about destiny. What excited Burl was throwing himself smack in the face of good sense.

Oh, how I love you, Dolly, he'd say at the oddest moments, in the middle of flossing his teeth, or while meticulously folding a bath towel in thirds.

The name's Evelyn, she'd say. He took that to mean she loved him back. Which might or might not be true. How could you recognize a love that wouldn't ruin you?

"Our girl's in good form today," Burl declared as they climbed the stands to find his lucky seats. Once they were sitting, she took his binoculars from around his neck and trained them on the track. There was Mary Lou, being paraded to the post by her jockey, as hopped-up as her one-sixteenth owner.

"You'll see, Peaches," Burl murmured. "It's gonna be great."

Mary Lou's Bluff didn't win the race and Evelyn didn't give Burl an answer. That evening, after Ruth dropped off Francie for a sleepover, Evelyn stood in the kitchen doorway, a cigarette in one hand, and watched Burl listening intently as Francie explained the politics of second-grade cliques.

"So, this Penelope is the top dog," he said.

"But everybody hates her," Francie clarified.

"Like most dictators," he said.

Francie might as well have been talking about the Cold War the way he took her so seriously. She'd started calling him "Uncle Burl" a year earlier. Ruth wasn't sure about it (she wasn't sure about Burl, either) and had tried to explain to Francie that he wasn't her real uncle the way Aunt Naomi's husband, Uncle Mitchell, was, but Francie didn't let up. Evelyn stubbed out her cigarette, then gave Burl a little signal. He got up from the couch and put on his sports jacket. He knew his place in the hierarchy of Evelyn's affections and never complained about having to give up a night with her when Francie slept over. Francie slid off the couch and put her arms around Burl's big middle. She loved him, Evelyn thought. Which might be a good-enough reason to keep him around.

"Bye," Francie said.

"Bye," he said.

"Bye."

He knew not to say more. Another of Francie's peculiarities: she had to be the last to say goodbye.

Evelyn attributed Francie's worries to Ruth. Ruth was unhappy. She wouldn't admit it, but Evelyn could tell by her restlessness. She couldn't sit at a dinner table for longer than it took to eat her meal before she'd be up, clearing her plate, and transferring leftovers into Tupperware. She didn't bother to ask if everyone else had had enough. *She'd* had enough. Not just of the meal, but before that of cooking it, and before that of shopping for the food, and before that of letting Tom talk her into staying in Cleveland so they could be close to Helene, even though there was no job for Ruth here, not at the university where she'd gotten her degree, and not at any of the colleges within driving distance. She'd begun to talk about looking for work at a local high school. None of them taught German, of course, but she could get away with teaching French. She hadn't done anything about it, though. All that pent-up energy and that big brain of hers and she had no idea what to do with herself. Just last week, when Evelyn and Burl had joined everyone at Helene's for one of her endless Friday-night dinners, Ruth had suddenly stood up from her chair as if it had caught fire. When everyone looked at her curiously, she made some vague excuse about a charley horse in her foot, but Evelyn caught something odd in her daughter's expression that had nothing to do with a cramp. The phrase caught Francie's imagination, and they all turned their attention to her. Tom asked Burl if a charley horse had to do with racing. Burl said no, it had to do with baseball, and the conversation moved on from there. As Ruth slowly sat down, Evelyn understood what she'd seen in her daughter's eyes: Ruth wanted to run but there was nowhere to go.

Evelyn didn't think her other girls felt this way. Back in Omaha, Naomi was happily overwhelmed by her twins. There was nothing more exciting for her than discussing Nathan's swimming schedule or the fact that Leah had moved up a level in gymnastics. Paula, single now, as Evelyn had predicted she would be, was a lawyer at a firm in Lincoln. She said she was very happy although her declarations always felt more like challenges. But what had happened to Ruth, Evelyn's independent, self-possessed daughter, who took a train all the way east to a college where she knew not one soul? Where was her girl who had gotten top honors on her PhD thesis, beating out all the boys? How had Ruth become so baffled?

"Don't you think it's a great idea, Mom?" Ruth had said when she asked Evelyn to move to Cleveland to help with the baby, her enthusiasm for her idea barely masking her terror.

Evelyn did not say that a girl with *Dr.* at the head of her name ought to be able to figure out how to manage an infant. She didn't say that, after a lifetime of raising children, she had no desire to take care of anyone else's and that she had no interest in living in Ohio when she had a perfectly good life in Omaha. She didn't say any of those things because the request had thrown her. Ruth had always been Frank's child more than hers. Evelyn would walk in on the two of them discussing some World War I battle or another, and Ruth would stop talking, her silence a way of letting Evelyn know she was not required. This was the first time her oldest daughter needed her.

"If that's what you think you want, Mom," Ruth said the following Saturday, when Evelyn brought up Burl's proposals. She'd never mentioned them before. Probably because she didn't take Burl seriously. Or maybe because she wasn't sure how Ruth would react. And how did she react? *If that's what you think you want.* Not exactly a seal of approval.

The two stood in the kitchen of Ruth's house. Tom and Francie were out buying art supplies for a school project about the Wright brothers. Ruth, still wearing her nightgown, her hair unbrushed, her face looking a little sleep-rumpled, forked scrambled eggs straight from the pan on the stove. The toaster popped. Evelyn's slice of rye was blackened just the way she liked it. Ruth dug at the crusty bits of egg stuck to the sides of the pan. She should have used more butter, Evelyn thought, but lately Ruth seemed suspicious of indulgence. The whole thing made Evelyn want to pinch her. "You're slouching," she said.

"I always slouch."

"No, you don't. I taught you girls to stand up straight." Evelyn put down her toast and put her hands on Ruth's shoulders to push them back.

"Mom!" Ruth said.

"Have you seen those old ladies hunched over walkers? They look like snails. That's what you'll look like if you don't stand up straight."

"Well, when that happens, you can say, 'I told you so.'"

"When that happens, I'll be dead."

"Very funny."

"You know, Ruthie, sometimes if you decide to be happy, you become happy."

"Did you get that from a fortune cookie?"

"I got it from life."

"It's as easy as that?" Ruth said. "You just decide?"

"Oh, I don't know," Evelyn said, her combative energy failing her.

"Anyway," Ruth said, "we're not talking about me. We're talking about you getting married to *Uncle Burl.*"

She leaned on the name with her usual skepticism. Ruth thought he was a little dull, for one thing. And she objected to the fact that he was twelve years Evelyn's senior. "I just don't know what you get out of it," she said now. "Except the opportunity to be his nurse. By the time he's—"

"I happen to be pretty good at math," Evelyn said. She studied her half-eaten toast then tossed it in the garbage. "I suppose if it was something I wanted I would already have said yes."

"Or maybe not," Ruth said, smiling.

"I'll admit I'm a bit of a cocktease."

"Jesus, Mom!"

"Oh, you people go on about feminism *this* and liberation *that*, but you still want your mothers to be virgins."

Ruth's laughter brought a light to her face that Evelyn saw so rarely these days. They both turned at the sound of the front door. A second later, Francie ran into the kitchen followed by Tom, who carried a bag from the hobby shop.

"Nana!" Francie said. "We're building *Kitty Hawk*!"

"We've got balsa wood. We've got Styrofoam. The whole nine yards!" Tom announced happily.

"What?" Ruth said. "But all she has to do is draw pictures and glue them onto poster board. That's what the assignment says."

"Extra credit," Tom said. "Right, Francie?"

But Francie wasn't listening. She was busy digging through Evelyn's purse, looking for the pack of gum she knew would be there.

"And then you know what's going to happen?" Ruth said. "You'll get a quarter of the way done and then tell me you have work to do, and I'll have to build the rest of it. And I don't want to build an airplane, Tom. I'm no good at all that artsy-craftsy stuff. I'll ruin it."

Was she about to cry? Evelyn looked at Francie, who was, thankfully, busy unwrapping a stick of doublemint, folding it in thirds, and then popping it into her mouth. Tom put down the bag and reached out to hold Ruth.

"I can't do it," she said.

"Okay," he said.

"I just can't."

Francie watched her parents, her mouth working slowly as she chewed. Evelyn took her hand.

"Let's see what's new in your room these days," she said, leading Francie down the hall.

In her bedroom, Francie showed Evelyn the little barn she'd made out of a shoebox she painted red that held the small plastic horses Burl had given her for her birthday. Evelyn praised the little snips of yellow yarn that were meant, Francie told her, to be hay. Francie went to work carefully placing the horses in what seemed like a finicky arrangement, spacing them evenly apart, their hooves lined up perfectly. Watching her make the small adjustments, Evelyn felt herself grow more and more agitated.

"Stop that now," she said when she couldn't stand it anymore. "It's fine the way you have it." From the worried look on Francie's face, though, she could tell that her precision had nothing to do with what the little diorama looked like. It had to do with why she had to snap her fingers the right way and all her other odd habits. Burl was sure she'd grow out of it. Well, she'd have to, Evelyn thought. A person couldn't spend her whole life making sure things lined up.

On the first Saturday in July, against all odds, or maybe because Burl had done up his pocket square in a flawless three-point fold, or because of his witchy incantations—who could say?— Mary Lou's Bluff won her race. Burl was so beside himself that he hired a local artist to paint the mare's portrait from the snapshot he kept in his wallet. A few weeks later, when Evelyn and

Burl went to the artist's storefront studio to pick up the finished product, she saw that the woman had altered the head-on view of the photograph so that now the horse gazed thoughtfully up and to the right, just the way every one of Evelyn's daughters had been posed for her high school graduation portrait. She stifled a laugh but she wasn't able to hide her dismay when, as she and Burl drove back to her apartment, he announced that he was giving her the painting as a gift.

"A filly for your filly?" Evelyn said, glancing in the rearview mirror at the absurd portrait, which sat in the back seat.

"That's clever," he said.

"A winner for your winner."

"It would look good over the television in the den," he said, ignoring her. "Or above your bureau."

She couldn't help herself. "That way you can think of riding her while you ride me."

"Cut it out," he said quietly.

They drove for a few minutes in silence.

"If you don't want the painting, you don't have to have it," he said finally.

"I don't want it."

"That's all you had to say."

He dropped her off in front of her apartment building. He wouldn't come up, he said. She didn't like to think she'd hurt him, but something in her wanted to know how it felt to take things too far, to see what would happen if she risked losing his interest. But as she stood alone in the elevator watching the floor numbers light up, she didn't feel anything. She took a shower. She heated up some leftover meatloaf for dinner. As she ate, she thought she'd been wrong: it wasn't that she didn't feel anything. What she felt was nothing, and nothing was a feeling just like happiness or sadness was. Nothing was eating this meatloaf. Nothing was washing the plate, then drying it with a dish towel, then putting it back in the cupboard. Nothing was using the same plate for the next meal because it was always on the top of the stack. Nothing felt like forever.

That night, she called him. She said she wanted the painting after all. Burl did the self-respecting thing and waited a week before coming over, and even then, he didn't bring the painting. She had to ask again. The possibility that he might not give it to her made her sure she wanted it and that she'd wanted it all along.

A week later, Ruth called at six-thirty in the morning sounding breathless and excited. She needed to come over right away, she said. She had news.

"It'll have to wait. I need to get to work," Evelyn said. She wanted to be in the office early. The end of the month was always busy with some contracts wrapping up and new ones starting. As secretary to the head of a company that leased hundreds of billboards across three states, she was responsible for the details.

But twenty minutes later, her doorbell rang, and there was Ruth, smiling with too many teeth. "Mom? What in the world?" she said, walking over to the painting of Mary Lou that Evelyn had left sitting on the living room couch. She was waiting for Burl to come over and hang it in the den. She didn't like Ruth's tone or her laughter. She was used to the painting by now. She was comforted by the horse's tender gaze and by the way the artist had painted the light falling across the white snip on the mare's snout. She'd gotten into the habit of greeting the portrait when she came home from work each day. *Hello, girl,* she'd say.

She headed into her bedroom to finish getting ready for work. Ruth followed. Her jumpy energy was irritating. She moved around the room picking up things and then putting them down—a perfume bottle, a framed photo of Naomi's twins, an eyeglass chain. Evelyn tried to ignore her. She found a new pair of L'eggs in her top bureau drawer, sat on the bed, and put on the hose, silently complimenting herself for the hundredth, or the thousandth time on getting the job done without her manicure snagging the nylon. Then she stood in front of her closet, deciding what to wear. Not deciding, really. She knew she was going to wear the brown linen skirt and the cream-colored blouse because this is what she wore every other Wednesday, but she thought that if she took her time, Ruth might get bored and leave. But she kept pacing around the room.

"Did you come over to watch me get dressed?" Evelyn said, grabbing the skirt and blouse off their hangers.

"We're moving to New York City!"

Evelyn turned around. Ruth's eyes were wide, as if she had just been given this surprising news, too.

"I'm standing here in pantyhose and a bra and you're telling me you're moving to New York?"

"What does that have to do with anything?" Ruth said, laughing. "But yeah. And soon! We'll be out of here by the end of August, if you can believe it. I know it feels spur-of-the-moment, but we've been talking about this for months. It's just taken a while to get Tom used to the idea. You know how responsible he feels for his mother. And then he had to get a new job, which happened much sooner than we thought."

She was talking fast. Too fast. A hundred already-made decisions spilling out at once. Tom's new job. Francie's new school. She and Tom would rent a furnished apartment for the first six months. She'd already arranged to keep all their things at a storage facility in Cleveland until they got the lay of the land and knew where they wanted to live. Evelyn turned away and quickly put on the skirt, taking none of the usual pleasure she did when she zipped it closed and felt the material hug her hips or when she ran her hand over her nearly flat belly. She put on the blouse and hurriedly buttoned it.

"What's in New York?" she said, staring at her closet floor, pretending to consider her choice of shoe.

"Well, for one thing, Tom will be handling bigger investment portfolios. There are a lot of rich people in New York."

"There are a lot of rich people in Cleveland."

"It turns out he has contacts in New York from business school," Ruth said, ignoring her.

"And what about you?"

"What about me?"

"What will you do?"

"What do you mean what will I do?"

"With your life. In New York City."

"I'll go see art. I'll go hear music. I don't know, Mom. I'll visit the Statue of Liberty."

"You're moving all the way to New York so you can see the Statue of Liberty?"

"Mom, you're being obtuse."

"Fancy word."

"Change is good. Look at you!"

"Look at me what?"

"You moved out here. You have a picture of a horse in your living room. You might get remarried!"

"I didn't move here to get married," Evelyn said, thinking of the hours she'd spent holding and rocking and feeding Francie or simply being with Ruth so that she didn't feel marooned in motherhood. That was the problem with children, she thought. They take what they need. They take what they need and then they move to New York.

Ruth sat down heavily on the edge of the bed. "Why can't you be happy for me?"

"I'm happy for you."

"No you're not. But that's okay." She looked at Evelyn. "Things could be better for me in New York. Don't you think?"

"Who are you?" Evelyn said. She heard the hurt in her voice and wished she hadn't spoken.

"What are you talking about?"

Evelyn wasn't sure. It was only that she had a clear memory of her mother shaking with rage and disappointment because Evelyn didn't take her life seriously. "Did I ever tell you that I had a teacher who said it wasn't worth his time to teach girls math?" she said.

"That's awful," Ruth said.

"What's awful is that I believed him." She slipped her feet into a pair of low heels. "I'm going to be late for work."

Ruth followed her back into the living room. Evelyn took her purse from the credenza and looked inside to make sure she had what she needed for the day—her glasses, her cigarettes, her pack of Kleenex, her gum. Her gum that made her purse smell so sharp and sweet that Francie would bury her face in it.

"But what about Francie?" Evelyn said, unable to control the alarm in her voice.

"She's coming with us, obviously!" Ruth said, happily. "New York will be a great place for her to grow up. All those people!"

Evelyn thought of Francie on a crowded street snapping her fingers, or doing whatever craziness she'd come up with next. There would be so much to scare her in New York City, so many things that would be out of her control.

By the end of the summer, Mary Lou's Bluff had placed in a string of races. Burl attributed this to the portrait, that somehow the horse knew her worth and was rising to it. This time, Evelyn knew he was joking. In his gentle way he was forgiving her for the business about the painting and for her cruelty.

Labor Day Monday was hot and humid. She'd showered and oiled her legs, put on her favorite sleeveless shift and slingbacks. She found a hat in the back of her closet and freshened it up with a ribbon. It was silly—this wasn't the Kentucky Derby, after all. But, for the first time in her history, Mary Lou was a contender.

Because of the holiday, the track was more crowded than usual, and it took a while for Evelyn and Burl to make their way from the paddock to the stands. Burl's lucky seats were taken but he didn't seem disturbed by this and they found spots two rows behind. Mary Lou and her jockey were announced over the loudspeaker and, as if she sensed the expectation, the mare high-stepped and swished her tail. Evelyn looked through Burl's binoculars. Mary Lou's jockey was having a time getting her into the stall at the starting gate and once he finally managed it, she wouldn't settle. Burl wasn't agitated by the horse's behavior. In fact, he seemed withdrawn. For all his swagger, Evelyn realized that he was a man who never thought he'd get what he wanted.

At first, she didn't realize what had happened. Only moments after the start of the race, the crowd let out a collective gasp and rose to its feet. Before she could ask what was going on, Burl stood up, maneuvered his bulk out of the row, then ran down the steps with surprising speed. She looked through the binoculars again. Mary Lou had fallen down on the track and was lying on her side. Her jockey had been thrown some yards ahead of her. His leg was bent the wrong way. Evelyn knew what a fallen horse meant. *Not Mary Lou!* she thought. *Not our girl!* She pushed her way out of the row, took the steps as quickly as she could, and found Burl at the fence. She watched as the other jockeys were being flagged. Little by little, the horses slowed, and the riders began to lead them off the track. Trucks sped toward the accident, and while doctors tended to the injured man, a vet inspected Mary Lou. The crowd was still quiet, waiting for the verdict. Burl didn't take his eyes off the motionless horse. And then suddenly the crowd roared as Mary Lou, in a series of powerful, frightening moves, rolled over, rose up, and started to run. The racecourse was empty. It belonged to Mary Lou now and she ran all out. Burl grabbed Evelyn's hand, brought it up to his chest, and held it there. She could feel his heart. His eyes were full. His jaw worked against some emotion. Together, they watched Mary Lou run the curve. The crowd whooped and applauded and Evelyn yelled along with them, urging Mary Lou to *Go! Go!* When the mare ran past, Evelyn felt the pounding of hooves inside her body. The outriders chased Mary Lou down and were almost on her when she turned and made a thrilling leap over a fence into the inner field. Evelyn felt—she didn't know what she felt. The horse's crazy freedom had unleashed something in her. She was outside her body, beyond herself.

The outriders brought their horses to the fence but went no farther. Everyone watched as Mary Lou ran around the grassy area. Her explosive energy began to wane. She seemed to become lost. She turned this way and that, not knowing where to go. Evelyn felt heartbroken for the horse who'd unknowingly run into her own trap. Finally, one of the outriders dismounted and climbed over the fence. After a few attempts, he caught Mary Lou by her reins. Slowly, the mare wound down, submitting to the man's control as he opened a gate and led her across the racetrack toward the stables. The fans applauded. How fickle they were, Evelyn thought bitterly. They'd wanted the horse to win. And then they wanted her to lose.

"Hey there, Sal," Burl said quietly. She'd nearly forgotten that he was there. He was still holding her hand to his chest. She felt the weight of his palm, the way his fingers wrapped around hers. Thick and gentle. It wasn't a perfect hand. It was too big. It was attached to a body that was too old, and to a person who might be, okay, a little dull at times. But she could hold this hand for a while, she thought, and maybe for a while after that.

"Yes," she said. She wasn't sure he heard her, or if he did, that he understood what she was telling him. It didn't matter. She'd tell him again when the time was right.

* * *

In January, Evelyn woke to an early-morning phone call from Ruth. She was crying. The building where she and Tom had stored all their belongings had burned down overnight.

"Everything's gone, Mom," she said. "Everything. It's just . . . There's nothing left."

After they hung up the phone, Evelyn called in sick to work. She took her photograph albums down from the bookshelf and pulled out pictures of Ruth when she was a baby and others when she was a little girl, playing with her sisters in the yard in Omaha. And another of her petting Fidelity, that ridiculously named dog whose loyalties were questionable given the number of times she ran away. Evelyn pulled out a scallop-edged photo of Evelyn and Frank wincing into the sun at Lake McConaughy. They'd been on their honeymoon. They looked like children themselves. Another photo of Ruth in her cap and gown at her high school graduation, leaning down to kiss her father, who was quite frail by then. She pulled out pictures of Francie when she was just born, when she was three months, then six months, then a year. Francie on a merry-go-round; Francie running through a lawn sprinkler; Francie in the Mary Poppins Halloween costume Evelyn had sewn for her. She would pack up the photos and send them to New York. Ruth would need evidence of who she'd been now that she was starting all over, too.

SIX

OTHER PEOPLE

Cleveland, Ohio, 1983

"What do you care about!" Marjorie Flamenco says. It's less a question than an insult. The tall, imposing woman who leads the self-improvement class has the rock-carved features and frozen shoulders of a military general. She tells the class to call her *Ms.* and she wears no makeup—two things that, in Helene's mind, go together. She stands, using the authority of her height to assert herself over the class participants, who have committed one hundred dollars and one hour a week for six weeks to wear name tags, sit in a circle of uncomfortable folding metal chairs, and learn how to, according to the circular that arrived with Helene's mail, "Grab Your Life by the Throat!" Ms. Flamenco begins each class by locking the library's double glass doors, which gives Helene a dubious feeling of inclusion in this group of strangers who know where to be on Thursdays at six p.m., but have no idea how to manage the rest of their lives.

MARISA SILVER

At last week's introductory meeting, Ms. Flamenco had announced that the sessions would be structured around six *essential questions*. That first evening's question was *Why are you
here?* From her tone, the participants seemed to have gathered
that if their answers weren't good enough, or dramatic enough, or
sad enough, they might be expelled from the class, and so Helene
found herself exposed to uncomfortably intimate stories about
job loss, marital antagonism, and confusion about sudden mone-
tary gain. That first night, the group was *not* exposed to the story
of a seventy-year-old woman who has a sense of foreboding upon
waking each morning that cannot be entirely eased by luncheons
or sorting through piles of donated clothing and toys for Jewish Family Services or helping children learn to read. Helene had
told the group only that she was recently widowed. That was as
much of her private life that anyone deserved to know. That Emil
died fourteen years earlier was not something she felt it necessary to add. Time was not the issue. Or it is exactly the issue, she
thinks now as she looks at the group cowering under the weight
of this week's new question. The issue is the years, the months, the
weeks. The issue is the alarming and perpetual tomorrow.

"What do you *care* about?" Marjorie Flamenco repeats.

A silence follows. Don, who won two hundred and fifty
thousand dollars in the Ohio state lottery, stares into the distance as if the answer to the question might be on the table
with the coffee urn and a platter of Rice Krispies treats. Peggy,
a teacher who lost her job because, she explained cryptically,
"of love," starts to inspect her fingernails. Helene looks at her
watch. Emil gave it to her. Or rather, she bought it, had it gift
wrapped, then put it next to her place setting at her fifty-sixth
birthday lunch, which is also the day he died. Fifty minutes to

126

go. She has never taken a self-improvement class before. She has never taken any classes, not the rug-hooking or painting classes that her friends recommended during those first seasons of widowhood. As if what were missing from her life was her ability to draw a pear. And yet somehow, when she sat at the kitchen table one morning after another awful night and read the circular, she thought that possibly a class was just what she needed to put a stop to this feeling she has when she's awake at two in the morning, or sitting at one of those luncheons, or boxing up cans for a food drive: the feeling that she can't draw a full breath. The feeling that she is about to die.

That she has nothing in common with these people is as plain as their clothing. Helene has dressed for the occasion in a skirt and a matching jacket, but the others wear wrinkled work clothes, or blue jeans or, in the case of Peggy, the lovelorn teacher, a pink terrycloth tracksuit. And the clothes are only part of the problem. In what other circumstance would Helene come across someone like Gina, a dark-haired mother of two who laughed when she announced she was considering having an extramarital affair, or Joanne, a middle-aged woman whose drug-addicted son steals money from her. Or Neil, a slight man with delicate hands who told the group that he was taking the class because his wife needs him and their son to get out of the house on Thursday nights so she can host her women's group. Earlier today, Helene called the library to withdraw from the class, but then her eyes traveled to her calendar and she saw that all her days were full of activities she'd arranged so that she would have something to write on her calendar.

"Come on, people," Marjorie says. "I can't help you if you don't help you."

127

Gina says she cares about her dog, an Irish wolfhound named Buzzy, which, coming from a woman with young children, seems, to Helene, a bit tasteless. Newly wealthy Don says he likes to go bowling and that Ronald Reagan seems like a decent fellow. Peggy, the teacher, admits that she is having a hard time getting over Elvis's death. Helene wonders if this is the love that cost the woman her job and if she is mentally ill. Connie Waddington, who is one of the librarians, says that she cares about books. She might as well have described the color blue as being blue.

"And Helene cares about . . ." Marjorie Flamenco says.

Helene feels an uncomfortable surge of adrenaline. She considers standing up, gathering her coat and purse, and leaving, but it's too late. "Bach," she says.

"Bach," Marjorie Flamenco repeats.

"The composer."

"I'm aware."

Helene doesn't care about Bach. She doesn't know anything about him. She rarely listens to any kind of music except for whatever happens to be playing in the car if she's gone to the car wash and the man who waxes the Chrysler has turned on the radio to keep himself entertained. She can't say what she does care about. Well, Tom, obviously. And Francie. Why didn't she just say she cares about her granddaughter? Who could quibble with that? But if there is one thing she absolutely does not care about, it's Wolfgang Amadeus . . . No, that's not it . . . Something, something Bach.

But now she will have to care about him, because the assignment for the following week is to engage with your *passion*, a word Marjorie Flamenco says with the slightest bit of distaste the way she might say "tongue" or "spatula." That over the course of one class, the woman has leapt from mere care to passion seems unfair to Helene, a punitive bait and switch. But she says nothing, because she knows that when she goes home, she will enter the back door into her shadowed kitchen, walk down the dark hallway, then climb the stairs. She'll change into her nightgown and lie down in bed. She won't turn on the bedside lamp, because more and more, when she's alone in the lighted house surrounded by the silent night, her heart flutters and her chest grows tight and she feels as if she's trapped inside her skin and that even if there were a way to break free there would be nowhere she could go because there is no way to escape her skin or her life and the only thing she can do is turn her face to her pillow and make the most awful sound.

After the class is over and Marjorie Flamenco leaves, librarian Connie offers to keep the building open for another half hour for anyone who wants to socialize. Helene has no desire to spend more time with these people than she already has but when she looks through the glass doors, she hesitates. It was only sprinkling when she arrived, but now it's really coming down. The sodium lamps in the parking lot make the rain look like a million sharp pins. She imagines herself walking out the doors, raising her umbrella, and making her way to her car, but all these perfectly normal actions feel suddenly impossible. She senses that it's about to come on: the flutter in her chest, the underwater sensation that makes sounds feel farther away than they are. *Not here*, she thinks. *Not in front of these people.* She takes a breath and the fact that the air doesn't get trapped in her throat and that her lungs almost fill helps her calm down. Still, there's the problem of the rain and the possibility of slipping and falling and making a spectacle of herself or worse.

She joins the others, who have gathered around the table with the coffee and the sweets. Without the presence of their instructor, the group has relaxed. Gina is happily admitting that she told her husband that the class runs for two hours instead of one.

"That way I get to skip dinner, bath, *and* bedtime," she says. "Mike and the kids can fend for themselves. Which probably means he's giving them cereal. But, whatever. My kids can mainline Cocoa Puffs if it means I get two hours to myself. Hey!" she says, suddenly, turning her gleeful attention to Don. "Did you really win all that money?"

Don nods.

"I bet you got a car. Or a boat. Everyone always gets a car or a boat," Gina says.

"I haven't bought anything," Don says apologetically.

There are jokes: I'll take that money off your hands! I'd buy a one-way ticket to paradise! But the energy peters out as everyone realizes that Don, with his sideburns, his sparse comb-over, and his gentle paunch, seems genuinely perplexed.

No one speaks. Joanne, mother of the drug addict, takes a napkin, wraps it around a Rice Krispies treat, then puts it in her purse. "I only took the one," she says when she notices Helene staring.

"Emergency! Emergency!" The call resonates through the room. Everyone turns to look at a bulky young man in a plaid hunting jacket who stands in the doorway of the children's reading room. He's holding his crotch.

"Coming, Son," Neil says, and hurries across the room.

Helene had thought that Neil's son was just a boy, but this person looks like he could be in his late twenties. Everyone watches while Neil takes his tall, hulking son by the hand and guides him to the men's room. Once they are inside, the others fall into an awkward silence.

"Eddie is one of our best customers!" Connie says finally. "Neil brings him to the library Monday mornings, first thing, rain or shine."

This releases a murmur of approval.

"By the way, Helene," Connie says. "We have a very nice classical music section."

Helene is taken aback by the woman's familiarity. Somehow, she hadn't thought her name tag would give others the right to behave as if they know her.

"We get kids doing reports for school," Connie continues. "And there are quite a few music enthusiasts like yourself in the area. I'd be happy to pull some volumes about Bach tomorrow and hold them for you behind the counter."

Helene would not like the woman to do this. She would like her to be quiet. And she would like the others, who are now waiting for her to respond, to mind their own business. "That would be fine," she says.

Just then, Neil and Eddie emerge from the men's room. Neil grabs his coat from the back of his chair and puts it on, then heads toward the glass doors. His son follows behind. At the doors, Neil waits while Eddie zips up his jacket. Then Neil reaches up and lifts the hood over his son's head, tying the strings so that it closes snugly around his face. There is some commotion between them. Eddie lets out a frustrated whine, then walks to the checkout counter and waits there as if the library were open for business. Connie makes a small unhappy sound, then goes behind the counter and takes a book from a nearby shelf. She opens the back cover, date-stamps the slip, and hands the book to Eddie.

"Thank you, Mrs. Waddington," Eddie says loudly, landing on each syllable with equal force.

"You're welcome, Eddie," Connie says.

Eddie follows his father out of the building. Connie returns to the group and starts to clean up the paper cups and napkins. She works quickly as if she's impatient for the night to be over. "We don't even shelve those sorts of books anymore," she says to no one. "The publishers call them fantasy, but they're just smut. I can barely stand to look at the covers of those half-naked— I don't know what they're supposed to be—Valkyries?—with those skimpy little outfits that hardly cover their hoo-has. But they're the only books Eddie will read. I told Neil I'd give him the books, free of charge. But you should have seen the look on his face. That poor man. I don't know about his wife, but it's always Neil who brings Eddie here and probably everywhere else, too. If he didn't have the library there'd be one less thing to fill the day." She takes a napkin and sweeps crumbs from the table into her hand. "You know, it doesn't even matter what date I stamp on the book. Eddie just likes to hear the sound. *Kerchunk*." She sighs and lets the crumbs fall into the wastepaper basket. "Does anyone want the rest of these?" she says, holding up the platter of treats. She looks at Joanne, whose cheeks flush.

"I could take them off your hands," Don says, coming to Joanne's rescue. "Not that I need it," he adds, patting his stomach.

Everyone goes to work. Gina finds the empty tin the treats came in. Peggy transfers them from the platter, taking care to hold each square with just the tips of her fingers. Joanne warns Don to keep the tin horizontal so that the treats don't get ruined. Helene feels like something is required of her but she doesn't know how to make herself a part of things. She puts on her coat and pushes through the glass doors, steeling herself for the rain, the cold car, her dark house.

During the following days, she puts the class out of her mind. On Friday, she spends the afternoon tutoring. Some volunteers try to get the children to like them, but Helene doesn't have time for tic-tac-toe or letting kids tell her fortune with—what do they call it?—*cootie catchers*. No one can quibble with her track record, though. All of her students' reading skills improve quickly. And she's nice enough, isn't she? While she's sounding out the long *a* in the word *baby*, little Darla rests her head on Helene's arm. Which is nice, although probably she's just tired. It reminds Helene of Francie when she was younger and would make little unintentional gestures—putting her hand on Helene's knee when she got up from the couch or backing into Helene in a crowded elevator. Thinking of Francie, whom she sees so infrequently now that all of them are in New York, Helene feels an emptiness take hold. She moves her arm so that Darla sits up and remembers where she is and who she's with.

By Tuesday of the following week, Helene has not engaged with Bach. She feels alternately angry at the Flamenco woman for giving homework, as if Helene were a schoolgirl, and a growing sense of anticipatory shame. She tunes into the classical station on the radio in the den, settles onto the couch, and listens to whatever is playing. The music seems nice enough but it turns out not to be Bach. According to the nasal-voiced announcer, who is surely putting on his British accent, the piece is by Schumann. The next selection, he says, is by Claude Debussy. She tries to *engage* with Claude Debussy as practice but she doesn't know what she's supposed to think about. The whole piece goes by in a smear of notes, and then suddenly, here is the announcer saying something about the Leipzig Gewandhaus Orchestra (and now he has a German accent!) and she realizes she can't remember one note of what she just heard.

She does not want to read whatever books Connie has put aside for her at the library but she worries that if she doesn't pick them up, the woman will notice and realize that Helene is not a serious person. Librarians are prissy with their constant shushing and their signs that tell you not to reshelve books as if an even moderately intelligent human being can't be trusted to alphabetize. When she arrives at the library, she's relieved that another librarian is on duty and that Connie is nowhere in sight. The woman collects the books from the hold shelf and nods to herself as if she approves of Helene's interest in—ah, now Helene sees, when the woman slides the books across the desk—*Johann Sebastian Bach*. Helene is disheartened by the girth of two of the books. They don't even have pictures on the covers, an indication of the dullness of what's inside. The third book looks more optimistically slim. But then she realizes that it's a children's book called *Little Johann*. When she turns it over to read the back cover, she learns that the book is the fourth in a series for children. The other titles are *Little Franz*, *Little Camille*, and *Little Giuseppe*. Helene feels that Connie is mocking her by imagining that she would want to read a children's book about a subject she is *passionate* about, but she also feels sheepish because she doesn't have any idea who Little Franz, or Camille, or Giuseppe grew up to be.

On Thursday night, Helene feels a nervy energy as the group settles into their chairs for their third meeting. She didn't make any headway with the tomes, but from reading *Little Johann*, she now knows that Bach was a precocious little boy, and that he probably composed music when he was very young, but that we (and she now includes herself in a special group of people who know things about the composer) can't be sure, because Bach did not make a habit of preserving his work. *Much*, Helene says to herself now, having rehearsed what she will say, *has been lost to history.*

But it turns out that Marjorie Flamenco doesn't ask the group about how they engaged with the dogs and dead singers they claimed to care about. Instead, she has another plan for the class.

"Today's question comes in the form of free association," she announces. "When I say a word, you say the first word that comes to your mind. Let's start with you, Don. When I say 'bowling' you say . . ."

"Bowling," Don says.

"That's my word," Ms. Flamenco says. "An association is a word that you think of when you hear my word."

"Lane," Don says.

"Not what it makes you think of, Don," the woman says with effortful encouragement. "What it makes you feel. I say 'bowling,' you say . . ."

"Fun?" Don says.

135

"We'll come back to you," she says. "Gina, when I say 'Buzzy,' you say . . ."

"Why am I the only one who cleans up the crap in the yard," Gina says.

"One word," Ms. Flamenco says.

"Pissed off," Gina says. "Pissed."

"Neil, when I say 'Eddie,' you say . . ."

"Tired," Neil says.

"Connie, when I say 'book,' you say . . ."

"Tired."

"That's Neil's word."

"It's my word, too."

"Books make you tired?" Ms. Flamenco asks.

"Yes," Connie says. "Very."

Ms. Flamenco turns to Peggy. "When I say 'Elvis,' you say . . ."

"Bill Foster."

"Just one word."

"Principal."

"A feeling, Peggy."

"Starving."

Helene is shaken by the brazenness of that word. Everyone is being humiliatingly honest. Their willingness, their *eagerness* to expose their emotions, even their most private ones, feels threatening. What can she possibly say about Bach that will match a woman who is starved for someone named Bill Foster? She read about Bach, or at least she read about his childhood. She did end up hearing a few Bach pieces on the radio. But did his music sound any different to her than Schubert's or Schumann's or whatever else she listened to? There were notes.

They were arranged one way or they were arranged another way and all of it sounded—

"And Helene, when I say—"

"Nice," Helene says, feeling defeated. "Bach is nice."

Principal Bill Foster, everyone learns during social time, was Peggy's lover for over a year. That is, until she went into his office one day after school hours, took an SAT test out of its sealed box, and gave it to a boy named Axle Mayhew.

"Who is a truly gifted artist," Peggy says. "But whether he gets into a college with a halfway decent art department that will give him a scholarship depends on whether he can memorize vocabulary words. I can't tell you the number of good kids I've seen who can't get ahead because they don't know what 'exacerbate' means."

"To make something worse than it already is," Connie says automatically.

"Oh, I see! You lost your job because of love," Helene exclaims suddenly, remembering what Peggy had said in that first, introductory meeting. She's surprised she's spoken, but Peggy doesn't seem offended. In fact, she offers Helene a grateful smile. "I lost love, too," she says.

No one speaks. The quiet makes a space around the word *love* so that it seems to float in their midst. Helene feels that she could reach out and hold it. She wonders what that would be like.

The fourth class is devoted to answering the question *What am I great at?* The members of the group have become comfortable enough with one another that when Don says that he's been told that he's generous with people, and Gina says, "Yourself excluded, Mr. Moneybags," he smiles in acknowledgment.

The question at the fifth meeting is *How do I get in my own way?* Helene offers that she stays up too late at night and needs more sleep. Which is a kind of truth, she thinks, proud to have participated.

"I gave my son money," Joanne says when it's her turn.

"And what do you think he'll use it for?" Marjorie Flamenco says.

"Probably drugs," Joanne says. She looks worn out.

"This is a pattern of behavior you need to break, Joanne," Ms. Flamenco says.

"I know," Joanne says.

"What is this behavior doing to you?" Ms. Flamenco asks, her uplift at the end of the question letting Joanne know there is only one answer.

"It's stopping me from getting what I want," she says dutifully. "I'm sorry."

"You should apologize to yourself. Yourself deserves more."

"I'm sorry," Joanne repeats.

"He's her son," Neil says quietly. He's sitting beside Joanne and he turns his body so he's facing her head-on. "You don't have to feel bad. No matter what anyone says. He's your boy. You'd do anything for your boy."

Helene looks toward the children's reading room, where Neil's son is probably deep into one of his Viking books. She misses Tom now that he's moved away and there is so much about his life she doesn't know. And when he comes to visit, and tries to fill her in, she misses him more.

Everyone arrives at the last meeting promptly at six, but Marjorie Flamenco is not there. The group is unsettled. Small conversations start up and then die down. Eddie begins to make some noises in the children's room, so Neil goes to check on him and then returns. Twenty minutes later, Ms. Flamenco arrives. She stamps her snowy boots on the mat, then strides across the floor. They all sit up in their chairs, waiting for her to take charge. But there is something different about her tonight, Helene thinks. Some overcompensating energy that makes her seem frenzied. Another unusual thing: the woman is wearing makeup, a thickly applied foundation that only partly obscures a bruise on her left cheek. Helene feels a dark recognition. Once, when she and another reading tutor were lifting boxes of donated school supplies onto a storage shelf, the woman's shirt rode up, and Helene saw a black-and-blue mark on her waist. The woman had made a quick excuse about having fallen. Helene pretended to believe her.

Ms. Flamenco announces the sixth and final question of the course: *What does fulfillment look like?* No one volunteers an answer. Maybe everyone has noticed the bruise and, like Helene, feels confused. Over the past five weeks, their teacher has told them what is wrong with the way they think about themselves. Don needs to believe that he deserves his fortune. Connie needs to stand up for herself when the library superintendent puts his hand on her backside while blaming her for the decline in attendance. Gina needs to stop fantasizing about having an affair and commit to her husband and her children. They've accepted her criticisms and promised to take her advice, but now it seems that Marjorie Flamenco is no more capable of *grabbing her life by the throat* than the rest of them.

"Maybe my husband and I could go away for a weekend," Gina offers quietly. "Maybe that could be good."

Everyone nods in agreement.

"I'm going to give my superintendent what for and quit my job," Connie says.

"Will that be fulfilling?" Marjorie Flamenco asks.

"It will feel good to see the look on his face, that's for sure," Connie says. "And don't worry, Neil, I'll make sure the other ladies know where I keep Eddie's books."

"I bought a lawn mower," Don says. "One of those fancy ones you ride around on."

Everyone applauds.

"But what if I don't know what fulfillment looks like?" Helene says, more loudly than she'd intended. Nothing has changed for her. She's still afraid of her lighted house and her dark house. She still can't breathe at night. She still doesn't know what to do with her time so that she feels like she's alive. She doesn't even know what feeling alive means.

Marjorie Flamenco doesn't say anything. Helene knows the woman has no answer and that she might not have answers to any of the questions she's asked during the last six weeks.

At seven o'clock, the class ends. No one suggests staying for coffee. Everyone seems eager to go home, to let these meetings and the intimacies they've provoked evaporate into the cold night air. As each person leaves the building, Helene feels an irrational stab of abandonment. She will never see these people again.

Neil helps Eddie with his jacket. Tonight, Eddie wears a hunting cap, and Neil lowers the flaps around his son's ears. When Neil starts to button up his own coat, Eddie reaches down to help his father, just as his father has helped him. Helene can't bear it.

"Neil, would you like to go to the symphony with me?" she says.

Neil looks startled by her invitation, maybe even a little fearful. She should stop but she can't. "I have three tickets for Saturday night. At eight o'clock. Do you think you and Eddie might like to join me?" She doesn't have three tickets or even one. She saw the advertisement in the newspaper earlier in the week. Bach was on the program, and she considered it for a moment, but decided that since the class was coming to an end, she didn't have to pretend any longer.

"Of course, you're probably busy," she says.

"We'd like to come," Neil says.

"Well . . . Well . . ." She's suddenly flummoxed. "Would you like me to get a ticket for your wife?"

"I think Erica would probably appreciate an evening to herself. She works a long day so that I can spend all this time with Eddie."

Helene envies the dependable affection she hears in his voice.

"At Severance Hall?" Neil says helpfully. "At eight?"

"That's right," she says.

"How about we meet you a half hour before at the box office," he says. "That will give us time to get used to things."

He means Eddie, of course. Neil has told the group that Eddie has trouble with unfamiliar environments and new people, which is why Neil and Eddie do the same things at the same times each week. And this is why Neil sometimes feels that his life is very small but that he doesn't know how to take that problem by the throat because Eddie will always be the way he is, and someone will always have to take care of him.

"Seven-thirty, then," she says.

"Sharp!" Eddie says.

* * *

Eddie and Neil are already standing outside the concert hall when Helene arrives. It's a mild night, and she feels the pleasure of being watched as she approaches them. She notices that Eddie is wearing dark pants, laced shoes, and an overcoat rather than his usual jacket. Neil wears a suit. She appreciates that the effort she's made with her own outfit—she's wearing her black velvet dress and her coral beads tonight—has been matched by Neil's sense of occasion. They greet one another and join the crowd heading into the lobby. When she bought the tickets, Helene was disappointed that the best seats available were on the second tier at the side, but once the three of them check their coats and find their seats, she's glad for the location. It might have embarrassed Neil to think she'd gotten the highest-priced tickets. A man takes the empty seat on the other side of her. He nods, and she gives him a brief smile in return. On her other side, Neil settles Eddie in and helps him to adjust to the new place and all the people. He opens the program and points out the pieces they will be hearing. He describes what it will sound like when the concert begins, that it might get loud, but that Eddie doesn't need to be scared. He explains how they will be quiet when the music is playing and clap when everyone else claps. When the musicians begin to file onto the stage and take their chairs, he explains what's happening, too.

"I guess you're familiar with this first piece," he says to Helene once Eddie seems at ease.

She opens her program. The concert begins with Bach's Concerto No. 1 in D Minor. She tries to read the program note quickly so that she can say something intelligent but it's useless. "The truth is, I don't know anything about Bach," she says. "I barely know anything about music at all."

Neil laughs generously.

"I don't know why I said that I did," she says.

"It was Ms. Flamenco. She could scare a bat out of hell. But we all survived."

She's relieved to have admitted her lie and she feels something else, too. They've been through an experience together, she and Neil and the others.

The concertmaster enters the stage, and the audience briefly applauds. As he tunes the orchestra, Neil whispers into Eddie's ear, explaining, making sure Eddie feels comfortable. The applause starts up again more fervently as the pianist walks onto the stage followed by the conductor. The soloist sits at the piano while the conductor mounts the podium. He pauses. A chair squeaks. Someone coughs. The music begins.

At first, Helene's attention is focused on the prowess of the pianist, who plays the notes with furious speed, barely moving his upper body as if his arms and hands have nothing to do with the rest of him. She reminds herself to think about the music. She remembers the kinds of things the radio announcers talk about and she tries to pick out little patterns of notes. *Motifs*, she thinks with satisfaction. But after a while, she tires of this and allows her attention to wander. There is only one woman among all the violinists. Ruth would have something to say about that. And frankly, Helene has something to say about it, too. It's ridiculous to think that out of all the women in the world who play the violin there are not more who are good enough to be part of this orchestra. She should bring this to someone's attention. She'll write a letter to the editor of the paper. That's exactly what she'll do. Something shifts in the music and her attention is drawn back to it. There's a dark atmosphere to the piece. Well, it's written in a minor key, she says to herself. That must have something to do with it.

Eddie becomes restless and he starts to make small, unhappy sounds. As Neil tries to quiet him, the man on Helene's right looks over to see what the problem is. When he catches Helene's gaze, he raises his eyebrows as if she is not connected to the noisy pair and that she, too, must be thinking: What kind of a man brings a person like that to a classical music concert? At first, she's embarrassed by Eddie's disruption and the man's growing impatience and disapproval. But when Eddie makes another noise, and the man glares at Neil, she becomes angry. No, she's enraged! How dare this man insinuate that Neil and Eddie should not be here? Or that Eddie should not be allowed to react to the music any way he likes? If she could speak, she'd tell this man that people are people. They are tired-out librarians and men who are stymied by unearned luck. They are widows who lie in bed terrified that they are lost in their noisy days and their noisy, pointless lives and that they are missing everything that matters. They are all these strangers in the concert hall who've come from across the city in order to listen to some notes arranged in particular ways that are different from any other ways they could have been arranged.

Look at them! she'd say to the man. Look at all these people! Look at all these lives!

SEVEN

WINDOWS ON THE WORLD

New York City, 1989

The window seat in her bedroom is Francie's favorite place to be. Maybe in the world. (*Hyperbole*, her mother would say and then tell her the Greek or Latin or whatever weird language the word comes from, and then her father would say, *I once met a girl named Hyperbole*, and then they'd all try to think up a good limerick.) She's not exaggerating though, she thinks as she tucks herself into the alcove. She remembers discovering the spot when she was little, and they'd first moved into the ninth-floor apartment. She'd never lived that high up. Sitting on top of the warm radiator cover and looking out the window, she couldn't tell who was bigger, she or the little kid roller-skating on the sidewalk below. She's fifteen and a half now and she knows about perspective but she doesn't think this exactly answers the question.

She can sit on her window seat for hours watching the traffic, or the delivery people pumping their bikes, or the panhandler who is always on her block and who once told her that her shirt was inside out. She had been embarrassed but also grateful that she could go back home and flip the shirt around before she walked into school looking like that. Still, it was weird to realize that all the times she tried not to notice that woman, the woman had been noticing her.

She looks at today's handout from English class. The essay counts for seventy percent of the grade. Which means, at best, she'll get a C because she barely participates unless Ms. Walker directs her radar gaze at her, which lets Francie know she is about to be destroyed. It's not that she doesn't have things to say. It's just that by the time she thinks of something, she's also thought of why it might not be true or not entirely true because really, everything depends, and then, when she's finally ready to speak, Ms. Walker has called on someone else.

Her teacher has given them a choice of three topics for their essay on *We Have Always Lived in the Castle*.

1. The Individual vs. Society
2. Isolation as Metaphor
3. Is It Real?

The first topic seems maybe the easiest because the two other books they've read so far this year—*The Scarlet Letter* and *The Crucible*—are also, according to Ms. Walker, about the individual versus society, and so Francie thinks she knows the right things to say to get at least a B on the essay. The second topic— well, isolation doesn't seem like a metaphor. Isolation is the feeling of standing in the hall at school along with a bunch of other kids and saying to herself, "You are one of the kids standing in the hall," even though she feels like she's behind a piece of glass looking at kids who talk and laugh and slam their locker doors and seem to know how to *be*. It's the feeling of walking down the street and watching everyone else move without having to think about it, while she can't take one step without being completely aware that she's putting her foot down here, and then the other foot down there, and then wondering if she put her foot too close to that dog turd, in which case she'll be anxious until she gets home and can wipe off the sole of her shoe with a wet paper towel and then wash her hands in the hottest water she can stand, which will make her hands really red. And then her mother will say, "Hands get more chapped in the winter," and she'll give Francie some moisturizer because she doesn't realize that Francie washes her hands so much or folds her clothes so that the edges line up in her drawers not because she wants to but because she has to.

Isolation is exactly what it is.

Topic three is confusing. Obviously, *it's* not real. *We Have Always Lived in the Castle* is a made-up story. People in real life don't even talk like that. And people don't poison their whole family and get away with it. Topic three is definitely a trick question, and she's bad at those. Marina says it's because she's gullible and believes the most obviously untrue things are true. Marina says this is her problem. *Among many*, Marina will add, and then Francie will say, *Look who's talking*, and then Marina will go, *Ha-ha*, and Francie will go *Ha-ha* back. Which is why Marina is her best (really her only) friend. Because she's not like the other girls in school, who pretend to be nice with their baby voices while they tell you that your breath stinks and then pout and fake apologize so that you'll forgive them because they're only being *honest*.

Suddenly, she startles and jumps off the window seat. Her heart is beating in her brain. It takes a minute before she realizes that something has struck the window. There's a small impression on the glass surrounded by tiny fissures. "Oh, shit!" she says out loud. The summer before, a bird flew into her window, leaving a smear of blood and feathers. Her father tried to clean it, but when he opened the lower window, it covered up the splatter on the upper one. Benny, the super, came to look at it, but he said there was nothing to do until the building's scheduled window cleaning in six months. At first, Francie was disgusted by the bird's remains, but as weeks went by, she became interested in the slow decay. The blood went from red to tomato paste to rust. Some of the feathers dried up and disintegrated, leaving ghostly imprints on the glass.

She doesn't know why birds keep dying on her window. Maybe they see a reflection and think they are flying into more sky. Or maybe they see themselves and think they are their own enemy birds that they have to attack. It's terrible to be so wrong about everything. She settles back onto the window seat and puts her finger to the scar on the pane. It occurs to her that the whole idea of being inside or outside doesn't really mean anything. It's hard to think of yourself as *here* and other people as *there* when all it takes is a confused bird to erase the difference.

Marina would roll her eyes and say, "*Heavy*, Francie." She'd say, "Thinking is overrated." But when Ms. Walker calls on Marina, she blurts out the first thing that comes to her mind and it's always right and even a bit unusual, just like Marina is unusual, the way she lines her lips with a dark pencil that doesn't blend in with her gloss because she thinks it's cool to be a little ugly and because she likes to see the way people stare as if there's something wrong with her.

There's a knock on Francie's door. It opens, and there are her parents, looking weird, like they're waiting for her to tell them that they did something wrong and give them a consequence. She gets a weird feeling in her body, the same thing that tells her even before she realizes it that the man she's about to walk past is pissing into a tree planter or not to sit next to someone on the subway because he's crazy. The same body knowledge that tells her she is about to get her period about two seconds before she feels wetness in her underwear, a useless warning that gives her no time to do anything about it. Her parents come into her room and sit on her bed. They pat the spot between them. She doesn't want what is about to happen to happen. But then she realizes that it already has, so she slides off the window seat and does what they ask. They each take one of her hands. She can't look at them so she stares at her poster of *The Queen Is Dead* on the wall. She wants to be that person, that French actor or whoever it is, lying back, looking calmly at whatever he is looking at, which is probably nothing, thinking about what he is thinking about, which is probably sex. She wants to be listening to Morrissey singing about how he doesn't care if he's in Liverpool or Leeds or Birmingham, or better yet, about time's tide smothering you, which is her favorite from *Meat Is Murder*, or really any song would be okay, just so she doesn't have to listen to her parents saying what they're saying, because she doesn't think she can bear the embarrassment of pretending to be surprised by something that she realizes she already knows. She never put it into words exactly, at least not the ones her parents are using now: *separate, temporary, space*. But in the last year, things have gone missing. At the dinner table her mother doesn't talk excitedly about her terribly brilliant or terrifically dim undergrads. She doesn't tell them about whatever translation she's been hired to do, and she doesn't try to explain to Francie how political and historical change can alter the nuances of language and *blah, blah, blah*, ideas that are sort of boring but also kind of interesting. And when her father does the dishes, he doesn't suddenly burst into a horrible rendition of "Octopus's Garden" or whatever goofy song he comes up with to make her mother laugh. She can't remember the last time they made up a family limerick. When Francie is in her bedroom doing her homework, she doesn't hear Tom Brokaw's nasal voice coming from the living room, which means her father is not watching the news, and she doesn't hear her mother giggling, which means she's not sitting on the couch next to him reading "Shouts & Murmurs." There is only quiet, and then her mother announcing that she has to *get some air*, and the sound of the overpainted front door unsticking, and then the heaviness of it closing. There are her father's stocking feet going *shush shush* against the wood floor as he heads to the kitchen. Sometimes, Francie joins him there and the two of them pick at a pint of Frusen Glädjé until they hear the front door open again, at which point her father puts the ice cream back in the freezer and washes the spoons like he wants to destroy the evidence.

"You see, honey," her father says now, coming to the end of the speech Francie has barely heard. "Mom and I, I guess we've been unhappy for a little while."

Of all the blurry words they've been using, *unhappy* is the one that finally makes its way through to her and thuds in her chest. She's never really thought about her parents' feelings. Sometimes they get on her case about cleaning her room, or talking to Marina for too long on the phone, or because of her report card. They yelled angrily at the TV when Dukakis was being such an idiot that he might as well have handed the election to Bush, and then they yelled some more when Bush won. Sometimes her father is remote because of something that happened in the stock market, but soon he's back to his regularly scheduled nice-guy self. When the talk is over, Francie lets her parents take her to the kitchen so that they can make hot milk with honey, something they used to give her when she was little and had nightmares. They say embarrassing things to her while she drinks. *Want a graham cracker to go with? You can make graham cracker soup!* They seem to need her to be young. What she feels, she thinks, when they finally let her go back to her room and she's sitting once more on her window seat, is that everything that will ever happen in her life has already happened.

She looks out her window. She didn't even get a chance to tell her parents about the bird. Now when she does, she won't be telling her parents. The word *parents* doesn't mean parents anymore. It's undergone what her mother would call a *semantic change*. When she tells them about the crack in the window, she'll be telling her mother. Or her father.

Everyone's parents are splitting up. She'll call Brian Strauss about the bio homework, and his mother will say, "Brian is at his *father's*," in a way that is too loaded considering Brian isn't even her friend, only a science brain she can count on to give her the answers to the hard problems. Marina's father disappeared when Marina was twelve and then turned up later in California. At first, Marina said she would be spending the entire summer in *El-ay*, a word that took up residence in her mouth as if it had always lived there. But that never happened. Marina and her younger brother, Evan, spend all of July at their aunt's house in New Jersey so that her mother can *take some time* for herself.

Take some time. Francie's mother, usually so anal about language and critical when it's sloppily used, had said the same thing. How in the world can a person take time? What is supposed to happen to everyone else without it?

Her father has already rented an apartment up by Columbia. He'll move out over the weekend. "You'll come up and visit once I have things set up," he said.

The word *visit* makes her feel like her insides are collapsing.

"It's a terrible thing," her grandma says when she calls early the next morning to check on her. "No one in our family has ever had a failed marriage."

"You'll be fine," her nana says when she calls ten minutes later.

"Have you spoken to your nana yet?" her grandmother asks.

Her nana says: "I can't imagine what Helene will have to say about this."

No and *Nothing really*, Francie tells them because by now she's learned to pretend that each has sent the better birthday gift or the bigger Hanukkah check.

"Bummer," Marina says when Francie tells her the news.

They are walking up Amsterdam toward school. Marina lights a Marlboro and hands it to Francie, who takes a drag. Her eyes fill.

"Are you crying?" Marina asks.

"Smoke," Francie says, waving her hand in front of her face. She passes back the cigarette.

Marina slips off the necklace she wears every day. It started off as a hollow silver heart suspended on a long chain, but the heart got caught in a taxicab door.

"A crushed heart," Marina says, putting the necklace over Francie's head.

"Ha-ha," Francie says.

"Ha-ha," Marina says.

"It's possible for a person to have too many feelings," Marina says thoughtfully. "You can be happy or sad or tired or awake, but everything else is pointless. My shrink is always, like, 'Tell me what you're feeling. Let's dig deeper into *that*, shall we?'" Marina shakes her head and her black bangs sway back and forth. Francie admires the certainty of Marina's looks, those blunt-edged bangs, her thick eyebrows that are just like Madonna's, the way she wears her ragged miniskirts and thrift-shop boots so effortlessly, like the girls in the East Village who look as if their clothes just happened to fall on their bodies without them noticing. The whole thing adds up to Marina. When Francie examines herself in the mirror, she's just disconnected pieces: dark hair that is not straight or curly, but that sort of lies there flatly, and embarrassingly plump lips that her mother says she'll grow into, but for now she just has to live with. Tall. Thin. Small chested like her mother. If someone was asked what Francie looks like, she's pretty sure they'd say, "Oh, you know, like some girl."

What she admires most about Marina is that she doesn't go through life having two conversations going on at the same time in her head the way Francie does. Like after Francie's parents explained to her which weekends she'd spend where and how they'd still do things together as a family, she was listening and nodding, but the whole time she was also thinking about the fact that her body was corkscrewing tighter and tighter and she had to do something to relieve that feeling, but she didn't know what, and she had to remind herself to say *Yes*, she understood, and *No*, she didn't have any questions, so that her parents wouldn't think anything was wrong.

And wasn't something wrong? All the time? Even when something was not, technically, wrong? Because, for instance, the whole time she'd been considering which essay to write about *We Have Always Lived in the Castle*, her parents were deciding that the words *parents* and *home* and *family* were about to undergo drastic semantic changes.

During the next week, life at home is pretty much the same. Or it's exactly the same as it was before Francie started to notice that things were different. Her alarm rings. She stays in bed until her mother yells at her to get up. She goes to the kitchen. Her mother stands at the stove eating eggs out of the pan while she reads the Arts section of the *Times*. Her father drinks coffee while he reads the *Wall Street Journal*. Francie grabs a yogurt from the fridge and finishes reading her history pages. Her mother asks her father to pick up the dry cleaning on his way home from work. He says he will. Later, at dinner, they eat chicken and cauliflower and rice and make the usual jokes about her mother's habit of cooking monochromatic dinners. Her mother says, "A soothing palette to soothe palates," because she likes figures of speech. Then Francie calls Marina and they talk while they do their homework and watch Tracey Ullman. The sheer normalness is so stressful that Francie can't wait to be in school because at least school, with all its accompanying self-consciousness, feels like it's actually happening, whereas home feels like it might be a TV show.

The only thing that makes the week different from any other is that her parents keep asking her how she's feeling. *It's okay to be sad*, they say with hopeful looks, as if without her misery as proof, they can't be sure what they've done.

Over the weekend, her parents want to replay the family's greatest hits. Her father wakes her up early on Saturday morning so they can go to Zabar's and buy the smelliest cheese they can find. Her mother wants them to go to an afternoon movie so the three of them sit in a mostly empty theater sharing popcorn and watching *High Hopes*. When it's over, they stand outside in the cold and debate whether to go for Chinese or Japanese, a discussion that always includes each of them saying what they'd order at either place. They end up sitting at a big hibachi table with people they don't even know, which is weird, Francie thinks, because those people probably assume that Francie and her mother and father are a family, when they are only watching the chef toss an onion into the air and slice it in eighths before it hits the sizzling grill *as a family*.

On Sunday morning, her mother puts on her long coat and her boots and goes out for bagels, while her father makes his "famous eggs," which aren't famous, only scrambled, but he always says that, and Francie's mother laughs when he does because it's some old joke between them. Francie once read an article in a magazine at the doctor's office called "Ten Things to Do Before You Die." It listed things like traveling somewhere you always wanted to go or looking up old friends you haven't talked to in a while. But what's the point of doing all those things? You aren't going to remember going to Paris when you're dead. You aren't going to be glad you got back in touch with your college roommate.

On Sunday afternoon, she and her mother stand at the door while her father waits for the elevator, a suitcase and duffel bag at his feet. When the elevator comes, he turns and gives them a little wave that doesn't really work.

The first week he's gone feels like he's just on a business trip or visiting Cleveland on his own. But it isn't really like that at all, because her mother doesn't stay in her bedroom like she usually does, correcting papers at her desk or talking on the phone. Instead, she wanders around the apartment straightening pillows and picture frames and complaining that she's too hot and opening windows and then saying it's too cold and closing them. When Francie goes to the kitchen to get some peanut butter, her mother shows up in the doorway. "You like peanut butter," she says, as if she got knocked in the head and had amnesia and now has to relearn everything she ever knew. Later that night, she comes into Francie's bedroom holding the *Voice* and telling her about a review she just read of the Replacements' new album. Her mother doesn't care about music. It was always her father who took her down to Tower Records and to concerts when she was too young to go on her own.

"I thought you'd be interested," her mother says, and then, after too much silence, Francie says that she is.

Or they'll be sitting across from one another at the dinner table the way they always have, but her father won't be at one end to balance the triangle, and this will feel a little bit like drowning.

She's almost relieved when the weekend comes and she takes the bus up to her father's for the first time. While he lets her into the apartment, he tells her that it belongs to a professor who's on sabbatical.

"A temporary situation for a temporary situation," he says cheerfully, but the minute he does, they both deflate. He tries to rescue the situation by showing her around. He points out the things that don't belong to him with pride, like the masks from the tribe in South America that the professor studies that hang on the living room wall. She thinks the masks are kind of scary, but her father doesn't seem to mind all those empty eyes staring at him.

He points out that he put a framed photo of her on the piano next to photographs of the professor's friends and family.

He's got the whole weekend planned out. They go to the Columbia campus and walk around admiring the buildings. They visit the Cathedral of St. John the Divine and Grant's Tomb. They eat Cuban food for lunch and Salvadoran food for dinner and they have breakfast at her father's new favorite diner. By Sunday afternoon, they are both overstuffed and exhausted. When it's time for her to leave, her father stands at the door of his/not his apartment and watches while she waits for the elevator, just like she watched him a week earlier, and all she can think of is whether she is here and he is there or if it's the other way around. And the whole time he is telling her that he loves her and she is telling him that she loves him, too, she is also thinking about the fact that, because he asked her to, she has left her pajamas and her extra T-shirt and a pair of socks in the room that he calls her bedroom, but that is really the professor's office that has a pullout couch. She starts to get that twisted-up sensation in her chest. Leaving her clothes feels the way not being able to wash her hands does, like she has to fix something or else she can't move on to whatever she's supposed to do next.

When she gets back home and opens the door to her apartment, her mother is standing right there in the entryway pretending that it's such a coincidence because she was just getting something out of the front hall closet. Francie wonders if her mother stood in that exact same spot all weekend long, waiting.

"I gotta work on my essay," she says.

"But what about dinner?"

"We ate," Francie says, and wishes she didn't see whatever it is that passes across her mother's face.

In her bedroom, she finds her headphones, sits on her window seat, and listens to "How Soon Is Now?" on her Discman. The familiar lyrics and the sound of Morrissey's voice settle something inside her. She had been so upset when the band broke up. Her parents tried to comfort her. They told her that once, everything they owned burned up in a fire. "We had nothing!" they said merrily. "We had to start all over from scratch!"

There's another mark on the glass. It's just a small fracture, not as bad as the first. She's relieved to think that maybe this bird got away with it.

* * *

Two months later, Marina turns sixteen. Her mother wants to take her to Windows on the World to celebrate.

"I know it's cheesy," Marina says when she calls Francie to invite her along. "But Mr. Mafia is paying."

Mr. Mafia is what Marina calls her mother's new boyfriend, who peels off twenty-dollar bills and gives them to Marina and her brother to get them to like him. He's not really in the Mafia; he's a surgeon. He does some kind of heart operation that is so hard to do that people come to him from all over the world. They're so grateful when they end up not dead that they give him fancy watches and solid gold cuff links. Marina said that one patient from Saudi Arabia sent him a horse, but he sent it back.

In the week leading up to the dinner, Francie and Marina discuss just how dumb it is that Marina's mother wants to celebrate at a tourist trap, and how this is proof that her mother has no idea of who Marina really is. But when Friday night arrives, and the elevator doors open onto the restaurant, Francie is amazed and she can tell that Marina, despite her decision to wear a black tank top with holes in it, is excited, too. Mr. Mafia has reserved a table by the window, and Marina's mother makes sure that Francie and Marina both have seats closest to it. The two of them exclaim about being able to see practically the whole East River and how pretty the bridges look all lit up, because, really, they are not that different from tourists seeing a place for the first time. Marina, who mostly can't stand her brother, lets him lean in close to her so that he can see, too.

She also allows her mother to say embarrassing things about being sweet sixteen and never been kissed. Marina blushes and gets fake-mad so that everyone can go, "Ooohhhh" because now they know that she has been kissed. She's been more than that, Francie's and Marina's private smiles say, but they won't tell Marina's mother about Billy Cunningham's self-proclaimed "magic fingers."

Everyone's having a really good time and at one point Mr. Mafia (who, Francie learns, is really named Bruce) takes Marina's mother's hand and holds it to his cheek. Marina's mother seems really happy with this person who is not Marina's father. Francie feels a swimmy, dangerous emotion fill up her chest and thicken in her throat. She turns and looks out the window. The thing about being so high up is that everything below looks like the exact shape it is on a map, only somehow it doesn't feel as real as a drawing. Maybe she should do topic number three for her essay. Maybe *Is It Real?* isn't a trick question after all.

When she wakes up late the next morning, she sees something glinting on her carpet. She rolls off her bed and crawls over to discover a silver pellet buried in the green shag. Something tells her to go to her window, where she sees that inches away from the other two cracks there is an actual hole in the glass, and that the hole is the same size as the thing she's holding in her hand.

"Mom!" she cries. "Dad!"

By the time her father gets to the apartment, her mother has already called the police. Two of them are in Francie's room along with the super. They say that the hole and the pellet are from a BB gun and that probably the other cracks in the glass were made by a BB gun, too.

"It looks like someone has been shooting at your daughter's window," one of the policemen says.

"But why?" her mother asks. Her voice sounds like a little girl's.

The police tell Francie's mother and father that an investigation will be opened and what they can expect next. Benny says that he'll put in an order for a new window right away.

"Oh, honey," Francie's mother says after Benny and the cops leave. "Why didn't you tell us?"

"I thought it was just birds," Francie says.

"You have to tell us when bad things happen so we can take care of you," her mother says.

Which means, Francie guesses, that she has to tell each one separately so that she can tell the "us" that isn't an "us." And none of it matters anyway. Because what could they do about misguided birds, and her spinning mind, and all the things she has to be vigilant about all the time because there are just so many ways that things can go wrong? There are so many things you can step on or brush against and so many answers you can give to questions that won't be right, because any answer is only right from one point of view.

"It's okay, Ruthie," her father says, putting his hand on her mother's back. "Francie's safe. That's all that matters."

Before they left, the police said that Francie should probably avoid her bedroom until they can figure out what's going on. Francie pulls her sheets and blanket and pillow from her bed, but her mother and father insist on making up the living room couch together. They stand on either end holding the corners of her sheet, snap it, and let it float onto the cushions. They do the same with the blanket and then they move around the couch, adjusting the bedding and plumping up her pillow. When they're finished, they look at her with anticipation, the way they used to when they gave her a present and were waiting for her to unwrap it. Her father sticks around all day, which feels weird because it's not like he can stop whoever is shooting from doing it again just by being there. Also, he acts like he's a guest, asking if he can use the bathroom or if anyone minds if he eats the last apple. At dinnertime, her mother orders pizza and the three of them eat, sitting on Francie's temporary bed while they watch one TV show after another, waiting for *Saturday Night Live* to come on. The next thing she knows, she's waking up. She must have fallen asleep in the middle of the show, and her parents must have tucked her into her couch/bed. Pale, gray light comes through the living room window. She hears the morning delivery vans trundling down the street and the pneumatic wheeze of a garbage truck. Her mother's bedroom door opens and then it closes quietly. She's about to call out to let her mother know that she's awake, but then she hears the unmistakable sound of her father making his way down the hallway, the familiar slide of his socks along the floor. The sticky front door opens. A moment later, it closes.

Her heart is beating too fast. She gets off the couch and walks quietly to her mother's bedroom. She's about to knock when her mother makes a wretched sound that reaches right inside Francie, takes hold of her guts, and squeezes. Francie doesn't think she's ever heard her mother cry before. She stays at the door for a moment longer unsure of what to do then goes back to the living room. She stands next to the window and looks down at the street below. A few moments later, her father comes out of the building. She can't tell from nine stories up but she imagines he's wearing his shoes now. He pauses in the middle of the sidewalk for a moment like he hasn't decided what to do next. Finally, he turns and walks toward Broadway. He'll probably catch the bus up to his apartment. Or maybe he'll take the train. Or maybe he'll just walk. He likes to walk.

In April, her mother decides that Francie should sign up for a language program in France for the month of July to improve her skills. Francie isn't so sure, but she doesn't have any other idea of what to do with her summer so on a warm Sunday morning, she sits on her window seat and fills out the application.

It turns out that the shooter was a kid. His parents got him the gun but didn't realize what he was doing with it. He'd shot at a few other windows in her building, but nobody ever said anything about it. A person on the second floor had thought it was just a fluke. The people on the fifth floor didn't deal with it, because they were renters and planning to move out anyway. Marina says the kid is a juvenile delinquent and that he'll probably end up being a serial killer. Francie isn't so sure. She thinks maybe he was only wondering what it would be like to be standing in one place and also be in another place at the same time.

Benny put in the new window. The glass is smooth and clear.

EIGHT

TEN

Cleveland, Ohio, 1991

And why, Helene thought, was Francie at the front door?

"It's just me, Grandma," she said. Her smile was brief, and then she lowered her head and looked down at her feet as if she were lying and only pretending to be herself. Helene had a view of her jagged part, around which the hair had been dyed black, while the rest of it was a shade of—Helene wasn't entirely sure—banana?

"Why aren't you in school?" Helene asked, but as soon as she did, she realized her mistake. She reached out and brought Francie inside the foyer, closed the door, then drew her in for a hug. Francie barely responded. Her body was limp. Whatever energy she'd summoned to get herself from her college in Pittsburgh to Cleveland had obviously been spent.

"Don't tell Mom and Dad I'm here, okay?" Francie whispered. "Please, Grandma."

Helene let go of her and took a step back.

"They'll just freak out, and I can't deal," Francie said. "Promise?" Before Helene could answer, Francie looked past her and her face relaxed. "Hi Erna," she said, then walked over and gave Erna a hug and a kiss.

Coolheaded as always, Erna didn't react to Francie's surprise appearance. Still, Helene had known the woman for half a century and she understood the variety of her silences. Erna agreed: something was wrong.

"How did you get here, darling?" Helene said.

"I took a Greyhound."

"A bus!" Helene said.

"People take the bus, Grandma."

"I know people take the bus."

"I was so tired. The second I sat down, I passed out," Francie said.

"That doesn't sound safe. With all those strangers."

"Grandma." Francie sighed.

"Franka can smell my cooking all the way from college," Erna said, using the name that had always affirmed the special bond she and Francie had. "She knows I'm making cabbage rolls for lunch."

"Oh wow," Francie said, "I'm starving!"

Helene had always scolded Tom when he used that word. Back then, she didn't like the idea that his declaration, especially if she was collecting him from school and they were within earshot of other mothers, shone a bad light on her ability to keep him well fed. As she and Francie followed Erna down the back hallway, she felt a stab of shame about the things she once thought mattered. She could still recall those photographs from

Biafra that showed the huge, helpless eyes of children who were actually starving. To think that she'd once worried that someone might think she couldn't feed her son. This was happening more and more to her, this reckoning with all of the versions of herself she'd ever been. She could be tender about an awful hairstyle—you could forgive a victory roll—but it was harder to excuse some of the things she once believed. To think that she'd voted for Eisenhower! She'd corrected her mistake with JFK, but she had to bear some of the blame for Nixon, didn't she?

In the kitchen, Helene got a good look at Francie. Her complexion was bad, her cheeks sandpapered with pimples. She'd ringed her eyes with heavy black liner so that she looked like a raccoon. Her T-shirt and one leg of her blue jeans were shredded as if she'd been clawed at by another raccoon. Her short leather jacket, which was hardly warm enough for February, had a vandalized look, too. Helene knew the whole getup might be the thing nowadays—she'd seen the magazines with those fashion models looking like death whenever she and Erna went to the grocery store. Well, Francie's outfit would be something the girl would have to forgive herself for when she'd lived for almost eight decades and had to come to terms with the person who once thought that walking around looking like a vagabond was a good idea.

Erna started to take plates down from the cupboard while Helene set the kitchen table. Five years earlier, she stopped eating her meals alone in the dining room. She hadn't made a decision about it, really, but one day when she was sitting down to lunch, she mentioned to Erna that the big room was awfully cold. Without saying a word Erna had picked up Helene's place setting, brought it to the warm kitchen, and laid it across the table from her own. The two ate tuna fish sandwiches and tomato soup together for the first time in forty-five years. Soon after that, Helene started arriving in the kitchen a few minutes before noon to set the table for the two of them. The promise of this small, pleasurable lunchtime routine gave shape to the mornings. She'd stopped tutoring a few years earlier. The drive to the east side became too much, and the people in charge kept changing up the rules. Lately, phonics had been thrown out in favor of something called "whole word." Forget sounding out the letters; now children were supposed to understand what they were reading without actually being able to read it. She could have adapted, she supposed, could have taken the two-day training course they were offering, but something in her let go. She'd had enough. She'd had enough of volunteering at the temple, too. Just that morning she'd gotten a call from the head of the Shiva Committee asking her to sit the next day. Helene had agreed to do it, but it would be the last time. She used to like the work. There was a quality of emergency to it. The last-minute phone calls coming in when someone's nephew decided not to show up made her participation a bit heroic. But she'd been saying yes for so many years to the Shiva Committee, and to clothing drives, and to food drives, and to so much else because she'd been terrified of an empty day. Now she wanted emptiness. She didn't want to fill time or pass time. She wanted to feel time's weight and its crawl. Let her look at the clock and see that the minute hand had barely moved since the last time she checked. Let the day be endless.

Francie slid into a chair, barely pulling it back far enough from the table to give herself room as if she thought she were made of air. "I didn't even know where I was going until I got to the bus station," she said. "I just had to get out of there, you know?"

Helene did not know, but she wasn't sure if she wanted to know, either. If she did, she'd be required to do something about it. She loved Francie with all her heart, but she didn't think that she was up to taking responsibility anymore. Not for students, or grieving strangers, or even for her family. Responsibility was dangerous. When Thomas was young and experienced sadness or defeat, she'd climb down into the dark well of anguish with him. And when she managed to bolster him and get him back out of that hole, she was left feeling his injuries as if they were her own. And then there was always the worry that she couldn't help him. A child could go so terribly wrong. Look at that Ramirez boy she'd read about! The Night Stalker, they called him. He was somebody's child once; somebody responsible for him had obviously made terrible mistakes. If Helene had failed the students she tutored then they would not read at grade level and would fall behind. And if they fell behind they might not graduate and they would be more likely to get into trouble. And all because she had not taught them to read. Well, there was more to it than that, she knew this. Still, all you had to do was read the newspaper to understand that something was terribly wrong in a country that boasted about equal rights and civil rights, but where a child could be one *whole word* away from disaster. Her friends hated when she brought up topics like these at lunch. They'd hear her out, but she'd catch them trading glances. And then, inevitably, someone would end the discussion with the great default: *It could be worse. We could be living in Russia.*

So, no. She did not want to know what was going on with Francie. What she wanted was to feed her, to let her stay the night, and then send her back to school, where she belonged.

Erna set down plates filled with cabbage rolls and rice, and the three of them ate, letting the business of cutting and chewing take the place of conversation.

"I smell like ass," Francie said finally.

"After you eat, you can take a bath," Helene said.

"In yours?" Francie said, her face brightening. Helene's tub had always been Francie's favorite because it was square-shaped. When she was little, Francie liked to pretend it was a swimming pool, lying on her stomach in the shallow water, splashing and kicking and making a mess. Helene took showers now. The slick tub was too treacherous and the possibility of, one day, not being able to climb out of it, of having to call for Erna, or worse, having to wait through the night until Erna showed up the next morning and found her naked and waterlogged—well, you had to anticipate the worst when the very worst was near at hand. Tom wanted her to turn Emil's study into a bedroom so she wouldn't have to risk the stairs. She refused. She could never be comfortable in that room.

"After you eat, you can take a bath," she said.

"You said that already, Grandma."

"I don't think so."

Francie looked at Erna for confirmation.

"You smell so bad, she had to tell you two times," Erna said.

While Francie bathed, Helene and Erna studied the contents of the refrigerator and discussed dinner. Erna said she had the ingredients for a coffee cake, a Francie favorite. They briefly reminisced about the pecan halves that Erna had let Francie use to decorate the cake. She'd made a happy face. A peace sign. To think that a girl who liked happy faces could turn into a girl who, by her own admission, smelled like a dirty rump.

Helene went upstairs to see if Francie wanted baked chicken or macaroni casserole, but Francie was already fast asleep in Tom's old room. Her ratty-looking backpack sat on the bedside table and her clothes lay in a pile on the floor. Her hair was wet. She'd not managed to wash off all her eye makeup and traces of it smeared the pillowcase. When she shifted positions, the sheet slid down her chest, and Helene realized she was naked, and worse, that one of her nipples was pierced with a tiny silver hoop. She quickly pulled the sheet over Francie's pale shoulders as if she didn't want Francie to wake up and see what she'd done to herself.

There was a muffled beeping sound coming from somewhere. Helene looked underneath Francie's clothes and then felt around in the pocket of her blue jeans, but finally realized that Francie's backpack had dislodged the handset of the telephone. How exhausted she must have been not to hear that incessant noise. Helene hung up the phone then gathered the dirty clothes and carried them down the hallway to the laundry chute, another feature of the house Francie had loved when she was young. She'd used it as a slide for her stuffed animals, despite the fact Helene had forbidden it. Back then, it had mattered to her that something like a laundry chute, or a melon baller, or a consommé bowl be used solely for the purpose for which it was intended. She'd believed there was a larger lesson in that, a respect for the way things were meant to be. She thought that a person who thumbed their nose at perfectly reasonable conventions—and yes, she'd really believed this!—was a threat to the way society worked. The ideas she'd gripped onto so tightly for so many years had made her feel that her life would always be admirable and safe. Yet what was a melon baller, after all, but fear? What was this laundry chute but something to put distance between her and her filth? Of course, it was useful for Erna, who would otherwise have to carry armfuls of dirty clothing and bedding down two flights of stairs into the cellar laundry room. But for Helene to throw her dirty clothes down a chute and wait for them to miraculously appear in her drawers clean and folded—that was something else, wasn't it? It was like eating alone at the dining room table. It was a lie she'd told herself for too many years.

She might write a letter to the editor about that. Years earlier, they'd printed the one she'd written about the orchestra, and ever since then, when she saw something she was convinced was unfair or wrong, she took out her personalized stationery and composed another piece. They didn't always publish her opinions, but occasionally they did.

She brought the clothes downstairs. She and Erna spoke about running the washing machine on its quick cycle since Francie didn't have a change of clothes. Helene had peeked inside that knapsack and there was nothing in it but a grim-sounding book called *Being and Nothingness*, a half-eaten Mounds bar, a child's wallet embossed with a Mickey Mouse face that held a five-dollar bill and some change, and a half-empty pack of Marlboro cigarettes. Inside a wrinkled baggie was, Helene knew, a different sort of cigarette altogether.

Erna washed and dried the clothes and left them outside Francie's door. At four o'clock, her husband, Paul, pulled into the driveway and she left for the day. Helene stood at the kitchen window and watched Erna get into the car. It bothered her that, for so many years, she hadn't given a thought to having Erna work through supper when the woman had a family of her own to care for. Paul was a piano tuner. Helene had always thought that must be such a satisfying job. To turn something wrong into something indisputably right. Francie slept and slept. Helene microwaved the macaroni casserole Erna had plated and left in the refrigerator, as she did with each evening's dinner so that Helene didn't have to bother with the stove. Helene had simmered a pot of soup a while back and even though she was certain she'd turned off the burner, when Erna arrived the following morning, the kitchen smelled of rotten eggs.

She was sitting on the couch in the den watching the seven o'clock news when Francie finally appeared. She looked not exactly rested. Maybe over-rested, Helene thought, as if so many hours of sleeping had exhausted her all over again. Her hair stuck out at odd angles, but at least her clothes, while still mauled looking, were clean. She sat down on the couch, tucked her legs underneath her, and leaned her head on Helene's shoulder. How startling to feel the press of a body. This was something no one told you about getting older, Helene thought: how rarely you were touched. On the TV, President Bush was wearing army fatigues and greeting soldiers at an airport hangar.

"He looks like a little boy playing dress-up," Helene said.

"When did you become a cynic, Grandma?"

Was it true? Helene wondered. She supposed it was a good thing, this invasion, after what Saddam Hussein did to those poor Kuwaitis. And Iraq was problematic for Israel. *Is it good for the Jews?* used to be the only question she or anyone she knew would ask and the answer would tell her how to vote and how to think. This had made sense once, she supposed. But she'd grown to believe that the workings of the world were too complicated to be reduced to a single guiding principle.

173

When the news was over, she and Francie went to the kitchen, where Helene microwaved another plate of food. Francie propped up her chin in one hand while she forked the macaroni with the other. She ate heartily for the first few bites, even made some appreciative noises, which Helene would have to remember to tell Erna about. Soon, though, indifference took over until Francie was only pushing food around her plate. Helene offered her a piece of coffee cake, but Francie said she was tired again.

"I haven't been getting a lot of sleep lately," she said.

Her eyes searched Helene's face, and Helene felt something was required of her. Francie wanted her to ask some sort of question that would allow her to say things Helene wasn't sure she wanted to hear. "Too much schoolwork?" Helene said.

"Not really."

"You shouldn't ignore your studies."

Francie's expression shifted. "Nana's in Florida?" she asked.

"That's right," Helene said, feeling the creep of an old resentment. She rarely spoke to Evelyn these days. She knew of her whereabouts only because Tom had mentioned it during one of their weekly calls.

"A beach sounds nice," Francie said.

"If you like that sort of thing," Helene said.

"Who doesn't like a beach, Grandma?" Francie said, laughing lightly.

"I just don't know what people do there all day."

"Nothing," Francie said. "That sounds really good to me."

Helene wanted to say that a girl Francie's age, a girl just at the beginning of her life, ought to aspire to more than nothing. Not knowing what you wanted could lead you into all sorts of trouble that you might not be able to get out of until it was too late.

As if Francie intuited what Helene was going to say, she stood up. "Is it okay if I go back to bed?" she said.

"Of course," Helene said. She should have been relieved. What she felt was that Francie had given up on her.

As she washed Francie's plate, she realized that she was exhausted, too. Maybe it was climbing up and down the stairs. Or the argument she'd been having with herself about whether she should call Tom and let him know that Francie had shown up out of the blue. She'd had very little to do with Ruth since the divorce, but recently, Tom had sent her a magazine with a poem in it that Ruth had translated. Helene hadn't really understood the poem, but she'd been impressed to read *Translation by Ruth Turner*, after the last line. She hadn't even been that bothered by the fact that Ruth had gone back to her maiden name. Helene missed her old name. To think that seventy-seven years ago, her parents held her in her swaddling clothes and said to one another: *Let's call her Helene Harker!* It was astonishing to think how much of her life her parents had missed.

Tom ought to know that Francie had played hooky and gotten on a bus with nothing but a few dollars and a marijuana cigarette. But if she called, she'd lose Francie's trust. The girl was fine, she told herself as she turned off the lights on the first floor and climbed the stairs. Nothing a good meal, some clean clothes, and a night in a comfortable bed couldn't cure.

When she reached the landing, she heard Francie's voice through her closed door.

"Please," Francie said in a high-pitched whine. "You have to talk to me. I don't understand. I thought you— But I love you," she wailed.

A silence. And then, "Tell me what I did wrong. Please. Don't hang up. Hello? Hello?"

Helene felt disoriented. Her heart was fluttering. She thought she might faint. She hurried into her room and shut the door. Had she ever heard that kind of desperation? Francie's craven suffering—the humiliation of it. She sounded as if she were begging for her life.

She sat down at the foot of Emil's bed. All these years later and she still referred to it that way. How many nights had she watched him sleep, wrestling down the yearning in her body? She'd paid attention to so much, to his expressions when he came home each day so that she could discern his mood, to the sound of the study door closing when he shut himself inside the room, to the noise of it opening again, which would quicken something in her. And oh! She could still summon his touch when she asked his help to zip up her dress. He would fasten the hook and eye, his doctor's hands nimble and precise, so that he never pinched her skin or pulled on the short hairs at the nape of her neck. Still, there was always a moment when his cool fingers brushed her skin and she felt . . . *something*, and then, when he took his hands away, she felt the loss. But had she ever experienced what Francie was going through? No. She had her consommé bowls and her butter pat mold. She had her rules about what Tom could and couldn't say in public. She had *The Doctor says this* and *The Doctor thinks that* to protect her from that kind of devastation.

She woke at seven-thirty the next morning, much later than usual. She lay in bed relishing the small disorientation of a changed routine, and then, with a start, she remembered that she was due at the shiva by nine-thirty. She hurriedly put on her bathrobe and left the room, pausing outside of Tom's bedroom door. There was no sound; Francie was probably still sleeping. Erna would arrive at nine and she could manage things until Helene returned. Then she'd see about getting Francie a flight back to Pittsburgh. No. Helene changed her mind. What Francie needed was to get out of bed and get back on her feet. In fact, she needed to do that right now. If the bus was good enough to get her here, it would be good enough to take her back. Helene could drop her off at the station on her way to the shiva. My God! You didn't miss school because of a broken heart!

"Time to wake up dear!" she said as she opened the door. The bed was empty. She heard the toilet flush in the bathroom and then the sound of the sink faucet. Well, that was a good sign. Francie was up, ready for a new day. The sheets and blankets had fallen to the floor, and Helene stepped into the room to pull them back onto the bed. She'd always taught Tom to make his bed right after he got up in the morning. Probably one more thing she'd cared about for the wrong reasons, but an unmade bed still struck her as uncomfortably suggestive.

"Dear?" she called out. "Francie?" When she got no response, she knocked on the bathroom door, then opened it. Francie, wrapped in a bath towel, stood at the sink.

"Grandma!" she cried out, turning around. "What the fuck?"

"Oh no!" Helene said. Francie's face was a mess. Her pimples were bright red and there were small pinpricks of blood where she'd picked at them. "Oh no!" Helene repeated, cupping Francie's cheeks. "Why would you do that to your beautiful face? You're only making things worse."

From Francie's look of resignation, Helene realized that this had been the point. She wanted to look worse. She wanted to stick needles in her nipples, and rip her clothing, and tear at her face. Helene was furious at whoever it was that had treated her granddaughter so badly. And she was furious at Francie, who didn't know how to protect her heart. "Get yourself ready," she said. "We're leaving in half an hour."

"I don't want to go anywhere. I'll just stay here. It's okay."

But it wasn't okay. Francie wasn't okay. "Get dressed," Helene said. "We have somewhere we need to be."

Francie was sullen on the drive over, each sigh meant to indicate the degree to which she believed herself to be a victim of Helene's whim. But maybe, after years of Friday-night dinners, she had an innate appreciation for ritual because she stopped sulking and became curious as soon as they walked into the shiva house. Helene hung her coat and Francie's horrible jacket in the entryway closet, then took two prayer books from a stack on a small table. She made sure no one was looking, then lifted the sheet covering the front hall mirror and patted her hair into place.

"Here are the rules," she said, handing a prayer book to Francie. "Don't ask anyone how they are. For that matter, don't ask anyone anything. Especially the widow. If anyone talks to you, you can say you are sorry for their loss or you can say, 'May his memory be for a blessing.' Nothing more."

"I don't even believe in God," Francie said.

"What does that have to do with anything? You're a Jew and you can sit. Those are the only requirements." She took Francie by the hand and led her into the living room. She didn't recognize anyone although she hadn't expected to. She had no idea who the dead man, Aaron Gelb, had been, or who the widow, Cherry Gelb, was either, only that they belonged to Helene's temple, and that one of the ten people who'd agreed to say the morning's prayers had something better to do. The mood in the room was less somber than weary. This was the seventh day. People were worn out.

Nearby, a man stood holding a plate filled with miniature pastries. He looked like most of the men at these things, wiry gray hairs poking out of places they shouldn't, a yarmulke clinging precariously to his balding head. A widower, obviously, from the looks of the suit he hadn't brought to the tailor when he shrank. Granted, a shiva was not a fashion show, but Helene had been mindful about what she wore. This morning, she'd put on a rust and navy tweed dress that was woven through with a bit of pink. Respectful, but not heartfelt. There was no sense in pretending.

The man hurriedly finished swallowing and set down his plate as if he were embarrassed by his greed. He introduced himself as Richard, a second cousin, once removed. They were already down to the once removed, Helene thought as she shook the man's hand. "I'm sorry for your loss," she said. He put his other hand on top of hers, holding her in his moist grip, and gave her a look of helpless resignation, which seemed a bit dramatic given his relationship to the dead man. Oh, Francie was probably right. She'd become cynical. Maybe that's what happened when you stopped believing in all the things you used to think were true.

The furniture in the living room had been pushed aside to make way for the stools, and ottomans, and even an overturned milk crate topped with a throw pillow, all of which the assembled mourners were now lowering themselves onto. Helene motioned Francie to a pair of chairs that had been moved against the wall. A shiva was important, but there were some aspects of the ritual she was relieved not to have to take part in, and sitting in such a way that a stranger would have to hoist her up at the end of the service was one of them. Someone started chanting, and the rest launched into the first of the prayers. Helene reached over, opened Francie's book, and pointed to the transliteration on the facing page.

"Pray," she whispered.

"Really?" Francie said.

"Really."

Before they'd left the house that morning, they covered the worst of Francie's blemishes with powder. Things looked passable in the forgiving yellow light of Helene's bathroom, but now she saw that the effort hadn't done much good. The powder was now clinging to the inflamed pimples, and clots of it had become lodged in the creases of Francie's nose and chin. Helene had a passing thought that she wished that Evelyn was not in Florida. She had always been so fastidious about her looks; she would have known what to do.

Helene opened her book, but this was just for show. She'd been to these gatherings so often that she knew the prayers by heart. She could recite them while thinking about other things, and now she turned her attention to the room, which was decorated like so many living rooms of people she knew: couches and chairs upholstered in mustard and rust and olive green. Heavy glass ashtrays and bowls. Some odd items from their travels; in this case, a samurai warrior doll glowered from atop an upright piano. The widow sat alone on a couch. She looked

impassive. She was probably tired. Grief was exhausting—
Helene remembered that. She judged the woman to be around
her age, possibly a few years older, even though she'd chosen
to wear a dress that showed her knees. She had terrifically thin
ankles. Helene had always admired a thin ankle.

Francie was trying to sound out the transliteration. This
pleased Helene. It had been right to bring her here. All the girl
needed was to stop brooding about herself. A bit of perspective
never hurt anyone. There was breaking up with a boy. And then
there was death. The mourners were getting through the prayers
at a nice clip. Helene started to think ahead. She and Francie
would stop by the pharmacy and find an ointment for her skin.
Then they'd go back to the house. Erna was probably making
their lunch already. The leftover macaroni. And maybe she'd
find something to do with the boiled broccoli from earlier in the
week. Chop it up and mix it with a little mayonnaise for a salad.
Helene and Erna enjoyed the puzzle of repurposing leftovers.
There was a pleasing tidiness in leaving no trace. After that,
Helene would call and see about the bus schedule. She'd make
Francie promise to sit up front near the driver.

The mourners began to recite the kaddish. Their voices grew
louder as everyone reenergized for the final push. Suddenly,
the widow seemed to become more alert. She sat forward on
the couch. She looked a little wild-eyed. Then, abruptly, she
stood up.

"Who are you people?" she said.

The chanting stopped. One of the mourners held out his
hand, as if to prevent the woman from stepping into traffic.

"It's just us, Cherry, darling," one of the women said. "It's
me, Sylvia, and Mel is here with me. And there's Ben and Rich-

ard. And Marion and Anna. And Jerry. And the Seldens are here. And"—she looked over at Helene and Francie—"there are some nice people from the temple."

"I'm sorry, but Aaron isn't here," the widow said. "You'll have to come back another time."

Someone let out a small gasp.

The second cousin once removed stood, walked over to the widow, and gently took her hand. "It's Richard," he said quietly. "You don't know me very well, but Aaron and I used to play when we were kids. Back in Buffalo."

"Aaron's from Buffalo," the widow said.

"Yes, he is," Richard said.

"Aaron's gone now, darling," Sylvia said. "He had a heart attack. We're all so sorry."

Oh, it was awful! Helene thought. These foolish people believed that the woman needed to be reminded that her husband had been alive at one moment and dead the next when what she really wanted to know—Helene was sure of it—was what in the world had happened to her life.

Francie reached for her hand. "Grandma?" she whispered.

Oh, poor Francie! How awful this must be for her. Helene turned to reassure her, but Francie was giving her an odd look.

"It's okay, Grandma," she said. "Don't cry."

"I'm not crying," Helene said. But then a tear slid into the corner of her mouth and she tasted salt. She was mortified. How embarrassing to have feelings for people she didn't even know.

The widow allowed the second cousin to help her back down onto the couch. He sat next to her while the mourners finished up the prayer. And then everyone rose and began to socialize and eat. Helene wanted to leave quickly but she had to pay her respects. She took Francie's hand and led her over to the widow. Helene introduced herself. "I'm sorry for your loss," she said.

The woman seemed herself again. She thanked Helene for coming. Then she looked at Francie.

"This is my granddaughter," Helene said.

The woman reached up and took Francie by the hand.

"May his memory be for a blessing," Francie said. "I don't really know what that means."

The widow smiled. "It means I was lucky," she said. "You'll be lucky, too."

The bus was scheduled to leave at three o'clock that afternoon. During lunch, Erna came up with a reason to drive all of them to the station. Some urgent need for a new mop, which Helene knew was not true. The old mop was perfectly fine. But Tom had been arguing with Helene about her driving, and more and more, Erna found excuses to take her to the places she needed to go. The three rode to the station in comfortable quiet. Erna parked, then she and Helene walked Francie into the depot. Helene bought Francie's bus ticket and handed it to her.

"Grandma," Francie said, "do you think that woman can really tell if I'll be lucky?"

"What woman?"

"From this morning. She doesn't even know me."

"Of course you'll be lucky," Helene said, and when she saw Francie's relief, she knew it had been the right thing to say.

Helene and Erna hugged Francie and then watched as she went outside to find her bus. She didn't look any different than she had when she arrived. Her clothes were still a mess. Her backpack sagged even with the addition of the sandwich and apple Erna had put in it. Helene had slipped twenty-five dollars into Francie's wallet when she wasn't looking. The pharmacist had given her a tube of something he said would help, but he told her that she should see a dermatologist. She would or she wouldn't, Helene thought. And she would either chase after this boy who didn't love her or she wouldn't. There was nothing Helene or anyone else in the world could do about it. Francie was a girl going out into the world with all her burdens and her needs, trying to get what she wanted. Helene hoped she would find some luck in her life, but she knew that, no matter what, she would suffer along the way. Maybe there was luck in that, too.

NINE

TINY, MEANINGLESS THINGS

Cleveland, Ohio, 1992

Wednesday is ironing day, a day of smoothness, the close smell of wet heat, and the satisfactions of erasure. How rewarding it is, Evelyn thinks, to work the tip of the iron into the wrinkled underarms of her favorite blouses and watch the creases disappear. Now that she is seventy and her skin has lost its elasticity, this trick of reversing time is no longer available to her.

It's like a head of wilted lettuce, she thinks as she mists the blouse with her spray bottle. All you have to do is put it in ice water and it springs back to life. These were lessons she'd tried to teach her daughters: the right way to store vegetables, to fold clothing, to wash their faces (never soap, only water). They'd ignore her, which only made her repeat her warnings two or maybe three times, until they screamed at her and slammed their bedroom doors. They were young. How could they know the disaster of carelessness?

She knew. She'd been at her cousin's wedding in Tulsa when Frank died—it was now almost thirty years ago. The doctor had told her that it would be safe to take those days off from her vigil, that Frank still had a little more life in him. Naomi and Ruth were away at school, Naomi in Kearney, Ruth all the way east at that private college that was so interested in her sharp and critical company that they'd given her a scholarship. It had been up to Paula to keep tabs on her father that weekend. Evelyn paid for a retired nurse to come in during the day to feed Frank, to keep him clean, and to give him his medications. All Paula had to do was peek into the bedroom once or twice during the night, just to make sure that he was resting easily. It wasn't a lot to ask of a sixteen-year-old who was up at all hours anyway, on the phone, whispering to boys. Evelyn had been surprised that Paula hadn't complained. She'd thought that, finally, her youngest was beginning to take pride in grown-up responsibility. She'd left phone numbers for Frank's doctor and a neighbor Paula could contact if something went wrong. She'd given her the number of the motel in Tulsa where she'd be staying and had made sure to tell the night manager to let calls through no matter the hour. But Paula hadn't called anyone. She hadn't even checked on her father when she came home from the party she'd promised to skip. The next morning, when the nurse phoned Evelyn, she said that Frank had been gone for "some time." Evelyn hadn't asked how long. She didn't want to know if the woman had found him with his mouth open, his last call for help unheard. Paula was still asleep, the nurse said. Should she wake her?

Thursday is the day when Evelyn clears the refrigerator of those vegetables that have been in the bins long past cold water's ability to revive them and when she tosses the slices of turkey that have taken on an oily sheen. She eats less now than before, but she hasn't gotten used to grocery shopping with this in mind. She watches the women who roam the aisles gripping baskets barely weighed down with a single chicken breast, two oranges, and maybe a child-sized carton of milk meant for lunch boxes. Walking advertisements for their own expiration dates. Who would want to die alone in her apartment and be left undiscovered for enough time that the smell of soured milk would be the giveaway? And here was another piece of advice that her daughters had ignored: always wear a good pair of underwear and a matching bra. Which was the opposite kind of warning, she realizes, one that wasn't about trying to make things last, but about the possibility of dying suddenly and violently and being discovered with your skirt up around your ears in a pair of sad panties.

"How's the wash going, Mom?" Ruth might ask if she calls from New York on a Tuesday. Evelyn knows she's teasing, but she also knows that her daughters can't figure out how she can make enough of a mess to account for this constant cycle of chores. "It gives her something to do," she once heard Naomi whisper to Ruth when they were visiting at the same time. She could have told them that jobs, marriage, raising children—all of it is just something to do. But she kept quiet. No more warnings.

It's when she's ironing the collar of her favorite lilac-colored blouse that she senses Scotty outside the apartment door. She's told him many times that he needs to ring the doorbell, or at least knock, but he never does. It doesn't matter, really. She always knows when he's there. She can feel him hovering. She lays the iron in its cradle and opens the door. There he is, swallowed up by his baseball uniform, which is spotless even though he's just come from practice. She knows his summer schedule by now. She imagines him on the field, mitt dangling at his side, staring at a bug in the grass or at a cloud, while the other seven-year-olds yell that the ball is heading his way. She's certain he doesn't care if he misses a catch. Scotty seems uninterested in his childhood. He's marking time, waiting for these years to go by, if possible, without his participation. He's skinny, and his ears stick out. His bangs fall into his eyes no matter how often he brushes or blows them away. Still, despite his slightness, there's something heavy about him she can't put her finger on. She knows not to greet him enthusiastically or to call him *honey* or *dear* the way adults address children they barely know. Something about Scotty doesn't encourage intimacy. Better for her to behave as if he is a worker clocking in for his shift. He stands, as he always does, at the threshold, waiting for her to walk a few steps into the room before he follows. He doesn't close the door behind him, so she doubles back to do it. This little routine has become so familiar that it no longer annoys her, although, at first, it did. She assumed that he was spoiled, and that no one ever made him clear his plate or make his bed. But then she remembered a news program she saw about a man who was released from prison after serving thirty-five years for a crime he didn't commit. When he reached a door, he always stopped and waited for someone else to open it. For nearly four decades, he hadn't been allowed to open a door on his own. During his years in prison, the man had lost something more than time. No, Scotty isn't spoiled. He asks for nothing and expects nothing.

He goes into her bedroom, humming quietly to himself. He often sings about what he's doing in high-pitched, aimless tunes that he makes up as he goes. "We're folding the sheets," he might sing, or "We're watering the plants." He doesn't seem to be aware of his habit, and she doesn't point it out. She thinks his lack of inhibition is proof of something about her that is undeniably good. Children know what's what. Children and dogs. Now Scotty's singing about hangers, and when he reappears, he's holding an armload of them. On Wednesdays, it's his job to put the pressed clothing back in her closet. She's taught him how to think of the hanger as a pair of shoulders so that he can arrange a blouse to hold its shape, how to fix a skirt on clips, or hang a pair of slacks so that the crisply ironed seams match up. He's too small to reach the hanging rod, so she keeps a step stool next to the closet for him. Forty-five minutes go by with them barely speaking to each other. "Here you go," she says when she hands him a piece of clothing. "Okay," he says when she reminds him to button a blouse once he's got it on the hanger.

When they finish their work, Scotty sits at the kitchen table eating a piece of cinnamon toast. She made it for him once, and now he prepares it himself, getting the loaf from the bread box, toasting a slice, spreading the butter, and sprinkling just the right amount of spice on it so that the cinnamon tastes sweet instead of bitter. He holds the toast with both hands and takes small bites along each of the four sides before starting around again. Finally, he's left holding the center, where the toast is thoroughly soaked in butter. She admires his patience. Most children would try to get to the best part as quickly as possible. But Scotty is not most children.

She knows almost nothing about him, not when his birthday falls, or what school he goes to, his favorite color, or the name of his little brother. She doesn't know what he wants to be when he grows up. It would embarrass them both for her to ask the kinds of questions people come up with to pretend they're interested in children's lives, and it would make what goes on between them unimportant. No, her relationship with Scotty is something else. They exist for each other only during the time when Scotty helps her with her chores and eats his toast.

He finishes the last bite and slides off his chair. She follows him to the door, opens it, and watches him walk to the far end of the hallway, where he disappears into his apartment. She closes her door, feeling a little bit wholesome, a little bereft.

It's only later, when she's changing for bed, that she notices that Scotty has rearranged her closet, putting her dresses on the left side, the skirts to their right, then her slacks, and finally the blouses. She organizes her clothes in reverse based on use—she almost always wears pants and blouses these days. Skirts are for the infrequent lunch out. Dresses are for funerals. She wonders what made Scotty change the order. Is this the way his mother's closet is set up? Occasionally, she runs across the woman in the hallway or the garage. She's always overburdened with children, or grocery bags, or plastic pails and shovels. She doesn't seem like a person who worries about how her closet looks. Once, earlier in the summer, just after Scotty started coming over, Evelyn shared an elevator with his mother. The woman didn't mention Scotty's visits or ask if Evelyn minded, as if she thought an old lady should be grateful for the company of a small, odd boy. Evelyn was about to say something to make it clear just who was doing a favor for whom, but then she saw that the woman's shirt was buttoned wrong and that her bra showed where the material puckered. Evelyn cleared her throat and touched her own shirt the way she would touch her lip to let a friend know about a crumb, but the woman didn't notice. For the rest of the day, Evelyn couldn't stop thinking about Scotty's mother walking around in public completely unaware of her embarrassing mistake.

It's Saturday, and Scotty helps her with the dusting. With the step stool he can reach the top of the refrigerator and the ledges above the doors with the chamois cloth. He hasn't begun the puff and stretch she noticed in her girls when they were about his age, the way they would gather weight around their middles right before a growth spurt, as if they needed stores of energy in order to blast off. She doesn't know about boys, though. For a boy, growing seems like an honest business. The bodies of girls are tricky things. They swell and shrink on a monthly schedule, which can be irritating, but can also be used to their advantage. This was something she never advised her daughters about. She didn't have to.

As Scotty follows her around the apartment, he hums one of his little tunes. He sings a word or two about a dust bunny he finds under the bed, then about passing the white-glove test, which is something she once told him about. Of course, she doesn't use a white glove. She doesn't even own a pair—who would, these days? But he was taken with the idea, probably because she told him it was a custom at Buckingham Palace, which is something that might not be true, but that sounds true. She tries to be straightforward with Scotty, but sometimes she can't resist the look on his face when he reconsiders her and wonders what other mysteries she might hold.

When they're done with the living room and the bedroom, they go into the den. It bothers her that the grass cloth above the television console is lighter where the portrait of Burl's race-horse once hung. The reverse stain feels like a scolding. He was so angry when she said she wanted a divorce four years after they married. No, he hadn't done anything wrong, she agreed when he drilled her with questions. No, he hadn't changed. Yes, she knew he adored her, that he worshipped her. What she couldn't tell him was that she'd never believed in all that. Maybe that was the problem. Frank had been gone for so long, but another man's professions of love still sounded phony. She'd begun to hope that when she returned home after a day at work, Burl wouldn't be there. She couldn't stand the patterns of their life together. *The fridge is making that sound again* meant that he was going to haul himself out of his chair with his customary grunt, put his shoulder to the refrigerator, and give it a silencing shove. *I sense an egg roll coming on* meant that he wanted to go to Pearl of the Orient for dinner. That was the explanation, wasn't it? she thinks now as Scotty moves things off the television console, dusts the wood, then puts the magazines, the ashtray, and the photographs of her grandchil-dren back exactly as they were: she couldn't pretend that her life with Burl mattered.

She stands in the kitchen while Scotty eats his toast. When he finishes the last bite, she takes a dollar out of the drawer where she keeps tip money for delivery boys and lays it next to his plate. "That's for you," she says. She's never given him money before.

"Why?"

"If someone wants you to do a job, they should pay you for it."

"Anybody could help you."

"But I don't let just anyone help me. I let you."

He stares at the dollar for another moment before he takes it and heads to the front door. She opens it, but then moves to block his passage. She feels the same welling anxiety that threatened when her daughters ignored her advice.

"Scotty, what I'm trying to tell you is that if you don't put a value on yourself no one else will. People will take advantage of you. It's not nice, but that's just the way the world works. Do you understand?"

"Okay," he says, which is a maddening non-answer, the kind that only increases her sense that he has not understood this important piece of information that will prevent him from making terrible mistakes in the future. She moves aside and lets him leave. Her heart is beating fast. It's horrible to care.

An eyeglass chain is the first thing to go missing. She hasn't thought about it for years, but the minute it's gone, she notices. The saucer on her bureau where it lived, coiled and unused, is empty. When she'd first seen the chain at the drugstore years ago, wearing it seemed like a reasonable idea, even nervy in the way it suggested the prissiness of a schoolmarm while, at the same time, drawing attention to her chest, where the glasses would rest. But after a while it became annoying to have her glasses bouncing against her whenever she wasn't wearing them, and she'd started to find the predictability of a man's roving eye more pathetic than exciting.

The next thing that's gone is a pack of tissues from the cabinet under the bathroom sink. She had just bought six of them at the market. She put one in her purse, but now there are only four left. She always keeps tissues with her to blot her lipstick. Oh, how Frank used to tease her about her lipstick! They'd be sitting at Ruth's or Naomi's high school graduation, and right when they called their girl's name, she'd take out the tube of her favorite red and redo her lips. Or in the middle of one of his doctor's appointments. She knew he liked her habits, though, just as she was comforted by the way he stored his shoes upright, leaning them against the wall, so they looked like tired-out men waiting for a bus.

There are some things so ridiculous they take your breath away!

The disappearances continue. A handful of Q-tips. One of the cedar blocks she keeps in her closet to stop moths from eating holes in her clothes. A thumbnail-sized shell from the collection that sits on the rim of the bathtub and that she adds to each year when she returns from her winter in Florida. Nothing that's gone missing is worth anything. The eyeglass chain was plastic and cost only a few dollars. On her last visit, Ruth had asked her why she didn't throw it out. But that was a different generation talking. Evelyn's daughters had been trained by advertising to get rid of perfectly good things and replace them with the new and (not much) improved. *Now look!* she says in silent conversation with her absent daughter. It turns out that the eyeglass chain was useful after all. It was something for Scotty to steal.

Because of course it's Scotty. Who else could it be? She and Scotty are the only two people who've set foot in her apartment all summer. She isn't angry—could a person feel angry about Q-tips? But she knows children are as devious as adults. They lie. They steal. They take what they need. They can be heartless. She was there when Paula, at eight or nine, told her best friend that she hated her. The girl's mother was standing nearby in the schoolyard, so Evelyn gave Paula a smack and made her say she was sorry. Paula's apology was bitter and unconvincing. She'd meant exactly what she said.

She should confront Scotty, Evelyn thinks one night while she's cooking a packet of instant rice. She'd be doing him a favor, stopping him before he shoplifts at the grocery store. She could reassure him that she won't tell his mother, that it will be a secret between the two of them. But does she want him to stop? In a way, the thefts are flattering. She feels chosen. Scotty, this peculiar child, wants to keep these small parts of her for himself. She looks around the apartment, wondering, with some excitement, what he'll take next. He's only a little boy, but he's managed to unsettle her. It has been a very long time since she's felt unsettled.

Scotty doesn't always steal something. A week goes by when everything is accounted for. He comes to the apartment and folds towels fresh from the dryer or helps her clean the windows with Windex and newspaper. He's dutiful and serious. He sings. He eats around the sides of his toast. During these dry periods, she sometimes places an intriguing object in plain sight—a small porcelain cat no bigger than a walnut, or a brightly painted Ukrainian egg. Scotty doesn't steal either of these, or the fancy pen Burl gave her one year. That he overlooks obvious treasures is tantalizing.

Another week passes during which she experiences a turbulent edginess that is relieved only when she discovers that he's stolen a travel-sized bottle of shampoo from the medicine cabinet. The following day, the golf pencil she keeps in the drawer of her credenza is gone. Her boss gave her a case of them as a joke retirement gift in recognition of her preference for them. At her send-off party, he toasted her, saying that she was the brains behind the whole billboard operation. It was the kind of lift-you-up-to-put-you-down thing that men said to women all the time, the exaggeration meant to imply the opposite. Only, in her case it was true. The man was fired six months after she left, unable to manage things without the reminder notes she'd written with her stubby pencils.

And then, one morning, she opens the silverware drawer and discovers that Scotty has stolen the last remaining corncob holder. She used to have six sets shaped like miniature ears of corn, but over the years they've met various fates, ending up in the garbage, or slipping into the narrow crevice where the counter and the refrigerator don't quite meet. The last one was useless without its mate, but she'd kept it. Frank loved corn on the cob and always challenged the girls to see who could eat theirs the fastest. He'd get out the typewriter and provide the sound effects. His silliness was the first thing to go once his heart started to give out. Playfulness took too much energy. Staring into the drawer at the empty place where the corn holder used to sit, she feels a quiet wrenching.

Any minute now, the phone will ring. It will be Paula, who calls every two weeks at eight-fifteen on the dot. She rarely visits. She's divorced with no children, so there isn't that obligation. She always calls right before she leaves for work so that she has an excuse to cut things short. She's a divorce lawyer in Lincoln. Naomi once called excitedly to say that she'd seen an ad for her firm in a local magazine featuring a glamorous shot of Paula. Evelyn had pretended to be impressed although she thought it was a little desperate for a lawyer to advertise like that.

Evelyn never mentioned anything outright to Paula about the night she failed to check on Frank. On the flight home from Tulsa, she had been consumed by anger and she rehearsed what she'd say to her daughter, how she'd be sympathetic about the fact that Paula had lost her father while making her understand what she'd done. But when she fit her key into the lock of the door, a different feeling took over. The silence in the house frightened her. The sofa, the coffee table, the spider and jade plants—they all seemed like imposter versions of the things she'd lived with for years. She climbed the stairs slowly. She was terrified, which was ridiculous—she'd given the nurse instructions to have Frank's body moved to the funeral home even before she'd boarded the flight. She stood in her bedroom doorway and stared at the perfectly made bed where Frank had so recently lain. She fought the urge to back away, to creep downstairs as quietly as she could and leave the house so that she could pretend she had not set foot in her future. But then she heard a noise, and when she turned around, there was Paula, peeking through a crack in her bedroom door, as if to protect herself from an intruder.

It was never easy between them after that. For the next year and a half, she and Paula did their best to avoid each other. Paula would come home at the end of the day and go straight upstairs to her room. At dinnertime, she'd call down to say that she wasn't hungry. Evelyn would leave a plate warming in the oven for her and eat her meal alone at the kitchen table, hoping that Paula wouldn't change her mind and join her. Any conversation between them, whether it was about the news, or Paula's college plans, or what dress she wanted Evelyn to sew for her prom, included not talking about that night. The house practically vibrated with the girl's impatience to get away from her mother as soon as possible. Which was why, not two months after Paula graduated from high school, Evelyn found herself converting the prom dress into a wedding gown. Paula, marrying at the courthouse, kissed a boy whose arrogance barely masked his insecurity. After the ceremony was over, Paula shot a look at her mother, her expression fierce and triumphant.

Evelyn looks at her watch. The phone rings.

"How are your spirits, Mother?" Paula says.

She begins every conversation this way, as if she can't imagine Evelyn's happiness. "Fine," Evelyn replies. "And yours?"

"I'm about to leave for work," Paula says, starting the timer on the call. "What are you going to do with your day?"

It's an innocent enough question, but still, Evelyn feels a pressure to make her life seem meaningful to her most disapproving child. "I've been robbed," she says.

"What? Mother? What do you mean?"

"I've been robbed," she repeats. It feels good to say it. The shock of the word in her mouth. The truth of it.

"Oh my God. Are you okay?"

Paula's worry seems sincere, and, for a moment, Evelyn wants to come clean, to confess what's been stolen and by whom. But she suddenly feels the threat of emotion and she can't speak. It's too much. The pack of Kleenex. The corncob holder. Somehow, if a real thief had stolen her television or her jewelry she wouldn't feel as bewildered as she does now. "It's nothing," she says. "Just some mail."

"Mother, mail theft is a federal crime. Did you report it?"

"It's fine," Evelyn says.

"It's not fine if they stole your Social Security check."

"Who said anything about a Social Security check?"

"They prey on the elderly, these people. And once they get your Social Security number, you've got a real problem on your hands."

"Are you charging by the minute?" Evelyn says.

"What are you talking about?" Paula says.

"You're not listening to what I'm saying."

"You just told me you were robbed."

But that's not what Evelyn was trying to say at all. Something has happened to her. Something terrible.

"I've got to get to work, Mother. Report the theft. Please."

Evelyn hangs up the phone feeling a sense of panic. She leaves the apartment, walks to the end of the hall, and knocks on the door. After a moment, Scotty's mother answers. Behind her, Scotty and his brother are sitting on the carpet, watching television.

"I need to speak with you," Evelyn says. "It's very important."

"All right," the woman says, opening the door farther. "Boys, turn off the TV." She leads Evelyn into the living room and motions for her to sit down on the couch. The cushions are unusually deep, and when Evelyn settles, her shoes barely graze the floor. Scotty's mother sits on a chair on the other side of the coffee table. She lifts her younger boy onto her lap. Scotty stands by her side. They watch Evelyn, waiting.

She straightens her back and tries to draw herself up, but the couch defeats her. "I thought you should know," she says, "that certain things have been stolen from my home."

"I'm sorry to hear that," Scotty's mother says.

She looks concerned, and Evelyn feels emboldened. "Many things," she says.

"Can I ask what?"

"Personal items," Evelyn says, enjoying the power that comes with the ambiguity.

"I wonder if there have been other thefts in the building," the woman says. "Maybe you should tell the manager."

"You don't understand," Evelyn says. "The only person who comes to my apartment is your son."

She glances at Scotty, who betrays nothing, his expression as unreadable as ever.

"What are you saying?" the woman says, her sympathy disappearing. "Are you accusing Scotty of stealing?"

"Ask him," Evelyn says.

But before the woman can do anything, Scotty leaves the room. A few moments later, he returns holding a shoebox. He sets it on the coffee table.

"Scotty, what is this?" his mother says. She moves her younger son off her lap, then leans forward and carefully lifts the lid, as if the box might contain a bomb.

Evelyn struggles to inch forward on the couch until she can see the contents, too. Everything that Scotty stole is there. She feels a small sense of triumph until she notices that Scotty's mother is giving her a strange look, as if she's reconsidering Evelyn and now thinks she might be disturbed, even dangerous. The woman picks up one of the Q-tips, then drops it back into the box, where it falls without a sound. She picks up the pack of Kleenex, looking not at the stolen item but at Evelyn, as if

Evelyn were playing some kind of trick on her, insisting on the value of this box full of trash.

"Those things belong to me," Evelyn says.

Scotty's mother puts the Kleenex back into the box, then covers the box with the lid. "Scotty, apologize to the lady," she says without much conviction.

"I'm sorry."

"There we go," she says to Evelyn. She hands her the box, then stands and walks quickly to the door and opens it. Evelyn feels the woman's impatience as she struggles to get up from the couch, then crosses the room, and leaves.

As she walks down the hallway cradling the box, she feels she's been cheated of something. Her justifiable accusation. The apology. None of that changes the humbling absence she felt when she looked at the space between her deodorant and the dental floss where the Pert shampoo once stood. Nothing makes up for the frightening sensation she had when she discovered that the corncob holder was gone, and she felt as if she were standing, once again, in that bedroom doorway all those years ago, staring at emptiness.

Don't wash your face with soap or you'll dry out your skin. Wear a bra or your breasts will sag. Check on your father.

Was there anything you could ever say to another person that would make a difference in the way things turned out?

Scotty never returns to her apartment after that. She doesn't expect him, but sometimes, when she's dusting the television console or hanging her skirts, she stops, thinking that she senses him standing outside her front door, but she doesn't. She distracts herself with activities. She plays bridge with her regular foursome, a competitive group whose games are fast and strategic and require her to be at her sharpest. She's put some of her retirement money into stocks, and she studies the business section of the paper carefully and makes small adjustments to her portfolio. There's another hurricane in Florida. A bad one, this time. She calls her friends down there. Some of their homes are damaged, one was completely destroyed. They all announce that they will use their insurance money to rebuild, as if the next storm will back down in the face of their bravery.

She visits Ruth and Francie in New York for a few days. Francie seems a little glum. She has a summer job scooping ice cream at a shop and comes home each day smelling like sugar and cigarettes. Over Labor Day, Evelyn visits Naomi and the Omaha grandchildren.

One morning in early October, she's waiting in the hallway for the elevator. She has a dentist appointment and then some errands to run. Scotty's apartment door opens. She feels herself grow hot; she has not seen the boy for months. But then a man, a woman, and a teenage girl she doesn't recognize emerge and head toward the elevator. The adults look dressed for work. The girl carries a schoolbag over her shoulder. Evelyn feels as if she's trapped in a dream. When the family reaches the elevator, the three acknowledge her, then talk quietly among themselves about who will be home at what time. The girl reminds them that she has practice. The elevator door opens. The family steps aside to let Evelyn get on first, but she backs away, hurries down the hall to the stairway exit, and pushes through the door. The stairwell is cold. Her hand, grasping the rail, looks pale and bloodless. Scotty's family must have left while she was out of town. How else could she have missed the moving truck and the racket of men carrying boxes and furniture down to the street? She reaches the first-floor landing and goes into the lobby. No one is there. The marble and mirrored entryway is furnished with black leather chairs and a glass coffee table, but it's all for show. She's never seen anyone sit in those chairs. The room is immaculate and useless.

There was a time, after Frank's death, when she found herself watching strangers—a man hosing down his driveway, a woman waiting in line at the post office, casually laying a hand on her little girl's cheek. Her fixation on these people was so intense that often they noticed, but she couldn't help it. She was perplexed by the way they went about the simplest tasks, those that had once seemed so minor to her that she hardly thought about them, but that she now had to talk herself through, step by step, as if she'd forgotten how to live. Once, when Ruth was home from college, she found herself putting a hand on her daughter's cheek just the way the woman at the post office had done. Ruth pulled back and gave her a funny look, which left her wondering if she'd ever been the kind of mother who did that sort of thing. She'd been prepared for Frank's death—his decline was slow, the end inevitable. When it finally came, she didn't feel lost the way people often said they did after a death. No, it was that she'd lost herself. She wonders if the person she's been for all these years is only an approximation of someone she never found again.

Scotty will forget what happened. He's seven, after all, and there is so much ahead of him that will occupy his attention. If he remembers her at all, it may be years or even decades from now. He'll eat a slice of cinnamon toast or feel the warmth of a freshly ironed shirt and have a vague impression of an old lady, or maybe a slight feeling of remorse. But before he can place the memory, something will distract him. And then he'll forget all over again.

TEN

A TROUBLED MIND

Cleveland, Ohio; Pittsburgh, Pennsylvania;
New York City, 1993

The doctor asks her why she is here.

"Where?" Helene says.

"Here, Mom. In this office," Tom says. He reminded her the day before and again that morning, told her she had an appointment just to check up on things, which was a vague and gutless explanation that now makes him ashamed. She resisted—she never liked a plan that wasn't hers—so he had reminded her that she sometimes forgot things, that sometimes she repeated stories. *Sometimes* was another evasion; these things are happening more and more.

"I'm an old lady," she said that morning. "If you want a new story, turn on the TV."

She's nearly eighty years old and still amusing in her haughtiness, but she's become sarcastic, as if she's in on the joke. She's even begun to mock herself, something that was unimaginable not so long ago. He wants to tell this to the doctor, to prove that the losses his mother experiences are far outweighed by the gains.

Dr. Gunther observes Helene, her smile blandly encouraging. Tom is sure that the woman is folding the seconds Helene takes to answer the question into her calculations.

"Remember, Mom?" he says. "We talked about it at breakfast."

"Let her answer," the doctor says. "Do you know, Mrs. Simonauer, why you're here?"

"Of course I do," Helene says.

"Can you tell me?"

"I don't sleep well."

"Anything else?"

"Tom was a terrible sleeper," Helene says. "He cried all the time. I don't know why he was so unhappy."

"I wasn't unhappy, Mom. I was a baby."

"I drove you around and around in the car. At all hours. I couldn't keep you in the house screaming like that. The Doctor needed his rest."

"Well, she remembers *that*," he says, trying for a joke as much for his own sake as for Dr. Gunther's. His mother hasn't referred to his father that way in a long time. He's noticed that she talks more often about the past, a time she must feel more certain about, a time that, perhaps, gives her more comfort than the present, where she often feels stranded.

Dr. Gunther doesn't laugh. The plaques on her wall attest to her fine education and her many fellowships. It suddenly strikes Tom as thoughtless to display evidence of her excellently functioning mind when her patients are in various stages of losing theirs.

"It's true, though, what she says," he continues. "She told me that sometimes she'd park in the driveway, but was too scared to move me, so we slept in the car." It's hard for him to picture his mother, never without heels and a matching purse, slumped in the front seat, her lips softly open, her cheek smashed against the window. "Remember, Mom?" he says. "'My mother is the best parents a boy ever had'?" When she doesn't react, he has the sick feeling that she's forgotten. The phrase had been a shorthand they used to soften the blow when his father wasn't available and it fell to her to take him to a ball game or to sit through *Creature from the Black Lagoon*.

Maybe it's just nerves, Tom reminds himself. He's nervous, too, which is why he's babbling now, explaining the reference to the doctor, telling her about the Mother's Day card he made when he was a boy. She smiles and raises her eyebrows at the implications. Now he and Dr. Gunther share something: the recognition of his mother's capability. He's brought the woman a little closer to his side, primed her to take his view of things, which is that nothing is terribly wrong with his mother. She's old and deserves her occasional repetitions and lapses. He's adept at the unspoken alliance. It's a strategy he uses when he meets new clients and wants them to feel as if they already know him, and that he and they have a history of mutual understandings. It's a way of convincing them to feel confident that he will maximize their investments. For the most part, Tom has succeeded in making people money, and lots of it, but he's grown to hate his ability to invent unearned trust.

"So, you're here to get help with sleep," Dr. Gunther says to Helene.

Helene doesn't answer. The doctor takes a pad of paper and

makes notes that seem much too lengthy given how little has transpired. It bothers him to think that she might already be making her diagnosis. If human beings were not that complicated, then what, he wants to say, is the point of all those diplomas?

Helene gazes at her lap. Whatever spirit she showed just moments ago has vanished. Tom resists the urge to tell her to sit up, look the doctor in the eye, to practice what she preached all those years ago when she was training him to be whatever sort of person she thought he should be, which is probably the one he's become. A man who radiates calm in the face of upheavals in the market, the one who didn't fall apart when his wife said she couldn't be married to him any longer. His mother had given him a great course in the brave face. Now he needs her to do whatever it takes to convince Yolanda Gunther, MD, PhD, who also found time to get a JD, that she's not losing her mind.

"Mrs. Simonauer," the doctor says, finally looking up from her pad, "I'm going to ask you some questions. There are no right or wrong answers."

"Then why are you asking?" Helene says.

Tom wants to hug her. The familiar aspects of her character that have always driven him insane are now the ones he cherishes. They are proof of her.

"How old are you?" the doctor asks.

"Seventy-nine."

"I'm going to say four words," Dr. Gunther says. "House. Telephone. Red. Shoe. Can you say those words back to me?"

"House. Telephone. Red. Shoe," Helene says.

For the next thirty minutes, Dr. Gunther runs through her test. His mother seems happy enough to do what she's asked. The doctor draws a square on a piece of paper and asks Helene to copy it. She draws a face and asks her to do the same. Helene lists all the words she can think of that start with the letter *p* in sixty seconds. She names the fruits she can recall in thirty. She doesn't seem bothered that she can name only eight fruits, although Tom is disheartened. She didn't even remember honeydew, her favorite.

Dr. Gunther shows Helene a drawing that looks to have been made in the 1950s. It shows an aproned mother pulling a tray of cookies out of an oven while her two Dick and Jane children play a board game at the kitchen table. The doctor asks Helene to say what is happening in the picture.

"I don't cook," Helene says. "And I don't have a daughter."

"These people are not meant to be your family," Dr. Gunther says.

"Well, I don't know who they are," Helene says.

"Can you make up a story about who they might be?" Dr. Gunther says.

Helene looks at the picture for a few moments. "A mother and children," she says.

"Mom," Tom says, but the doctor has already taken back the picture.

The questions continue. Helene knows her birthday, but she can't remember the name of the sitting president. Clinton has been in office for less than a month. How long after the New Year, Tom wants to ask the doctor, did it take her to stop writing 1992 on her checks?

"Mrs. Simonauer," Dr. Gunther says, "when we began, I gave you a list of four words. Can you remember them?"

Helene looks vaguely at the opposite wall. Tom doesn't know if she can't remember the words, or if she doesn't remember having been told them, or, even worse, if she can't understand what the doctor is asking her to do. *House. Telephone. Red. Shoe,* he recites to himself. He inches forward in his chair, hoping his movement might unstick her memory, just as he did all those years ago when Francie fumbled through a fourth-grade piano recital, hoping he could will her to the other side of humiliation.

"Can you remember one of the words?" the doctor says.

"I don't know," Helene says.

"One word was a color," the doctor says.

"A color?" Helene looks at Tom in confusion.

"One word was an item of clothing," the doctor says.

Helene's eyes dart back and forth. Tom feels a surge of adrenaline.

"An object you have in your home," the doctor says.

"I don't . . ." Helene mumbles.

"Or a place where people live."

"Stop!" Tom says, more forcefully than he'd intended. "Just stop."

"We're almost finished," the doctor says.

"No. I'm sorry," he says. "We are finished. We're done. This is so . . ." He can't find the word he's looking for to describe the cruelty that is taking place. It's the doctor's methodical demeanor. It's his proud mother submitting to this woman's demands. It's that he's put this whole thing into play, having been alerted one too many times by Erna about Helene's forgetfulness, and having finally admitted to himself that she does repeat stories, and that sometimes when he calls her, it takes her longer than usual to remember that he lives in New York, and that he and Ruth are divorced, and that Francie is away at college in Pittsburgh.

"This just feels so unkind," he says finally. He's demoralized. "I know you're doing your job. But I need to take my mother home."

As he and Helene leave the clinic, Tom tries to think of some way to salvage the disaster of the afternoon. He suggests they go out for an early dinner. She agrees, but almost as soon as he starts driving, she falls asleep, and so he heads straight to the house. She's disoriented when he wakes her, but once they're inside, she returns to form. She bustles around the kitchen and microwaves the plates of food that Erna left in the fridge. She orders him to set out the place mats and silverware.

"Did I tell you I'm taking a drawing class?" he says once they've sat down.

She doesn't answer. He's talked about this before. She doesn't remember.

"Well, I am, if you can believe it," he goes on. "I found an art class near my apartment. I go every Saturday morning. I'm no good at it. Actually, compared to everyone else in the class, I'm awful." He's never pursued a hobby, but the combination of his increasing uninterest in his work, the fact that Francie is at college, and his lack of enthusiasm for dating leave him with too much time on his hands. He laughs to himself. "Sometimes the teacher looks at my work and I can tell she's just stupefied."

"You told me this already," his mother says.

"Did I?" he says.

"Maybe you need to go see a doctor."

He thinks about when he was a teenager and she slapped

him across the face. He has no idea what impertinent thing he said, but he remembers his shame. "I'm just trying to help, Mom."

"House. Telephone. Red. Shoe."

"Why didn't you say that at the doctor's office?"

"I didn't remember it then. And now I do. It's a foolish thing to remember. A lot of things are."

Last week, Erna told him that his mother forgot that Erna has a daughter. When she was a child, Eliana came to the house with Erna during her school vacations. His mother always made a fuss about her. She bought her birthday presents. She went to Eliana's college graduation from Cleveland State. She attended the christenings of her children.

"I'm going to bed," Helene says, pushing back her chair.

"I'll walk you upstairs."

"Why?"

So you don't fall? So you don't lose your way? So you don't get to your room and not know why you're there? "To keep you company?" he says.

"I don't need company," she says and leaves the kitchen.

He washes the dishes, turns off the lights, then climbs the stairs and taps lightly on his mother's bedroom door. He hears nothing. He hopes she's remembered to take her sleeping pill. When he's in New York, he calls her every morning to make sure she's made it through the night without a mishap. When she answers the phone with a groggy *Hello*, he can tell that she's forgotten to take her pill, and that she's still tangled in the fog of a wakeful night. Often, when he's in a meeting or having lunch with a client, the sound of her scrabbling for mental clarity comes to him, and he feels momentarily unstrung. He'll return to the conversation, but the disturbing sensation remains. He and his mother are both lost, she in her mind, he in his life. He's frightened by the fact that all it takes is a shift in an attitude or a synapse or a stupid choice to make everything you once took for granted suddenly seem unconvincing.

He goes into his bedroom, but he's too agitated to sleep. He wishes he could talk to someone. He could call Ruth, but she's recently met a man named Michael, so he doesn't want to bother her. It's been almost five years now since his affair, but he still thinks of himself primarily as a man who cheated on his wife. All his attempts at explaining to Ruth why he'd done it captured nothing about the loneliness he felt in his marriage. Ruth had made the transition to life in New York with ease. She became fluent in the lingua franca of the city, referring to the subway as *the train*, knowing which Italian deli on Ninth Avenue made the best soppressata, a food he hadn't known existed and wasn't sure he liked. The city was as restless as she was, and its distractions suited her. And somehow, she was able to locate herself within them in a way she hadn't been able to in Cleveland. She found part-time jobs teaching at Manhattan Community College and Pace, and then, finally, a full-time position at CUNY. She made choices, while he followed a path that he'd stumbled onto when he got an A in the economics class he took in his senior year of college. Once he graduated and finished his year in Guatemala, and because he didn't have any better idea, he went to business school, after which he continued along a frictionless path to where he is now. Daily, he takes part in the vaunted worldliness of being able to walk down the street and feel the thrum of so many disparate lives. But all of it serves to remind him that he exists at the periphery of himself.

Was that the point of Delia? Some misguided way of trying to prove otherwise? That he could step off that path and follow an irrational impulse? The affair had made him feel more isolated than ever, and he ended it two months after it began. He will never forget the look on Ruth's face when he admitted what he'd done. His betrayal was not so much a shock to her as a fulfillment of an expectation that she would, once again, be abandoned. First by her father. And now him. They tried to find their way back to each other, but she couldn't reinvent her trust, and the marriage was over. They admitted as much when they drove from that town on the Mediterranean coast back to Paris to find Francie. Something about their daughter's choosing to ignore the fact that they'd traveled so far to meet up with her after her summer in France made their pretense of reconciliation too obvious to ignore. And why would Francie want to spend a week at the beach with her parents when she'd spent the previous year watching them flail as they tried to convince themselves that their separation was merely a step toward repair?

He's still astonished by how quickly the marriage dissolved. Not simply because he and Ruth didn't argue over the terms of the divorce, but also because it turned out that marriage was like any sort of faith. It was made real by an almost daily decision to believe in it. When he and Ruth decided that they didn't, the thing they'd conjured into being vanished almost as quickly as it had arrived all those years earlier, when he'd come home from business school to visit his recently widowed mother and saw a striking-looking girl getting into a beat-up car.

* * *

Dr. Gunther phones the house early the next morning. Tom takes the call and is grateful that she is willing to give him the news, but at the same time, her disregard for the rules of privacy lets him know what she's about to say even before she says it. She's as cool as she was in the office, but in this case, he's glad for it. His mother's memory is significantly impaired and will continue to decline. There's no way to know how quickly. There is nothing they can do. The doctor listens when he tells her that his mother remembered the list. House! Telephone! But even as he says this, he feels embarrassed, knowing there is no trading one fact for another. Both are true. His mother remembered some words. She has dementia.

"You need to be prepared," the doctor says.

He finds his mother in the kitchen eating her morning oatmeal, which, he notes, she's made on her own without calamity.

"Good news, Mom. The doctor says there's nothing to be too worried about."

She nods and continues to eat. He wonders if she knows he's lying. When he was a boy, she would listen to him claim he'd brushed his teeth, or done his homework, or later, that he hadn't been out drinking with the wrestling team, and she'd say nothing. It was her silence that broke him. She could wait him out for days until the tension did him in, and he'd admit to everything. She finishes eating, takes her morning pills with her orange juice, then goes upstairs to dress for the day. She's left her empty bowl and glass on the table. He doesn't know if she's forgotten to rinse them or if it's her habit to leave them for Erna. As he cleans up, he realizes that this is what things will be like now: he will analyze everything she does or says, looking for signs.

Erna shows up at nine. Her arrival calms him as does her equanimity when he tells her what the doctor said. She listens, then does what she's done every morning since he's known her: she goes into the walk-in pantry, pulls the chain that turns on the light, and closes the door. A few moments later, she emerges, having changed from her slacks and sweater into a pair of sweatpants and an oversized blouse. He's embarrassed to think that, when he was younger, she wore a maid's uniform. She hasn't worn one for years. Whether this was her decision or something his mother encouraged, he doesn't know. He suspects it happened without their discussing it, the way so many things have altered in the two women's relationship. Now it's Erna who makes the decisions about what to cook, or what instructions to give the gardener, or when to call a repairman. She always behaves as if these are Helene's choices. *Your mother thinks it's time to reseed the lawn*, she'll say to him when he calls. He knows that she doesn't do this out of a sense of station, but because this is her way of taking care of his mother's pride. Although it's all tangled up, isn't it? he thinks as he watches her make a grocery list. Class is baked into even the smallest details. He used to have the impression that Erna was much younger than his mother, but it turns out that they are separated by only six years. Erna is seventy-three now, but she seems to get sturdier as she ages.

On the airplane ride home, he feels numb. The doctor told him that he had to pay attention. His mother is alone in the house at night and on the weekends, and although he's begged her not to, he knows she still occasionally drives. Soon, that will have to change. Not yet, though. Not now. She's fine, he convinces himself. She made her oatmeal and didn't burn down the house. When he left for the airport, she and Erna were already discussing the order of the day's errands.

He takes a taxi from LaGuardia directly to his office. His assistant, Philip, hands him his messages. Ruth has phoned six times in the last few hours.

"Francie's in trouble," she says the minute she picks up his call. She tells him that Francie's roommate left a message on Ruth's answering machine. "Eliza said Francie hasn't left her room in weeks."

"But I just talked to her on Sunday," he says. "She sounded good." Hadn't Francie told him about a sculpture class she was loving? That she was thinking of majoring in art?

"I tried to call her, but she's not answering the phone," Ruth says. "I think we need to go there, Tom. I mean, maybe now?" she adds, her voice rising. It's her uncertainty that frightens him.

Philip books them on a flight that evening. Once they land in Pittsburgh, they pick up a rental car, then drive straight to the university. A student on his way out of Francie's dorm holds the door open for them. His disregard for safety makes Tom even more anxious than he already was. They climb the stairs, find her room, and knock. They wait, then knock again.

When Francie finally opens the door, Tom reaches for Ruth's hand to stop her from reacting. Francie's skin can't even be described as pale. It's simply drained of color. Her gaze is similarly washed out. She looks like the opposite of the girl he holds in his mind, his tall, dark-eyed daughter. His serious, careful girl given to smiling only after she's gone through a mental checklist of the potential hazards of momentary joy. Most disturbing is that she's lost weight. A lot of it.

"I think I have the flu or something," Francie says. The

room is stifling, but Francie sits on her unmade bed and pulls a blanket around her shoulders. Ruth sits next to her and holds her hand. Tom pulls her desk chair up close.

"When we talked last week . . ." he says. "Why didn't you say anything?"

"I mean, I felt okay that day," she says. "But it just comes and goes, you know?"

"What comes and goes, honey?" Ruth says. She puts her hand on Francie's forehead. "You don't have a temp."

"It's not like that," Francie says. "It's like, I get ready to go to class and stuff, but then I just can't. Like I don't think I can walk across campus. I just feel scared. Like maybe I'll faint or something."

"You're so thin," Ruth says, almost in a whisper.

Francie tells them that, at first, Eliza was helpful, bringing Francie meals from the dining hall. She let Francie read her notes from the two classes they share so Francie wouldn't fall behind. "But she's with this guy now and she stays over there most of the time," Francie says. "And sometimes I just feel too, I don't know, like I can't go to the dining hall. Like all those people . . ." Her voice trails off.

Tom thinks that the close, unwashed smell of Francie's body and the stiff orange rinds, brown apple cores, and crusty tissues she's dropped by the side of her bed might have chased Eliza away. He suspects, too, from the look of his daughter, that the flu is not the culprit. He's seen drugged-out kids on stoops and on the subways. There's something particular about their gazes that reminds him of Francie now, a kind of looseness, as if their brains aren't connecting to what they see. While Ruth takes

Francie down the hall to the bathroom to help her shower, he focuses on the immediate problem. He cleans up the garbage on the floor. He starts to make the bed, but the bedsheets reek of sweat. He opens the window. Ruth used to accuse him of not showing anger when she knew he was angry, or sadness when she knew he was sad. He supposes she was right. When his dad died, or when he and Ruth finally decided to call it quits, his mind did what it is doing right now: it slowed down and figured out the steps. He greeted an ending the way he approached a radical shift in the market: as a fact that needed to be plugged into a fresh equation so that he could quickly act on the new result. He looks out the window. Down below, a kid slips on a pair of headphones, then steps onto his skateboard and pushes off. Francie had a Discman in high school. She'd bring it to his apartment when she stayed over. Tom never got used to hearing her suddenly burst out singing for a moment before withdrawing back into her intense and private listening.

When Ruth and Francie come back to the room, Francie is wearing jeans and a button-down that swims on her frame. Ruth brushes her wet hair and then goes to work on it with a blow-dryer. He turns back to the window. It's too much for him—Ruth's tenderness. Francie's submission. Once her hair is dry, the three of them drive to a Burger King to get Francie some food. Then they check into the hotel Philip booked. The woman behind the desk gives them keys for two rooms, but the three of them stay together. They lie in the dark on top of the covers of the queen-size bed, Tom and Ruth on either side of Francie. After a while, she begins to talk. She started taking pills she got from a friend named Lila, she tells them. They make her feel like she can do a hundred things at once. She stays up for days, writes her papers and studies for her tests. They make her feel good at parties, too.

"Less worried about things," she says. "Less weird."

Tom wants to ask what she would have to worry about at a party. She's pretty and smart and she can be slyly funny. But he keeps quiet.

"But, you know, sometimes," she continues, "Lila won't share her prescription, or she runs out. And then, like, I can't do anything. I can't even stay awake. I just sleep all the time." She misses deadlines and skips lectures, she says. "And then, you know, it's all just—like, there's too much I have to do to make up for everything and I can't do any of it. I'm failing two of my classes," she says.

For a long time, they lie together in silence. None of them moves, but he knows they are all awake, wondering what comes next.

Six months later, Philip pulls him out of an early-morning meeting. Erna is on the phone. She's agitated, almost in tears.

"Your mother. She's gone."

Tom thinks he's going to vomit. His recent visits with his mother have been dispiriting. She's worse each time. But the idea of her dying has never crossed his mind.

"She took the car," Erna says.

It takes a moment for his body to catch up, for everything inside him to stop shaking. "But she doesn't drive anymore," he says weakly. He'd finally convinced her to stop. She gave him her license. It's in his wallet now.

"I was doing the laundry," Erna says. "When I came upstairs, she was gone."

After he hangs up, he calls the Shaker Heights police. The officer who answers asks where he thinks his mother might be. *Where did you lose it?*—the world's most inane question. "Usually they go someplace they know," the woman says. "Someplace familiar."

They. His mother has joined a club of the demented, wandering around towns and cities everywhere.

He tells the officer where his mother gets her groceries and what drug store she uses. He calls Erna to get more ideas, then calls the station again to add to the list.

The trip to Cleveland is miserable. The whole time he's in the air, he can't convince himself that the plane is going anywhere, that the stillness of flight is matched by the tremendous speed of the engines. Right after his mother's diagnosis, he hired someone to come in on the weekends so she wouldn't be alone. A month later, realizing how quickly she was deteriorating, he arranged for someone else to cover nights. He thought he had everything under control. When he lands, he calls Erna. His mother is still missing. He rents a car, and when he reaches the house, he calls the police station. "We've got a car on it," the officer on duty says.

"One car?" Tom says. "That's it? My mother is eighty years old. She's senile. She's been gone for five—almost six hours."

"Sir, we know how to handle this type of situation. You sit tight, and let us do our job."

After Tom hangs up the phone, he and Erna try to think of more places his mother might be. The dry cleaner? Would she have tried to see one of her friends?

"Most of them are gone now," Erna says, and this time, he knows what the euphemism means. "Your mother always talks about things from a long, long time ago," she says.

The recognition overwhelms them both. Did she go to the hospital where his father worked? To Tom's elementary school? Did she get on the highway thinking she was going to drive to Wheeling to visit her parents? Panicked, they head out of the house together. They know it would be better if one of them stayed in case his mother returns, but Tom is too agitated to wait, and Erna knows more about his mother's life than he does. They drive to the school where Helene used to tutor kids. They check the library in Shaker Heights. They go to a park where Erna says she and Helene sometimes sit on a bench with a bag of stale bread scraps and feed the birds.

"She loves the birds," Erna says, as they head down a path.

"I didn't know that." He thinks of his proud mother taking pleasure in tossing crusts of day-old bread to wrens and cardinals and he feels miserable. The bench is empty.

On their way home, Erna lets out a gasp. "Look!" she says, pointing to a row of shops.

And there is Helene's silver Taurus in front of a video store. Tom parks, and he and Erna hurry over to the car. Helene is sitting in the front seat. He taps lightly on the glass so that he doesn't startle her. She looks over, smiles, and lowers her window.

"Debbie won't cut your hair, darling. You're not a little boy anymore. You need to go to a barber."

Tom is confused, but Erna understands. She calmly reminds his mother that she gets her hair cut by someone named Steven now. "On Warrensville Center Road," she says. "Debbie closed her shop a long time ago."

"She did?" Helene says. "Oh, that's too bad."

Erna helps Helene out of the car. "You must be bursting," she says as she leads Helene into the video store to find a bathroom. When they return, Tom drives his mother home in his rental car. Erna follows behind in the Taurus. Helene is quiet. Tom reaches for her hand.

"Ten and two," she says.

"You're right, Mom," he says, putting his hand back on the wheel.

Once they're home, Erna takes Helene up to her bedroom while Tom calls the police station to let them know he's found his mother. Later, he and Erna sit at the kitchen table and plan. Erna will always keep the car keys with her and she'll take them home at night. Tom will have door alarms installed so that Erna will know if Helene tries to leave the house.

"Sometimes she doesn't recognize me," Erna says quietly. "When I come in the morning, she thinks I'm a robber. She looks so scared."

She's doing her best to appear composed, but Tom can see how much this pains her. She's known his mother longer than anyone else alive.

He calls Ruth and Francie to tell them what's going on. Francie withdrew from school and is home now. She divides her time between his and Ruth's apartments. They leave the schedule up to her. The first few months she was back were awful. She cried a lot. When she wasn't distraught, he worried that she'd taken something. She didn't do much with her time.

All the people she knew from high school were at college. The ones who'd gone to school in the city were busy with classes and new friends, and even when they invited her to join them at a bar or a party, she didn't go. Her solitude had made him ache. She seems stronger now. She sees her therapist and goes to NA meetings. She's waiting to see if she got the part-time job at a health food store that she applied for.

"I want to come see Grandma," she says now. He books her a flight for the following morning.

His mother wakes up just as Erna leaves for the day and Alice, the night nurse, arrives. Alice brings Helene downstairs, and the three of them eat together. Sometimes his mother is lucid. At other times, she drifts. The fact that he knows she will not remember much frees him to say things he once hid from her. He's never told her about Francie's troubles, but now he tells her about the anxiety and about the drugs.

"I mean, it's something she'll have to deal with, maybe for her whole life," he says. "But she'll be okay," he adds, more for his own sake than his mother's.

"That's nice," Helene says absently.

"She's taking classes at the Art Students League," he says. "It turns out she's the artist in the family."

"That's nice," she says again.

Francie arrives the following afternoon. She looks good. She's wearing her favorite outfit of the moment—a white miniskirt, black leggings, and an oversized shirt. She's gained some weight back, and even though she's lithe like her mother, there's a solidity to her that gives him confidence. He brings her into the den, where Helene sits on the couch. The television plays at a low volume, but she's not watching.

"Mom, look who's here!" he says. "It's Francie," he adds quickly, when his mother doesn't react.

If Francie's upset by her grandmother's diminishment, she doesn't show it. She sits next to her and gives her a wonderful hug. "Oh, Grandma, you smell exactly the same," Francie says.

Helene doesn't say anything.

"L'Air du Temps, right?" Francie says happily. "Your favorite."

"It is?"

"Yep. Whenever I go to a department store, I spritz a little on. Here and here," she says, tapping her finger on both sides of her neck. "Just so I can smell like you."

He feels a rush of emotion, not simply because of his daughter's kindness, but also because she seems so much like herself. She's patient when Helene traces her finger over the tattoo on her arm.

"It's a rose, Grandma," Francie says.

"Roses are red," Helene says.

"Violets are blue," Francie says.

"You love me," Helene says.

"And I love you," they both say together. A shared ditty from Francie's childhood.

Helene notices the newer tattoo on the inside of Francie's wrist. *Darlin' Jenny*. Tom and Ruth thought it was ill-advised for Francie to get that one. Jenny is great, and Francie is as happy as Tom's seen her, but Francie's only twenty. It's hard to imagine that the relationship will last as long as the tattoo.

"Jenny's my girlfriend," Francie says.

He waits to see how his mother will react. She rubs her thumb across Francie's wrist.

225

"She's really nice," Francie says. "I love her."

"Is she Jewish?" his mother says.

And there she is, he thinks, his throat rising. Oh, how he adores her!

Francie gets a couple of photograph albums down from the bookcase and brings them back to the couch. She and Tom sit on either side of Helene as they look through them. He points to a picture of himself and his mother in a rowboat. He looks to be about three years old and he sits on her lap as she handles the oars. "I think this was in Wheeling," he says. "Remember? You used to take me there?"

"I don't remember," Helene says.

"Oh, look at that," he says, pointing to a photograph of her childhood home with its wraparound porch. "That's where you grew up. Remember?" He turns the pages excitedly, stopping on a picture of him standing in front of his first car. "Oh my God, Mom. The Bel Air. Remember?"

"Dad," Francie says quietly.

"Remember how much you hated teaching me to drive?" he says.

"Dad," Francie repeats. "She doesn't have to remember. It's just fun to look. Right, Grandma?"

She's right, of course. Does he really think that asking his mother if she remembers will make it so? Francie opens the other book, which holds older photographs. She stops on a formal picture of the Harker family. Tom's grandmother sits in a high-backed chair, her hair piled on her head in the style of the day. His mustachioed grandfather stands to one side wearing a straw boater. The children are ranged around their mother. Victor leans into her side; Louisa's hand drapes over her shoulder.

Helene sits at her mother's feet. She wears a big bow in her long, luxuriant hair.

"Poor Louisa. Poor Victor," his mother says.

Her expression is unreadable. The prick of a thorn. A fall (a leap?) from a rooftop. A tree crashing down on a car. How has she borne it all?

Later that afternoon, Erna and Francie take Helene upstairs so that she can lie down for a bit. Tom finds a couple of blankets and a pillow in the linen closet and puts them on the couch in his father's study. Francie can take his bedroom; he'll be fine down here. When he's done, he goes upstairs to look for her and finds her in the attic, sitting on the floor surrounded by boxes and dusty furniture.

"Look at all this stuff!" she says brightly. She's found a box filled with his old wrestling trophies and another full of his high school yearbooks and other remnants of his youth. She opens one and pages through it until she finds a picture of him and his team.

"Really sexy, Dad."

He sits down and takes the yearbook from her. He'd shot up that year and he looks gangly, barely filling out his singlet.

"In third grade, you got a B in penmanship," she says, reading an old, yellowing report card she's found. "'Tom should pay closer attention to his forward ovals, especially the letter *p*.' It's true," Francie says, putting the report card back in the box, "you still have shitty handwriting." She opens another box. It's filled with LPs. Francie pulls one out, looks it over, and hands it to Tom. *The Brandenburg Concertos*. His only memory of music in the house is when he would play "Hound Dog" on the old cabinet stereo in the den, and his mother would tell him to turn it off because the noise was bothering his father.

"Ooh," Francie says. She's opened a round box and put on a hat that makes her look like Jackie Kennedy. She pulls out some papers from the box and looks them over. "Ah-ha," she says. "Secret letters! Go, Grandma!"

"Let me see," he says, although he doesn't need to look at them to know what they are. He can't read them, of course—they're written in German. He'd believed his mother when she said she'd thrown them away. Or maybe he hadn't believed her, but he'd wanted to protect her, and himself.

"What is it, Dad?" Francie says. "What are they?"

He tells her what he knows. Which is not enough. There is no way to say if the child was his father's. There is no way to know if his father was a hero who tried to save this woman, or if he was a cad for keeping his wife in the dark, or if he was both those things, or neither. Tom remembers when his mother had gone to Wheeling on her own and left him in Erna's care. He'd woken up in the middle of the night to find his father sitting in the dark by his bedside. He was just making sure, he explained, that Tom was safe. What, Tom wonders now, was the danger that his father imagined might befall his American son?

"Poor Grandma," Francie says.

Of course she's right. His mother had put on her characteristic brave front, marching ahead in her determined way. But she must have felt so alone.

Francie continues poking through different boxes. She finds a pair of kid gloves and slips them on. The hat, the gloves—she's trying on her history. He has no idea what it means to her.

Once, when she was thirteen, she'd begged to be allowed to go hear the Smiths play at Pier 84. The lead singer was her obsession. Her bedroom walls were covered with pictures of him she'd ripped out of magazines. Her desperation to see the concert was almost frightening, and he and Ruth finally agreed that he'd take her. He doesn't recall much about the music, but he remembers that she held his hand the entire time without inhibition. He had known that this might be the last time she'd do such a thing, and that soon, she'd put distance between them in the ordinary way of adolescents. She'd memorized the lyrics of every song and sang loudly. She paused when the singer paused, hit the next word exactly when he did. She seemed so happy. And then, suddenly, she was sobbing, her face so racked with pain that she couldn't keep up with the lyrics any longer and she just gave over to her tears. He hadn't been sure what to do. He asked her if she wanted to leave, but she didn't seem to hear him. She didn't lift the collar of her T-shirt to wipe her eyes or get rid of the snot from her nose, a habit Ruth was trying to wean her of. He wondered if Francie even knew that she was crying, or if she was aware of herself at all. He realized in that moment, possessed as she was, she was becoming a new version of herself. He had no access to what was stirring inside her, and he knew that, in fundamental ways, he never would.

It's unbearably sad what's happening to his mother, he thinks as Francie starts to investigate another box. But his mother isn't sad. It's only that something is happening to her. She's in the process of becoming, too. It turns out that it takes a lifetime.

ELEVEN

THE MEMORY WING

Cleveland, Ohio, 2000; Cagnes-sur-Mer, France, 1989

Evelyn hadn't wanted to visit Helene. The women were no longer related, and it had been years since there was a reason for their performance of friendship. In this way, Ruth and Tom's divorce had come as a relief. But there was shame, too, for Evelyn, an inner collapse when she admitted to herself that she had spent nineteen years of her life with that woman shadowing her every thought and decision. Nineteen years! To think that this could count as one of her longest relationships. And then, with one phone call—*Mom, Tom and I are divorcing*—the years of clench-jawed diplomacy with Helene vanished, as if they'd never happened.

Afterward, Evelyn had taken a small pleasure in ignoring Helene's friends when she saw them at the market or the nail salon, feeling absolutely no reason to make nice. She liked the thought that these well-dressed busybodies would report back to Helene about Evelyn's rudeness or the fact that she'd kept her figure when the rest of them had settled into their battle-ready girths. But the truth was, Evelyn hadn't been released from the woman at all. She avoided Weybridge Road on the off chance that Helene would be looking out her dining room window at the exact moment Evelyn's Honda passed and might think that Evelyn was checking up on her.

During Evelyn's time in Florida, Ruth had kept her up to date, reporting first that Tom had moved his mother out of the big house into an apartment, and then, when Erna retired, into a nursing home. "She doesn't even recognize him anymore," Ruth explained sadly, the last time she called with news about Helene. It was late March then, and Evelyn was coming to the end of her yearly stay. It had been unsettling to know that Helene had taken such a bad turn. But it wasn't until Evelyn came back to Cleveland that the information truly sank in. Her first night home, she lay awake in bed, troubled by thoughts of Helene stashed away at Willowdale and vexed to be, all these years later, bothered on the woman's account. She'd show up at those Friday-night dinners and have to listen to Helene fuss over the roast. Even in the seventies, when people were lining up for gasoline and frying up liver and onions, Helene insisted on serving a pretentious hunk of meat surrounded by puckered and feeble-looking potatoes that reminded Evelyn of those gumball-sized beads the woman wore so tightly that they pinched the loose skin at her neck. How often had she kept her mouth shut while Helene implied that Francie's troubles must have come from Evelyn's side because *there is no mental illness in the Harker family*, even though, Evelyn knew, Tom had an uncle who jumped off a roof.

Willowdale was not surrounded by willows or nestled in a dale. It sat on a heavily trafficked street and looked like the nursery school that Francie had gone to. What was it called? Miss Hilda's? That Hilda woman painted her house red, put a couple of skinny goats and some chickens in her backyard, and called the whole thing a farm. She dressed in overalls, for God's sake. For Evelyn, who had been born on an actual farm, the whole thing was phony-baloney. As a matter of fact, she realized as she pulled into the circular driveway, it *was* the same place. The planter in the center of the roundabout that held impatiens had replaced the flagpole and the sun-bleached flag that the children had raised and lowered each day, their little hands placed uncertainly over their chests as they stumbled through the Pledge, unsure where their hearts were.

So, the nursery school had been turned into a nursing home, she thought as she parked the car. One babbling population exchanged for another. She'd been having a lot of these thoughts lately. Mean thoughts. Morbid thoughts. She'd see a man's bloated face and imagine his heart attack. Or she'd notice one of her friends looking gaunt and then think about what dress she'd wear when she stood at the woman's grave site, watching the casket being lowered into the ground. It was necessary to think of the worst things when the worst was so near at hand. She was seventy-seven. Reasonably healthy, but as the Floridians, those wrinkled prophets, reminded one another: all it took was One Bad Fall.

Nursery school to nursing home. Cradle to grave. She wondered whether, when Helene had first moved in, she was still with it enough to be aware of the irony. Well, even if she was, she probably wouldn't have found it funny. She had refused to set foot in that school after Francie caught a bad case of fleas. It was one more thing she blamed on Ruth. Well, Evelyn supposed she was right. The school had been an idiotic choice. Ruth had been delighted by the idea of Francie's spending time in a "rural" environment, as if cars weren't shooting past the school, making the goats shriek. As far as Evelyn could tell, the children learned nothing except how to fling dirt at one another and lick paint. Francie had started kindergarten behind. It was Evelyn who had made the girl sit on her hands when she added two plus two so that she wouldn't count on her fingers.

But, oh! Francie's little hands! The dusty, bodily smell of them. It was disgusting to think where they'd been during the day—inside her nostrils or scratching a badly wiped bottom. And yet, when Francie slept over, Evelyn couldn't help but give them a little sniff before making the girl submit to a good scrub with a nailbrush. She'd taught Francie how to care for her nails and her skin. Both things that Francie forgot. She'd had terrible acne as a teenager. And then she'd gotten involved with those drugs. Evelyn had visited her at the place outside of New Haven where she went when she was twenty-five and had fallen back into her bad habits. They'd played Boggle. Francie looked good, although her nails were bitten down to the quicks. They had a nice visit. But, after it was over and Evelyn took a taxi back to the airport, she thought, *I have just visited my granddaughter at a drug rehabilitation facility.* There were so many words she'd never imagined she'd have use for.

Florida was supposed to help. A land of forgetting. People there gloried in reinvention, marveling at how they were suddenly able to leap around a tennis court or walk eighteen holes without resorting to the cart. But Evelyn never forgot, not during aggressive rounds of canasta, not while she lay out in the sun, enjoying the scandal of her bikini. Florida was just a sunny place to worry about Ruth, or Francie, or about Naomi, who called too often, or Paula, whose two-minute weekly check-ins could hardly be counted as calls at all.

Entering the lobby of the nursing home, Evelyn was relieved to see that the room that had once housed pint-sized tables and chairs and cots for nap time had been turned into a decent-looking lounge, where peach-colored Naugahyde couches were adult-sized and stain-free. She spoke to the young receptionist about visiting Helene. The girl told her that it might be a while.

"Sometimes the clients have to be encouraged," she said, curling her fingers into air quotes, "to see visitors."

Evelyn thought instantly of cattle prods. She couldn't remember. Had Miss Hilda kept a cow?

The problem with memories, she thought as she sat down to wait, was that they were as exasperating as children: totally uncontrollable and always interrupting you when you were trying to think of other things. Like right now, as she sat in a room perfumed by Comet and Windex with a sharp undertone of decay, there was also, incomprehensibly, the smell of the sea and the sound of room-service carts clattering over a carpeted hallway. And here, in the waiting room of a nursing home at the beginning of a new millennium with its promise of a fresh start, it was also the summer of '89, when Francie had spent a month at that language school in France. *It will be so good for her!* Ruth had told Evelyn when she explained Francie's plans, although Evelyn suspected the reason had less to do with Francie and more to do with Ruth and Tom, separated half a year by then, throwing money at their daughter's unhappiness.

And then, midway through Francie's month away, Ruth and Tom came up with the idea that they should all, Evelyn and Helene included, fly to France in order to meet up with Francie on the Riviera when her classes finished. A family vacation! Ruth said, trying to convince her mother that this was a good idea. Evelyn had been skeptical. First of all, the last-minute ticket prices were ridiculous, and even though Tom was paying for the whole thing, she didn't like to be a part of frivolous waste. For another thing, it was the tourist season, and the only decent hotel Tom could find had just two available rooms. Evelyn knew the trip was a last-ditch effort on Ruth and Tom's part to repair things, so she went along with it. But then, after two endless flights and an uncomfortable car ride, the four of them arrived at the hotel only to find that Francie had left a message for them saying that she wasn't coming, and that she would meet them at Charles de Gaulle in a week for the flight home.

So, there they were at a fancy hotel perched above the Mediterranean Sea dumbfounded by the exhaustion of travel and the fact that their grand gesture had been met with a shrug. Ruth and Tom went off to make a phone call to the couple Francie had lived with in Lyons during her time at the school in order to track her down. Meanwhile, Evelyn and Helene followed a porter wearing a red fez to the room that they would share, which was, Evelyn discovered, outfitted for romance. Luxurious curtains plunged to the floor like half-shed gowns. Sculptures of fat, nasty-looking cherubs peered down at them from the corners of the room. And then there was the problem of the single queen-size bed.

"No, no, no!" Helene had shouted at the blank-faced porter. "WE NEED TWO BEDS!"

"There's nothing he can do about it," Evelyn said. She went into her purse and produced a dollar bill, which the young man examined as if it were a piece of smelly fish.

"The French," Helene muttered once he'd left. She dialed the front desk, but failed to secure a double room or, she said after she hung up, an apology. Evelyn laid her purse on the side of the bed nearest the phone. She wanted to be the first to receive news of Francie when Ruth and Tom called.

For the next ten minutes, the two of them unpacked, taking turns hanging their clothing in the armoire and laying out their toiletries in the bathroom. The awkwardness could be managed only if they didn't talk, but when Evelyn glanced into Helene's open suitcase, she couldn't help herself.

"What in the world?" she said, pointing at a miniature flag that was anchored in a silk pocket meant for delicates.

"Have you never seen an American flag before?" Helene said.

"But why do you have one in your suitcase?"

"I know who I am," Helene said.

Watching Helene refold a pair of underwear and then place it in a drawer, Evelyn suddenly felt overwhelmed by the intimacy of the situation. She announced that she was going to the front desk to see about changing money.

At lunch, Ruth and Tom reported that the phone call to the couple turned up nothing. Francie had left two days earlier. They had no idea where she was going.

"They made it seem like we were bothering them," Tom said. "They're supposed to be her French family. That's what it said in the brochure."

"That's a little sentimental, even for you," Ruth said. "I'm sure they do it for the money."

"Of course, you're right," Tom said deferentially. "I'm sorry."

"I'm sorry. I didn't mean that. I'm just worried," Ruth said.

"I know," Tom said. "I'm sorry."

Evelyn looked away. It was embarrassing to watch them trip over themselves trying to salvage the marriage.

"But what do we do?" Helene cried out suddenly, as if she'd just understood the situation.

"We wait," Evelyn said.

"Wait here?" Helene said, staring at her scallops Saint-Jacques as if she would have to take up residence in one of the shells.

"Whatever she's up to, Francie will be fine," Tom said.

"How can you know that?" Ruth said. "She's alone in a foreign country and she doesn't even speak the language."

"We don't know if she's alone," he said. "And after what we paid for this program, let's hope she speaks at least a little French."

His small joke fell flat.

"Just because you want something to be okay doesn't mean it will be," Ruth said quietly.

Tom looked down at his food. "Francie's smart," he said. "And she's already been on her own for a month and nothing went wrong."

"She probably made some friends," Ruth said hopefully. "They're probably bumming around, right?"

"And it could be worse," Tom added, looking at everyone, trying for optimism. "We're on the Riviera. The sea is right there."

All four of them dutifully turned in their chairs and looked out the arched picture window at the dark water below. The boundless world, and the fact that Francie was lost in it, silenced them.

Evelyn had never been to Europe. The truth was, she wasn't interested in overseas travel. She didn't like to admit this, because people considered you closed-minded, or fearful, or cheap, none of which she was—well, she was a little cheap. But she'd been forcibly marched through enough vacation albums to know that it was a waste of time and money going to places you'd already seen in photographs just so you could come back and show people a set of worse photographs of the exact same places. And then there were those *magical* encounters her friends were always bragging about. How they ran into a nice local man in Spain who brought them to a darling hole-in-the-wall, where they had a kind of ham that's *illegal* in the States! Or how they happened upon the most wonderfully friendly Berber nomads in Morocco, who invited them to their yurt for tea! The idea that people made a big to-do out of coincidence was ridiculous. Coincidences happened every single day, whether you were there to take a picture or not.

She might not have been much of a tourist, but she knew how to lie out with the best of them, so that afternoon, she put on her blue swimsuit and her paisley caftan, followed the signs, and climbed down a treacherously pitched stairway to the shore. She was disappointed to find that the beach was rocky and uncomfortable to walk on, but she didn't mind one bit when the cabana boy, who wore a jaunty neckerchief, set her up with a lounge chair and a wide blue umbrella, and gave her, she was sure, a little wink. After she lathered herself with Coppertone, she slid a cigarette out of its pack and was pleased when the boy rushed over to light it. She gave him a franc, lay back, closed her eyes, and exhaled into the sea air.

"You are groaning."

The voice was, unhappily, familiar. Evelyn opened her eyes. Helene was standing over her, wearing her traveling dress and pumps. Her pocketbook was lodged in the crook of her elbow.

"You got down here in those heels?" Evelyn said. "You could have broken your neck."

"Tom and Ruth are driving back to Paris," Helene said.

Evelyn stood up quickly. "I need to pack," she said.

"They've already left." Helene did not hide the pleasure she took in being in the know. "That couple called. Apparently one of the other children they are being paid to house knows where Francie is." Helene took a step backward, and her heels got trapped in the pebbles, throwing her off-balance. Evelyn reached out to steady her and, for a moment, the women held one another awkwardly. The cabana boy arrived with a second lounge chair and set it up under the umbrella. Helene sat, slipped off her shoes, brushed sand from the leather, and then, after an indecisive moment, lay back and placed them on the mound of her stomach. Her only concession to the idea of leisure was to cross her ankles. Grit, Evelyn noticed, had become lodged in the mesh of her stockings.

"Don't you want to put on something . . . cooler?" Evelyn asked, sitting down.

"I'm fine," Helene said.

"I feel like I'm sitting next to the abominable snowman. They have a dressing room down here. Let me run up and get your suit."

"I don't have one."

"We came all the way to the Riviera, and you didn't pack a swimsuit?"

"I don't wear a swimsuit."

"Ever?"

Helene's silence was her answer.

"What about when . . ." There were so many ways to finish that sentence. What about when Tom was young? What about when *Helene* was young? But Evelyn said nothing. Helene's acknowledgment might have been the most private thing she'd ever shared, a confession that she'd lived her life at a remove from her body. In all the time Evelyn had known the woman, she'd never once seen her with a man. "Why eat hamburger when you've had steak?" she'd heard Helene say more than once to explain her uninterest in finding another husband. Now it appeared she hadn't had much steak, either. "Well, you're better off," Evelyn said. "The sun is probably bad for you."

"Obviously not something you concern yourself with."

"I don't want to get skin cancer, but I want to get a tan. I don't want to get lung cancer, but I want to smoke. I do more than I don't, I guess."

"That's foolhardy."

So is wearing high heels on a beach, Evelyn wanted to say, but she kept her mouth shut, and lay back on her chaise.

They were quiet for a while. Evelyn was conscious of the sound of the water, the rhythmic crash and suck punctuated, every so often, by the shouts of a child or the caw of a seabird. The unpleasant noise of a motor grew louder until a biplane appeared, dragging a banner behind it that showed a model smiling hugely, her red lips open to reveal a set of gleaming white teeth. A moment later, the airplane released what looked like a flurry of confetti, but turned out to be small tubes of toothpaste. Evelyn and Helene both sat up on their elbows and watched as children scrambled for the treasure as if money had dropped out of the sky.

"The French," Helene said.

"I'm going for a dip," Evelyn said.

"I will hold down the fort."

Evelyn couldn't be certain if Helene was making a joke. She might, in all seriousness, be promising to guard Evelyn's towel and cigarettes from the marauding beachgoers, who were, right now, congratulating their children on their prizes and turning lazily onto their stomachs to bake their other sides.

Evelyn waded into the freezing-cold water up to her shins and reconsidered. She didn't want Helene to think she was lily-livered, though, so she kept going until the water reached her knees, then the tops of her thighs, and then her waist. Finally, she gathered her courage and dove in. When she surfaced, she instinctively turned and waved toward the beach, realizing, as she did, how stupid that was. Even if Helene was looking at her, she would not be impressed by Evelyn's courage. Evelyn started to swim back and forth parallel to the beach. She tried different strokes—the crawl, the breaststroke, even the sidestroke, which always seemed silly to her, invented for ladies who didn't want to sacrifice their hairdos. She flipped onto her back and moved her hands in figure eights. The sun was still high, and she closed her eyes. It occurred to her that, with Ruth and Tom heading to Paris, Helene was the only person in the whole place that she knew. She understood that it was possible to feel so barely tethered to the world that with one snip, you could fly away.

For the first time all day, she allowed herself to worry about Francie, and then she felt like an idiot for playing around in the water. She should go check with the concierge. There might be news.

She opened her eyes. She looked toward the beach, but it wasn't there. She tried to stand. Her foot scraped against something, but she couldn't touch bottom. Fighting a rising panic, she spun herself around. Now she saw the beach, but it was far away. The sculling of her hands had been no match for the tide, and she'd floated much farther out than she'd intended. She started to swim toward shore, but somehow, in her agitation, her accomplished strokes deserted her, and she crashed around sloppily, making little progress. Her body started to feel strange. This was not exhaustion. It was something more thick feeling, as if her bones were turning to cement. Soon, she could barely move her arms or kick her legs. She called out, but no one heard her. Her thoughts became gluey. For a moment, she considered how nice it would be to stop moving, but then she swallowed water, and the shock of it reminded her that she was about to drown.

By the time she was within reach of the shore, a crowd had gathered. Some people waded in, took her by the arms, and dragged her out of the water. She tried to tell them that she could walk on her own, but she couldn't make her mouth work and, in any case, even with people on both sides holding her up, her legs buckled. Then someone lifted her in their arms, carried her up the beach, and laid her on a lounge chair. Bodies hovered above her, blocking out the sun. People were talking at once and she had no idea what they were saying. She started to shiver.

"*Méduse!*" someone shouted. And then someone else said, "*Médecin.*"

Yes, she thought slowly, *I need medicine.*

"What is this? What is happening? Let me through!"

The perfume was familiar. And then the face.

"This woman needs medical attention!" Helene bellowed to the crowd. "Someone call an ambulance. AMBULANCE! I am the wife of a doctor. Do what I say!"

Evelyn tried to speak, but her tongue felt like an eel. Had she swallowed an eel? Oh, look! There was that cabana boy standing at the foot of the lounge chair. Such a nice boy. But why was he unzipping his pants? She was going to die, and the last thing she would ever see would be the self-satisfied smile on Helene's face as she watched the boy urinate on Evelyn's foot.

"I'm sorry, but Mrs. Simonauer doesn't want to see you." The receptionist was speaking to her in a near whisper, as if she were sure Evelyn would not want anyone else in the waiting room to hear this humiliating news.

"I find that hard to believe," Evelyn said.

"That's what they tell us to say," the girl said, her face reddening. "It's just that the nurse can't get her out of bed to bring her to the solarium."

"Then I'll go to her room," Evelyn said, standing.

"You have to either be on the list or the patient has to request a room visit," the girl said anxiously. "You know. Because of privacy and stuff."

"Oh, for God's sake," Evelyn said. "How would she request a visit if she doesn't remember anyone?"

"It's the rules."

"Do you have a supervisor?"

The girl's eyes widened. She was about to cry.

"Listen, dear," Evelyn said calmly. "I've come all the way from Florida." And then, throwing in a bit of Helene for good measure, "And I demand to see her right now!"

A few minutes later, she was following an orderly down a series of hallways until they reached a door of the kind, Evelyn thought, you'd find in a prison. Wire mesh covered the small window and there were two sets of locks. A small placard announced that they were entering the Memory Wing.

"Flight risk," the man said as he sorted through his key ring. He opened the door, then led her down an empty hallway that was painted beige, which might, Evelyn thought darkly, be a bit too suggestive of the minds of the patients behind each closed door.

"Here you go," he said, and left her in front of one of them. She knocked lightly, turned the knob, and went inside.

She hardly recognized the person in the bed. Helene took up so much less space than Evelyn remembered. Her body, once stubbornly thick, barely formed a shape beneath the sheets and blanket. Her skin was almost translucent. Her hair looked recently done, the style she'd favored all these years holding its own. Well, Tom had always been an attentive son, Evelyn conceded. She couldn't fault him for that. It would be like him to get a hairdresser to make a house call, knowing his mother would never go without her weekly wash and set. Maybe he'd even tracked down Helene's favorite hairdresser from ages ago. The woman had done Ruth's hair once, and Ruth still said it was the best cut she'd ever had. Suddenly, Evelyn missed her daughter terribly. She hoped Ruth would invite her to New York for a visit. Francie wasn't living in the city anymore. She said the place was bad for her. Too many temptations. When Evelyn last talked to her, she was tapping maple syrup in Vermont.

The room was small and overheated, but from the looks of things, Tom had tried his best with the decorations. A small painting of a countryside scene that Evelyn remembered from Helene's dining room hung above the bureau that had been in her bedroom. Her vanity and stool sat against another wall. The furniture could have no use here, and Evelyn wondered if Helene would even recognize the pieces. But maybe the shape of them or a barely detectible scent coming off the wood was familiar enough to give her a little comfort. Evelyn pulled the stool close to the bed and sat. Helene's eyes were closed. She was breathing evenly. Her hands rested on top of the covers. The joints of her fingers were arthritically askew, the knuckles swollen and painful looking. Evelyn took one of the hands in hers. The skin was satiny and warm, a heat that seemed to come not from the temperature of the room but from Helene's body. The determination of her blood that continued to pump so fiercely despite everything was a loyalty that made Evelyn's throat tighten.

Tom might have been keeping on top of his mother's hair, but Helene's nails were a mess. They'd been cut short and blunt, probably to keep her from scratching herself, but the cuticles were ragged. Evelyn reached into her purse and found the small tube of moisturizer she carried with her. She poured out a generous dollop and massaged the cream into Helene's skin.

Helene sighed deeply and slowly opened her eyes. She stared at the ceiling. Evelyn couldn't tell if she was aware that anyone was in the room with her or that someone was holding her hand.

"It's Evelyn," she said quietly. "I've come to see you."

Helene's gaze fell vaguely in her direction.

"Have you had a good rest?" Evelyn said.

For a moment, Helene seemed to focus. Evelyn squeezed her hand a little tighter. "It's me," she said. But then Helene's eyes shifted away toward whatever marked the outer limit of her view.

Evelyn fainted after the boy peed on her, either from shock or from the effects of the jellyfish poison coursing through her system. Apparently, a man carried her all the way up those perilous steps to the room she and Helene shared. She must have slept for a long time because when she woke, it was night and Helene was beside her, snoring gently. Evelyn's foot throbbed. She lifted the cover to try to see what was going on, but the room was too dark. She reached down and felt the bandages and pain shot through her body. She wondered who had wrapped her foot. Had a doctor been called? She was wearing her nightgown, although she had no memory of changing her clothes. It must have been Helene who pulled off her swimsuit. She would have had to lean Evelyn against her so that she could fit the gown over her head and shoulders and pull her arms through the sleeves one after the other. Just the way Evelyn had done when Francie was little and slept at her apartment, the drowsy girl so sweet in her floppy exhaustion. Just the way Helene must have done, too, Evelyn thought, when Francie stayed with her. She looked at Helene now. Her breasts were loose underneath her nylon gown, and Evelyn could see their flattened, oblong shapes. *Bosoms.* It was something Francie had said once when she had laid her head on Evelyn's proudly firm chest. She'd said that Grandma had soft bosoms, and that she hoped, when she grew up, she would have soft bosoms, too.

The phone woke them both the following morning. Evelyn grabbed it and listened.

"They found Francie," she said after she hung up.

Helene made a frightened noise, shot out of the bed, and crossed the room with uncommon speed. Frantic, she opened the door to the armoire and began to pull her dresses off their hangers, then went into the bureau drawers and pulled out her underwear. But then, suddenly, she seemed to lose her will. She stopped moving and held the wadded mass of her clothing, as if she wasn't sure what to do with it. "Poor Francie," she said.

"Poor Francie?" Evelyn said. "Poor us!" She felt a sudden rage toward the girl who had dragged them across an ocean. All this worry. All this money. Who knew how long it would take for Evelyn's foot to heal? Ruth and Tom's marriage was not going to make it, and the daughter they'd raised, the girl the four of them had doted on, and praised, and loved, had turned out to be nothing more than a selfish teenager. Poor Francie, indeed!

Evelyn got out of bed and hobbled across the room. The pain was awful. She took Helene's clothes from her and began to fold them and put them in the suitcase. Then she went to work packing up her things. Helene stood where she was.

"We need to get a move on," Evelyn said, rattled by Helene's uncharacteristic incompetence. But then she realized Helene was staring at her opened case and that her lips were moving. Evelyn heard "allegiance." She heard "the United States of America."

* * *

Evelyn gently put Helene's hand back on top of the bedcover. She remembered exactly how she'd felt watching Helene cling to her patriotism in that moment. She'd thought the woman was naive, as if the fact of a foreign country, and not a petulant teenager, or even her son, who had stupidly cheated on his wife, had turned everything upside down. But now she wondered if there hadn't been something—well, okay—holy about it. Evelyn had never believed in anything that she couldn't see with her eyes or hold in her hands.

"Helene," she whispered gently.

Helene stirred. Her eyes opened softly, then closed again. Evelyn slipped off her shoes, lifted the edge of the cover, and slid into the bed. She lay on her back and stared at the cracks in the ceiling paint, tracing their jagged pattern with her eyes. The two of them had spent so many years in an undeclared competition. Who got more time with Francie? Who was the better grandmother? How thrilled Evelyn was when little Francie told her that she liked to go to Grandma's for the food, but Nana's for fun.

She turned on her side and looked at Helene's profile. "I know who I am," Helene had said when Evelyn had made fun of her paper flag. Evelyn wondered if Helene's thoughts included the word *I* anymore. How awful that she might no longer exist for herself. But then Evelyn thought about the years people spent making marks on the world, trying to prove that they were alive and that they mattered. *Pay attention to me! Show me that you love me! Here I am!* My God, she thought. It was so exhausting.

"It's like she's not even there," Ruth had said when she called Evelyn in Florida to tell her about Helene.

But here she was. And what if there was no more *I* for her? What if her thoughts didn't include herself at all, but only the sensation of darkness or light, or warmth, or the feeling of being lifted up by strangers, or the fleeting image of a woman with a gleaming white smile floating across a cloudless sky?

TWELVE

AT LAST

Waldron Island, Washington, 2015

"You know this story, Ruth," Evelyn says. "Of course, you do. The one about Fidelity and those puppies."

Evelyn and my mother are sitting in the main room of the cabin where Jenny and I live, on an island off the coast of Washington. We can see Canada from our backyard. It's a worn-out joke, but Jenny and I don't get tired of it. We have a generator, a woodburning stove, and an ATV. We have a small motorboat that we use to get to and from Orcas Island, where Jenny grew up and where we keep our car in her parents' driveway near the landing. I run the art program at the high school there. Jenny teaches kids with special needs.

Something else we tell each other too often: the *Darlin' Jenny* tattoo on my wrist hadn't been a mistake after all. Well, it had been for most of our twenties when she bailed on my chaotic life as I tried to get sober. But we found our way back

251

to one another. I like to remind her that I never had the tattoo removed because I knew things would eventually work out. Which is not true. I kept it there as a sign of what I'd lost when my other desires led me so disastrously astray. What is true is that, whether it works out or not, love is not so easy to erase. Look at my parents. Since the divorce, neither of them has sustained a relationship beyond a few years. I'm not sure they try very hard. They still talk on the phone every day.

"I remember Fidelity," my mother says now, tucking her legs underneath her. At seventy, she still has long hair, a wonderful cascade of gray, which somehow makes her look younger than her years. "I loved that dog."

"You loved that dog when you felt like it," Evelyn says. "All you girls did. You begged us to get her and then half the time, you forgot she was there." Her voice is thin and weaker than it was even four months ago, when I visited her in Cleveland.

My mother and I sit on the couch, Evelyn in the armchair. It's the furniture from my grandmother's den that I kept after my father and I emptied out her house. I've carted that couch and chair with me to every place I've lived—the city-mouse-infested studio on West Forty-Ninth, where I made art and took any job that would pay the rent; the country-mouse-infested farmhouse outside of Burlington that I shared with four other students while I finished getting my degree. The springs are giving out, and the material is patchy. Still, it gives me so much pleasure to see the furniture each time I walk into the cabin.

I glance from my mother to Evelyn. They don't look alike. They never have. But there is something similar about them I can't quite name. I wonder whether, if I painted them, the likeness would come through. I doubt they'd let me try. The idea of the two of them agreeing to pose together and allowing me to look at them the way I'd need to—no, neither of them would be able to manage the intimacy of that. After I finished school, fueled by all the critical theory that captivated me, I made mixed-media installations. Recently, though, I've started to paint portraits. It's more challenging than I could have imagined. The more I think I understand a face, the harder it is to put it on the canvas. I've begun to layer my attempts one on top of the other so that the earlier iterations show through. I don't believe in the idea of the final version.

Jenny's lying down in our bedroom. Three months pregnant with our first child, she's exhausted and nauseated. This is our second try. We lost the first one at eight weeks. She's thirty-nine. I'll be forty-two in a few months. We tease each other about our geriatric pregnancy, which is the charming term our OB on the mainland uses. We chose an anonymous sperm donor, and there was not even a discussion about who would carry the baby. I don't need to pass down my predispositions. Jenny's DNA seems to make her vulnerable to sunniness and optimism. And she's beautiful. She'd say the same about me, but as much as I've made big strides in the self-worth department, I can't see it. I don't trust a mirror to give me an accurate representation of who I am.

This morning, I took our boat to Orcas, picked up the car, and rode the ferry to Anacortes. Once there, I drove an hour-plus to pick up my mother and Evelyn at the airport. A cumbersome trip, but I have come to appreciate a sense of journey.

I was anxious waiting at baggage claim, but when my mother and Evelyn appeared, I was relieved to see that Evelyn looked better than I'd expected. For the last year, my mother and my aunts took turns living in Cleveland while Evelyn underwent her treatments for lung cancer. She didn't hide the fact that she preferred Paula to the others. Naomi was too fussy and solicitous. My mother couldn't hide her discomfort with the bathing and the toileting Evelyn needed when she was weak from chemo. Paula, as it turned out, was detached enough to be the perfect caretaker. She didn't make herself the center of the drama. She did what Evelyn asked and kept to herself when her mother wanted to be alone. Evelyn's current remission is considered, even by her doctors, to be a small, if momentary, miracle. Evelyn doesn't believe in miracles, large or small. "I'm ninety-two," she likes to say. "I'm going to go now or not much later."

"I remember that dog, but I don't know anything about her having puppies," my mother says. "And I'll never forgive you for putting Fidelity down after I went to college," she adds, smiling mischievously; it's a score that was settled a long time ago.

"Fidelity went to live in the country with some nice people who had a farm," Evelyn says.

My mother laughs. "Half the kids I grew up with? When they left for college, their pets mysteriously went to live with some nice people on a farm."

"I can't help it if you don't believe me," Evelyn says.

When I was twenty-five and had relapsed, I went to a treatment center in Connecticut. Evelyn came to visit me there. I'd gotten to the lowest place I'd ever been and I was ashamed for her to see me that way. We sat at a round table in the dayroom, not making much progress on an aspirational collage that the staff psychologist wanted me to make. Magazines were spread out on the table between us, and we were lazily looking for images to cut out with dull children's scissors, pictures that were supposed to represent a future I wanted for myself.

"How about this?" Evelyn said, showing me a photograph of a fancy thatched-roofed villa perched over the turquoise waters of a Polynesian island.

"Not my dream," I said. It seemed precarious to me then to trust that a set of stilts would keep me from going under. And I was far from believing that I deserved any kind of luxury.

She looked around at the other tables, where patients played solitaire, or read, or sat staring at nothing while they waited for the next therapeutic event of the day. I started to feel a familiar agitation. I asked the monitor on duty if I could go outside for a cigarette. It was the one vice we were allowed so long as we smoked in the walled garden that was topped with concertina wire. We patients were told this safety measure was in place because of the not-great neighborhood, but we had our suspicions. Every so often, you'd catch someone looking at those spikes and you knew they were thinking about how much pain was worth it.

Evelyn watched me light up. "I hate that you smoke," she said.

I didn't know whether to be angry or grateful. Of all the things I'd done that she could have hated, cigarettes seemed to be the least offensive. "You smoke, Nana," I said.

"I'll make a deal with you," she said. "If you stop, I'll stop." She was suddenly captivated by the idea, as if she'd seized on a solution no drug counselor had, something that might cure me. It broke my heart to think of how I'd disappointed her, how I'd disappointed everyone. I didn't stop smoking then, but eventually I did. And, keeping her promise, she quit, too. But she was eighty by then, and a lifelong habit had done its damage. When she got sick, I was angry at myself for not quitting sooner.

In the garden, she watched me smoke the cigarette, then we headed back into the dayroom. When it was time for her to leave, she gave me a strong hug, as if she wanted me to absorb her resilience.

"I know I went too far, Nana," I said when she let me go.

"Oh, Francie!" she said with what I can only describe as delight. It was as if she'd finally understood something important, not only about my life but hers as well. "If you don't go too far, how will you know what's far enough?"

When she said that, I felt that maybe I'd be able to pull myself together, if only because she thought I could.

Evelyn starts coughing. My mother leaps up from the couch and goes to her side. I head to the kitchen, but by the time I come back with a glass of water, Evelyn's cough is under control, and she waves me away. She's stoved-in from all the treatment. Her famously straight back hunches. She uses a cane and not only for walking. The last time I visited her, I tried to help her out of a chair, and she jabbed the stick into my chest to hold me off. My mother and I were against this trip, but Evelyn insisted. She wants to see where Jenny and I live, and she wants to see Jenny pregnant. What she doesn't say is that she's not sure she'll be around for the birth. She's decided not to continue treatment when the cancer returns.

"It's just embarrassing," she said when I argued with her about that, but I understand. I think she means that, at a certain point, hope is unseemly. She still eats a breakfast of burnt rye toast. Some days, she'll eat that for lunch and dinner, too. She wants that bitter, frank taste in her mouth.

"It all started with a pair of socks," she says now, settling into her story. "Fidelity pulled them out of the second-floor hamper. She was a very curious dog. You couldn't go from the kitchen to the dining room without her running over to see what the fuss was about. She knew when one of you girls forgot to shut the pantry door, or when somebody didn't close the toilet lid. And then, before you know it, she's torn through a box of Ritz crackers and is slurping water out of the toilet bowl. I tell Frank to close the hamper lid after he tosses in his clothing at the end of the day. But that man has such a restless mind. He barely finishes one thing before he's on to the next."

She's telling the story as if it's happening now, pulling her past up to the present. I look at my mother to see if she's noticed, but she's rapt, waiting to see what comes next.

"So, Fidelity takes my socks into the backyard and digs a hole," Evelyn says. "She gets into a frenzy, dirt flying everywhere. She's not interested in the hole, only in digging." She stops talking. She closes her eyes.

"Mom?" my mother says. "You okay?"

I find a blanket and lay it over Evelyn's lap. Our cabin is surrounded by trees, and it never gets hot, even in summer. Just as my mother and I are about to leave the room to let Evelyn sleep, she opens her eyes and starts talking again.

"Ruth has a tantrum at three o'clock each day. On the dot. It's like she can already tell time, even though she's just a baby. The only thing is to lay her on top of the washing machine and start a cycle. Finally, she calms down and sleeps. Oh, my God! What a relief it is when the little girls sleep. I love it when they're sick. Not too sick. Just a little cold, or a slight fever—enough for a tablespoon of cherry cough syrup. Maybe a little bit extra. Then, they sleep. Three or four hours at a time. Heaven."

"So, what you're saying is that you drugged us," my mother says. She tries for a laugh, but I can tell that her mother, so lost in time, distresses her.

"Fidelity takes socks from the hamper," Evelyn says, ignoring her. She closes her eyes. "One of the girls' stuffed bears, tissues from the wastebasket. She takes it all outside and drops it into the hole. Then she settles down to guard everything. You can't get her to move. I tell Frank we'd better plug up the hole because one of the girls is going to break her ankle or worse. And then who is going to have to sit with her for hours in the emergency room? And who is going to have to keep her entertained for weeks when she can't go outside and play? Frank fills in the hole, and I put the socks and toys back where they came from. But the next morning, Fidelity's got everything and is back in the yard, digging. Oh, I'm so mad! I run outside and grab her collar to pull her away, and you know what she does? She turns on me and bares her teeth. I'm the one who feeds her. I'm the one who dries her off when she comes in out of the rain. But I know if I don't let go, that dog will tear me apart." She opens her eyes. "It's nice here, Francie."

"Thanks, Nana."

"Very quiet."

"What about Fidelity, Mom?" my mother says.

"Oh, Lord, that dog," Evelyn says. "She wouldn't come inside at night. And you girls were so hopped up about everything that you wouldn't go to bed. Oh, you girls begged to stay up. *Five more minutes! One more minute!* You know, there is such a thing as too much time." She clears her throat. "Francie, I'll take that water now," she says.

I bring her the glass. She takes a long drink. She closes her eyes again. "You know what I do?" she continues. "I go outside with a piece of steak and shake it in front of Fidelity's nose. She follows me into the kitchen just like I knew she would. But then she starts crying. You know that sound dogs make when they cry? That horrible yowl? She won't stop. Just like when you girls were babies. You'd lie in your cribs at night and cry and cry. Ruth cried three nights straight until she gave up. But you know what? A person has to learn how to be alone. The sooner the better."

I look at my mother. Everything about this is upsetting to her. She never talks much about her childhood. I know that she was ahead of her elementary school peers, and that her teachers didn't know what to do with her, so they sent her into the hallway to read. She always tells this story with pride, but I think she was lonely.

"And then," Evelyn says, "Fidelity got so fat! How did she get so fat? Who fed her table scraps? Well, of course, your father did. He'd wink at you girls while he snuck his arm underneath the table to feed that dog a piece of chicken. And you know, I always get so mad at him when he does that, because who is going to have to explain to you girls about dying when Fidelity gets so fat her heart can't pump her blood? Who is going to say, 'No, she's not coming back. Not ever'?"

She stops talking, and the three of us sit in silence. Jenny comes out of the bedroom looking soft and comfortably disoriented from her nap. She's hardly showing, but there's a change in her all the same. Some deep privacy, I guess I'd say. Which was intimidating when I first noticed it, but it amazes me now. It's not that she's leaving me out, but her body is giving her instructions, and she's paying attention.

"My favorite person," Jenny says, leaning over to kiss Evelyn's cheek. She means it. She's always loved Evelyn and finds her forthrightness refreshing. Back in our early twenties, when I was so besotted and called Evelyn to tell her about Jenny, and, for the first time, about me, she asked the sorts of questions I'd prepared myself for. What about such and such a boy I'd mentioned to her when I was in high school? Was I sure? How did I know? I tried to explain to her that I'd felt this about myself even before I was able to put words to it. I told her about the time I was sixteen years old and went to Paris to party with some friends instead of joining my family on the Riviera like I was supposed to. I'd met a boy at a café and went with him to his room in a shabby apartment, where we started to fool around. I tried to explain to her that I didn't dislike what was happening, but that I was aware that I ought to be feeling things, and that I wasn't, and so I got out of there before I had to do something I didn't want to do. She was quiet for a while, and I thought maybe I'd told her too much.

"It's good that you left when you did," she said finally.

She said that she loved me no matter what, which was a kind of backhanded acceptance, but I took it. Still, the next time she came to New York to visit and met Jenny, the first thing she said was "You're a girl." It wasn't a question. It was more as if she hadn't quite believed me, or as if she didn't think I knew what I was talking about. Jenny didn't blink, said that she was, indeed, a girl. "All right, then," Evelyn had said.

My mother gives Jenny her seat on the couch next to me. She sits on the floor by Evelyn's feet.

"You look green around the gills," Evelyn says to Jenny.

"I'm still low-level sick to my stomach. But I haven't vomited in a week," she says. "I think that part's over."

"It was terrible," I say. "Morning, afternoon, and night sickness."

"A girl, then," Evelyn says. "Girls make you sicker than boys."

"Lovely," my mother says. "Also, untrue."

"Says the person who called me in tears every time she upchucked. Why do you think I moved to Cleveland?"

"Because you were tired of Omaha," my mother says. "You wanted a change."

"Because I thought: If she can't handle a little vomiting, how will she handle a baby?"

"Girl or boy, we'll take whatever we get," Jenny says.

"What happens next?" my mother asks Evelyn.

"What next?" Evelyn says.

"With Fidelity."

"Oh that. Well, she's fat and her nipples start to swell," Evelyn says, picking up the thread of her story. "And now I know what's going on. Of course I know. She has that look, like there's nothing she can do about it now. And you girls, you are so excited. It's all you can talk about. Puppies! Puppies! And then one morning, Fidelity comes in from the yard carrying the socks in her mouth. And then she goes back and gets everything out of the hole. One by one, she brings it all into the house and puts the stuff on that ratty old blanket she used to sleep on, remember that thing? She stays on that blanket all day long for days. And then, little by little, her belly shrinks. And then, a few days later, she gets up off her blanket and doesn't bother about those stuffed animals and socks and whatever else anymore."

She stops talking.

"And?" my mother says.

"And nothing. That's it. End of story."

"What about the puppies?" my mother says.

"What puppies? She was never pregnant in the first place. It was just some strange thing dogs do. Like a—what do they call it?—phantom limb."

"So that's the whole story?" My mother is practically whining, as if she's been cheated out of a promise. "She was going to have puppies, but she didn't?"

"She was never going to have them in the first place," Evelyn said.

"I don't get it," my mother says.

"There's nothing to get. It was just a thing that happened. Other than that, she was a fairly normal dog."

We eat lunch, and then Evelyn lies down for a nap in our small guest room, which will be the baby's room soon enough. My mother packed the monitor from the apartment in Cleveland. She sets it up, and when she, Jenny, and I take a walk, she carries the receiver. She keeps holding it up to her ear and asking me if I think we're still within range. Occasionally, Evelyn coughs, and then we stop and wait, staring at the receiver, wondering if this is the last moment before everything else happens.

"I don't remember anything about that business with Fidelity," my mother says once we start walking again. "I mean the dog, yes. But the rest of it . . . I just don't understand why she would make up something like that." She seems hurt, but I think she's only trying not to be scared.

"Also, maybe not a great story to tell an expectant couple," I say.

"We're past that now, honey," Jenny says, taking my hand. "I can tell. This one's sticking around."

Maybe it's silly how much assurance I get from her certainty, but I believe her. Jenny radiates capability. I attribute this to her having grown up on an island with parents who let her pack a lunch and roam around in the woods, who taught her how to sail, and who didn't stand in her way when she was eighteen and announced that, before heading to college in New York, she was going to take a two-week solo trip up the Strait of Georgia. From Jenny, I have learned the names of trees and birds and wildflowers. I've learned how to fix almost anything that can go wrong with our house, and how to take apart and put together the boat's motor. I'm going to design and build the crib. But despite all my newfound abilities, Jenny has something I'm not sure I'll ever have, which is her belief in her ability to manage whatever comes her way. It's not even a belief, for her. It's in her bones, this sense that she and the world are not at odds with one another.

"But what do you think she meant by it?" my mother says, still focused on the business with Fidelity. It's as if she feels that whatever message is encoded in the story of a hormonally imbalanced dog will tell her something about her life that she's never been able to understand.

"Maybe it doesn't matter what it means," I say. "Maybe it only matters that she wanted to tell us about it."

"You would say that," my mother says. We've had these

arguments before. I'm less inclined to care about what things mean, in art or in the way people behave. Maybe it's a reaction to all those years of therapy. I could name a slew of reasons why I was so anxious and self-destructive when I was younger, but the neat arithmetic of cause and effect doesn't make me any more legible to myself. My mother thinks my attitude is intellectually weak, maybe even morally corrupt. But she also grew up with Evelyn and has had to try to understand the impulses behind her mother's subtle and not-so-subtle insinuations her whole life. My mother will still reach out and pull my hair from behind my ears the way her mother did so that she wouldn't end up with jug ears, which might have been Evelyn's way of telling her that she was not beautiful enough to risk inattention. But it could also have been Evelyn's version of care. Who knows?

"What are you working on these days, Ruth?" Jenny asks.

My mother cheers up, as Jenny knew she would. She likes nothing more than for someone to recognize her work. She talks about a poet she's been asked to translate for a small press. "She's known in Germany, but no one knows her here. It will get some attention."

"That sounds great, Mom," I say. It's hard for her to come to terms with the fact that I make art in a shed on an island in the Salish Sea and don't care whether my work is recognized by the New York art world or not. I think she sees this as an abdication of responsibility. One of the few stories she told me about her past had to do with those men in her PhD department who were so rattled by a smart woman that all they could do was make sexist remarks about her looks.

"I don't know," she says. "I might not do it. I'm not sure it's worth it."

I don't think she's talking about the money, or the size of the press. She's talking about time, and her sense that there's a certain amount of it that can be used one way or another, and that any choice she makes will always lead to regret.

Evelyn and my mother spend five days on the island. In the mornings, when Evelyn's energy is pretty good, we take very short, very slow walks. We talk about the trees, or the light, or we say nothing at all.

When it's time for them to head back to Cleveland, we retrace our steps. I take them by motorboat to Orcas, where we get the car and drive onto the ferry for the ride back to Anacortes. On the boat, we stay in the car. Most people do. Motors off, the ferry captain in control of getting us from here to there, it's as good a place as anywhere to grab an hour of quiet or sleep. Even though the visit was relatively calm, and we mostly sat around and ate and slept, I'm exhausted.

"I need to use the ladies'," Evelyn says.

"I'll take you, Nana," I say, opening the car door.

"To the bathroom?" Evelyn says. "I think I can manage that on my own, thank you very much."

"It's up a flight of stairs," I tell her as I open her door. "I don't mind."

She shakes her cane at me.

"Mom?"

My mother shrugs. She's worn out, too.

"If you don't mind, I'd rather not wet my pants," Evelyn says.

I help her out of the car, give her directions about which way to turn once she's on the deck, then watch her disappear into the companionway.

"Jesus," I say when I'm back in the car.

"You don't have to fly across the country with her," my mother says, although I'm pretty sure she would like to never leave her mother's side.

We sit for a while until sitting turns into waiting, and then we take turns wondering why she hasn't gotten back and reassuring each other that she's fine, that it takes time to pee at her age, and that she deserves her privacy and her dignity. And then we decide we can't give her either and we're both out of the car and running up the stairs. Once we're in the passenger cabin, we find the women's bathroom. We push open the doors of the empty stalls as if we imagine she's forgotten how to use a lock. Then we stand uncertainly in front of the one stall that's occupied.

"Nana?" I say quietly, knowing just how irritated she must feel to be called out in a public restroom where people make an effort to not notice one another. But then I imagine her slumped over on the toilet. This can't be her end, I think. Not like this. She wouldn't stand for it. I bang on the door while my mother bends over to look beneath it. Finally, it opens, and a teenage girl emerges.

"Fucking freaks!" she says as she blows past us.

Once we're back in the passenger cabin it takes me a minute to orient myself. There are exit signs leading to different stairways. Evelyn must have gotten turned around and gone to the wrong one. She's probably lost with no idea where she is or where we are. My mother and I run back down to our deck and search the rows of cars. When we don't find her, we head to the level where the delivery trucks and flatbeds are parked. We split up to search. I can't find Evelyn on this deck, either. When I connect back up with my mother, she's talking to a man in a reflective vest, gesticulating wildly, trying to make him understand the urgency of the situation.

"It's a boat," he says. "She can't go far."

But can she? She's decided to refuse more treatment. Is it possible that she's also decided that she's had enough of everything else? I race up the two flights of stairs until I'm back in the passenger cabin. And then I see her. She's outside on the deck, standing alone by the railing.

"Nana!" I call out to her once I'm through the glass doors.

She turns around, sees me, and waves.

"Oh, my God. What are you doing here?" I say when I reach her. "We've been looking for you all over the place."

"You didn't look very hard. I've been here the whole time."

"Mom!" my mother cries out. She and the crewman have come onto the deck. Once he sees the problem has been solved, he goes back inside.

"We nearly broke down the bathroom door," my mother says when she reaches us.

"Oh, I didn't have to go. I just wanted to get out of that car. The two of you are so gloomy."

"Jesus, Mom," my mother says. "I thought I was going to have a heart attack."

"You're not going to have a heart attack," Evelyn says. "That business with your father was only on the male side of the family. You girls will have to find your own ways to go."

We stand on the deck for a while longer, three abreast at the railing, the wind on our cheeks.

"It's very pretty, your island," Evelyn says to me. "But it's an idiotic place to have a baby. That's all I'll say."

"I'm sure you'll have more to say, Nana."

"We'll see."

I think about Fidelity, and her socks, and the hole she kept digging and re-digging in the yard, and how she just had to go through something until she didn't have to go through it anymore. *There, Mom*, I say to myself. *There's your meaning.* But does it clarify anything? As Evelyn said, it was just something that happened.

I think about Evelyn and about Helene, too. Their lives were full of so many things that just happened. I'll want to tell my child about these women, but there is so little I will ever know. A grandparent, a parent—it's not their job to explain themselves to their children and grandchildren. But it does seem to be the job of children and grandchildren to wonder, to weave together the bits and pieces that come down to them, to ask over and over, *Who are you?*

I know that Evelyn let a boy try to shoot an apple off her head, because she told my mother, who then, as a way of explaining her mother's stubborn and vexing character, told me. I know that Helene always traveled with a small American flag in her suitcase because I saw it when she visited us in New York. I know that my parents' wedding was rained out, but not before everyone had gathered in a park. Everything was ruined, the flowers and some paper hearts and streamers that Naomi had hung on the branches of a tree, decorations my mother thought were tacky, but also, she admitted later, sweet.

What will I tell our child about my life? Will I tell them that when I was very young, I broke my arm, and that when Helene drove me from the hospital to her house, she looked at me in the rearview mirror and said, "You love me more than you love your nana, don't you?" I didn't know how to answer. I was just a little girl. It had not occurred to me that love was something you could measure.

It seems to me now that loving more makes it impossible to love less.

"This is taking forever," Evelyn says, staring across the water.

She doesn't sound impatient. I was foolish to worry. As if she would make some final rash, dramatic gesture and fling herself into the sea. The women who I come from are not fanciful. They are blunt, easily offended, and resolute in their self-deceptions. But at the end of the day, they take life at its word.

Evelyn will wait it out, however long it lasts.

ACKNOWLEDGMENTS

Thanks to Anna Solomon, Amity Gaige, Megha Majumdar, Janice Nimura, and Sarah Shun-lien Bynum. Our ongoing conversations about writing helped me imagine this novel. Sarah—special thanks for your limitless willingness to talk through issues big and small. Your gifts for shaping character and narrative steered me right to the heart of the book. I'm indebted to my early readers Peter Blauner, Janet Meyers, Cathleen Schine, Dina Silver, and Claudia Silver. Thanks to Nicola Sweeney for important conversations. Thanks to *The New Yorker* and *The Atlantic* for publishing excerpts from the novel, and to Deborah Treisman for such heartening support. Thanks to MacDowell, the Corporation of Yaddo, the Ucross Foundation, and the Dora Maar House for the time, space, and quiet. Enduring gratitude to Henry Dunow. How lucky I am to be able to thank you with every book. Huge thanks to Kate Lloyd for your work on the book's behalf. My deepest gratitude to everyone at Simon & Schuster who embraced and supported this novel, including Julia Prosser, Anne Tate Pearce, Brittany Adames, and especially to my remarkable editor, Olivia Taylor Smith. Olivia, you asked exactly the

ACKNOWLEDGMENTS

right questions and made essential suggestions that helped me bring the novel to fruition. I am grateful for your insight and wisdom.

And always, thank you to Ken, Henry, and Oliver, who are constant inspirations and reasons for hope.